Wide Awake

a novel

SHELLY CRANE

Wide Awake 🜊 *Shelly Crane*

Reference: Useless facts found in *Uncle John's Monumental Reader*, www.dbmproaudio.com/facts.html, and the world wide web
Cover design by Okay Creations

Printed in the USA
1 2 3 4 5 6 7 8 9 10

Paperback available, also in Kindle and E-book formats through Amazon, CreateSpace, Barnes & Noble, Apple and Kobo.

More information can be found at the author's website:

http://shellycrane.blogspot.com

ISBN-13: 978-1483912646

ISBN-10: 1483912647

"IT DOESN'T MATTER WHO YOU WERE OR WHAT YOU'VE DONE. THE ONLY THING THAT MATTERS IS WHO YOU ARE RIGHT THIS SECOND." - MASON ,WIDE AWAKE,

OTHER SERIES BY SHELLY CRANE

SIGNIFICANCE SERIES
COLLIDE SERIES
DEVOUR SERIES
STEALING GRACE SERIES
WIDE AWAKE
WIDE OPEN
SMASH INTO YOU

Useless Fact Number One

A duck's quack doesn't echo and no one knows why.

Someone was speaking. No, he was *yelling*. It sounded angry, but my body refused to cooperate with my commands to open my eyes and be nosy. I tried to move my arms and again, there was no help from my limbs. It didn't strike me as odd until then.

I heard, "All I'm saying is that you need to be on time from now on." Then a slammed door startled me. I felt my lungs suck in breath that burned and hissed unlike anything I'd ever felt before. It was as if my lungs no longer performed that function and were protesting.

I heard a noise, a gaspy sound, and my cheek was touched by warm fingers. "Emma?" I tried to pry my eyes open and felt the glue that seemed to hold them hostage begin to let go. "Emma?"

Who was Emma? I felt the first sliver of light and tried to lift my arm to shield myself, but it wouldn't budge. Whoever was in the room with me must've seen me squint, because the light was doused almost immediately to a soft glow. My eyelids fluttered without strength. I tried to focus on the boy before me. Or maybe he was a man. He was somewhere in between. I didn't know who he was, but he seemed shocked that I was looking up at him.

"Emma, just hold on. I'm your physical therapist and you're in the hospital. Your..." he looked back toward the door, "parents aren't here right now, but we'll call them. Don't worry."

I looked quizzically at him. What was he was going on and on about? That was when I saw the tubes on my chest connecting my face to the monitors. The beeping felt like a knife through my brain. I looked at the stranger's hazel eyes and pleaded with him to explain.

He licked his lips and said softly, "Emma, you were in an accident. You've been in a coma. They weren't sure if...you'd wake up or not."

Of everything he just said, the only thing I could think was, 'Who's Emma?'

He leaned down to be more in my line of sight. "I'll be right back. I promise." Then he pressed a button on the side of the bed several times and went to the door. He was yelling again. I tried to shift my head to see him, but nothing of my body felt like mine. I started to panic, my breaths dragging from my lungs.

He came back to me and placed a hand on my arm. "Emma, stay calm, OK?"

I tried, I really did, but my body was freaking out without my permission. His face was suddenly surrounded by so many other faces. He was pushed aside and I felt my panic become uncontrollable.

I thrashed as much as I could, but felt the sting in my arm as they all chattered around me. They wouldn't even look me in the eye. That man...boy...was the only one who had even acknowledged me at all. The rest of them just scooted around each other like I wasn't important or wouldn't understand their purpose, like it was a job. Then I realized where I was and guessed it *was* their job.

My eyelids began to fight with me again and I cursed whoever it was that had stuck the needle into my arm. But as the confusion faded and the air become fuzzy, I welcomed the drugs that slid through my veins. It made the faces go away. It made my eyes close and I dreamed of things I knew nothing about.

My eyes felt lighter this time when they opened themselves. The fluttering felt more natural and I felt more alive. I could turn my head this time, too, and when I did I saw something disturbing.

There were strangers crying at my bedside.

The woman caught me looking her way and yelled, "Thank the Lord!" in a massive flourish that had me recoiling. She threw herself dramatically across the side of my bed and sobbed. I shifted my gaze awkwardly to the man and waited as he stood slowly, never taking his eyes from mine.

"Emmie?" When I squinted he said, "Emma?"

When I went to speak this time, the tubes had been removed. I let my tongue snake out to taste my lips. They were dry. I was thirsty on a whole new level and glanced at the coffee cup stuck between his palms. He looked at it, too, and guessed what I wanted. He sprung to set the cup down quickly and fill an impossibly smaller cup with water from a plastic pitcher. I tried to take it from his fingers, but he must have sensed I needed help, because he held my hands with his and I gulped it down in one swig with his help. My arms ached at the small workout they were getting and again I wondered what I was doing there.

I made him fill it three more times before I was satisfied and then leaned back to the bed. I decided to try to get some answers. I started slow and careful. "Where am I?" I said. It felt like my voice was strong, but the noise that came out was raspy and grated.

"You're in the...hospital, Emmie," the woman sobbing on my bed explained. She smiled at me, her running mascara marring her pretty, painted face. "We thought we'd never get you back."

That stopped everything for me.

"What do you mean?" I whispered.

She frowned and glanced back at the man. He frowned, too. "What do you remember about your accident, sweetheart?"

I shook my head. "I don't remember anything." I thought hard. Actually, that statement was truer than I had intended it to be. I couldn't remember...anything. I sucked in a breath. "Who are you? Do you know something about my...accident?"

The woman's devastated face told me she knew everything, but there was apparently something I was missing. She threw her face back onto my bed and sobbed so loudly that the nurse came in. She looked at the man there. He glanced to me, a little hint of some betrayal that I couldn't understand in his eyes, before looking back to the nurse. "She must have amnesia."

The nurse ignored him and took my wrist in her hand to check my pulse. I wanted to glare at her. What the heck did my pulse have to do with anything at that moment? "Vitals are stable. How do you feel?" she asked me.

How did I feel? Was she for real? I rasped out my words. "I feel like there's something everyone isn't telling me."

She smiled sympathetically, a side of wryness there. "I'll get the doctor."

I looked up at her. She was short and petite, her blond hair in a bun and her dog and cat scrubs were crisp. I watched her go before looking to the man again.

"I don't understand what's going on. Did I..." A horrifying thought crossed my brain. The gasp I sucked in hurt my throat. "Did I kill someone? Did I hit them with my car or something? Is that why you're all being so weird?"

The man's own eyes began to fill then. I felt bad about that. I knew it was my fault, I just didn't know why. He rubbed the woman's back soothingly. He shook his head to dispel my theory and took a deep breath. A breath loaded with meaning and purpose. "Emmie...you were in an accident," he repeated once again that I was 'in an accident'. OK, I got that. I wanted him to move on to the part that explained the sobbing woman on my bed. He continued after a pause, "You were...walking home from a party after the football game. Someone...hit you. A hit and run, they said. The person was never found. They left you there and eventually someone else came along and helped you. But you'd already lost a lot of blood and..." He shook his head vigorously. "Anyway, you've been here for six months. You were in a coma, Emmie."

I took in a lungful of air and uttered the question that I somehow knew was going to change my world. "Why do you keep calling me Emmie?"

He grimaced. "That's your name. Emma Walker. We always...called you Emmie."

"My name... Emma," I tasted the name. "I don't feel like an Emma."

He smiled sadly. "Oh, baby. I'm so sorry this happened to you."

The woman raised her head. "Emmie." She tried to smile through her tears. "Try to remember," she urged. "Remember what your favorite color is?" She nodded and answered for me, "Pastel Pink. That's what you were thinking, right?"

Pastel pink was the last color I would have ever picked. She tried again. "Or purple?"

Uh... "Are you sure I'm Emma?" She started to sob again and I felt bad, I did, but I needed answers. "Who are you?"

"We're your parents," the man answered. "I'm...Rhett. And your mother is Isabella. Issie..." he drawled distractedly.

"Rhett?" I asked. "Like in *Gone With the Wind*?"

He smiled. "That was your favorite movie when you were little."

I closed my mouth and felt the weight bear into my chest. I wasn't me. I had no idea who I was. These people claimed to know me and be my parents, but how could I just forget them? How could I forget a whole life?

I tried really hard to remember my *real* name, my *real* life, but nothing came. So, I threw my Hail Mary, my last attempt to prove that I wasn't crazy and didn't belong to these strangers, however nice they may be. "Do you have some pictures? Of me?"

In no time, two accordion albums were in my lap - one from the man's wallet and one from the woman's. I picked up the first, trying to sit up a bit. The man pressed the button to make the bed lean up and I waited awkwardly until it reached the upright position. I glanced at the first photo.

It was the man, the woman, two girls, and a boy. They were all standing in the sunlight in front of the Disneyland sign. The man was wearing a cheesy Mickey Mouse ears hat. I glanced at him and he smiled with hope. I hated to burst the little bubble that had formed for him, but I didn't recognize any of these people. The pictures proved nothing. "I don't know any of those people."

The woman seemed even more stunned, if possible. She stood finally and turned to go to the bathroom. She returned with a handheld mirror. She held the picture up in one hand and the mirror in the other, and I indulged her by looking. I have no idea why I was so dense to not understand what they had been implying, and what I had so blatantly missed.

I was *in* the photo.

I looked at the mirror and recognized the middle girl as the girl in the mirror. I took it from her hands and looked at myself. I turned my head side to side and squinted and grimaced. The girl was moving like I was, but I had no idea who she was. She looked as confused as I felt. I looked back at the picture and examined…myself. She was wearing a pink tank top with jean shorts. Her hair was in a perfect blonde ponytail and she had one hand on her hip and the other around the girl's shoulder. One of her legs was lifted a bit to lean on the toe. *Cheerleader* immediately rambled through my head. I almost vomited right there. "I'm a cheerleader?"

"Why, yes," she answered gently. "You love it."

My grimace spread. "I can't imagine myself loving that. Or pink."

It hit me then. Like really sank in. I had no idea who I was. I had forgotten a whole life that no longer belonged to me. I felt the tear slide down my cheek before the sob erupted from my throat. I pushed the pictures away, but kept the mirror. I turned to my side and buried my face in my pillow, clutching the mirror to my chest. My body did this little hiccup thing and I cried even harder because I couldn't even remember doing that before.

The man and woman continued to stand at the foot of my bed when the doctor came in. I looked at him through my wet lashes. When he spoke, his voice sounded familiar. "Emma, I'm sorry to have to tell you this, but it appears that you've developed amnesia from your accident. We'll have to run a lot of tests, but the good news is that in more cases than not, the amnesia is temporary."

I jolted and wiped my chin clear of tears. "You mean I could remember one day?"

"That's right."

"Don't get her hopes up," I heard from the doorway and turned to find the man-boy. My heart leapt a little. He was the only person that I remembered. Well, from when I woke up at least. He felt like some awkward lifeline I needed to latch onto. He shook his head. "Every case is different. She may never remember anything."

"Mason," the man yelled, making me jump at the volume of it, and shot daggers at him across my bed, "this doesn't concern you."

"She's been in my care for six months," he growled vehemently and then glanced at me. He did a double take when he saw that I was awake and looking at him. I had no idea what the expression on my face may have been, but he softened immediately and came to stand beside…my parents.

"Isabella. Rhett," he said and nodded to them as they did in turn. He was on a first name basis with my parents. He wasn't wearing scrubs like the nurse. He was in khakis and a button-up shirt, the sleeves rolled almost to his elbows. His name tag said "Mason Wright - Physical Therapy Asst.". He looked at me with affection that showed the truth behind his words. "I'm Mason, Emma. I've been doing all of your physical therapy while you've been…asleep."

"You look a little young," my mouth blurted. I covered my lips with my fingers, but he laughed like he was embarrassed.

He swiped his hand through his hair and glanced around the room. "Yeah… So anyway, I'll be continuing your care now that you're awake. You'll have some muscle atrophy and some motor skills that will need to be honed again." I nodded. "But, from what I've seen from working with you these past months, I'll think you'll be fine in that department."

"Working with me? Like moving my legs while I was asleep?"

"Mmhmm. And your arms, too. It keeps your muscles from completely forgetting what they're supposed to do." He smiled.

I wanted to smile back at him, but feared that I didn't know how with this face. Plus, my body was exhausted just from this little interaction. He must have seen that, too, because he turned to the tall man who had yelled at him before. "She needs her rest."

"I know that," he said indignantly. "However, the news crew will be here later on." He turned a bright smile on the woman that was supposed to be my mother. "She'll do an interview with them and tell everyone all about her ordeal. I'm sure you could even get a deal on a big story to the-"

My father spoke up, putting a protective hand on my foot. "You set up an interview with the press the day she wakes up...and didn't even get our permission first?"

They all kept talking around me. Mason started defending me along with my parents. The man apologized half heartedly and I assumed he was the head doctor or some hospital administrator from the way he was acting.

My mind buzzed and cleared in intervals. I lost all track of time and eventually just turned to let my cheek press against the grainy pillow. My throat hurt from the tubes that had been keeping me alive.

Only to wake up to a reality that was more fiction than non.

My eyes still knew how to cry though and I tried to keep myself quiet as I let the tears fall. I thought I'd definitely earned them. Eventually the room quieted and the lights were turned off, all but the small lamp beside my bed. The phone on my bedside stand had a small list of numbers, for emergencies I assumed, but the name on the top of the card was what caught my eye. 'Regal City Hospice'.

Mason had been right. I wasn't even in a real hospital. They hadn't expected for me to wake up.

I wondered if that fact had put a kink in someone's plans.

Useless Fact Number Two

You burn more calories sleeping than watching television.

The television was on. It woke me with screams and I looked up to find some women yelling at each over a scrawny man. Jerry Springer was still going strong after six months apparently. Six months…

I tried not to cry again.

It had been over a week since I woke up. My body was alive, but my brain just shut down. It was as if I was still asleep, but aware of what was going on around me. My eyes were open, and I just lay there and tried not to remember that I *couldn't* remember anything. My parents told me I was nineteen years old. I'd had a birthday only a week after the accident. Nineteen years of my life were gone, as if they never happened.

After they told me, I just turned on my side and refused to move. Refused to participate. Refused to be the person they told me I was. It made no sense. I could remember who Shakespeare was. I could remember what eight multiplied by eight was. I could remember what happened on September eleventh and the Twin Towers. So why couldn't I remember what color hair I had, or who my friends were, or even my own name?

The days blurred, the minutes pressed into hours.

The doctor came in and yelled at me, told me I was being a child. The police still had yet to 'interrogate' me, he said, like getting run over was my fault. My parents defended me, said that I'd been through enough. They begged me to eat and when I didn't, they had someone come in and put cloudy liquids into my IV to sustain me. I knew I was reacting. Whether it was *overreacting* or not, I wasn't sure. But wasn't I due a little bit of that after everything I'd been through?

But one factor was constant. Mason.

He never scolded me, he never gave me pleading looks to eat, and he never looked on me with disappointment. He just looked. He came in every day, more than once, and he'd stand in the corner or by the door. He watched me in a protective manner that no one else possessed. But his eyes also held an understanding in them, like he knew that I needed to have this time to just…be nothing.

Sometimes I stared back at him, sometimes I just closed my eyes. But today, as I looked over to find the woman — my mother — asleep in the chair with her head awkward and laid over the back of it, I knew it would be different.

Today, I was going to start trying. I couldn't be a vegetable forever. And I felt bad. My mother looked wrecked. I knew they worried about me this week.

I moved my arm slowly and shakily to the buttons that made my bed sit up. It hummed softly as it lifted me. I had no strength at all and it scared me a little to think about therapy and eating and…going to the bathroom.

I groaned a little in distress at that. I was going to be solely dependent on someone for who knew how long to help me while I got myself back together. I felt so undignified and I hadn't even started yet.

The door creaked as it swung open and Mason came in with two cups of coffee in his hands. He used his hip to close the door and looked like he was about to tip toe before looking up and seeing me sitting up. He looked startled, but relieved. "Well…hey there."

"Hey," I answered, my voice still so rough. I cleared it and he set the cups down. He poured me a glass of room temperature water and lifted it to my lips with a gentle smile. I held onto his wrists while he helped me and then licked my lips before trying to speak again. The rasp of my voice was embarrassing, but it was all I had. "Thanks…Mason. Or should I call you Mr. Wright?"

"I'm only a few years older than you, Emma," he teased. "Mason is my name, so call me that."

"How old *are* you?"

"I'm twenty-three, but enough about me. You're the star here." He grinned and took a big swig of his coffee cup. "So…ready to get to work?"

"Work?"

"Therapy. Aren't you ready to start walking again?"

I sighed. "How long will all that take?"

"It's different for everyone. You should be feeding yourself and brushing your own hair in just a couple weeks. You could be walking as soon as a month if we work hard."

"We?"

"Yes, we," he said through a smile. "I'll be here the whole way."

"Wait, what month is it?"

"It's February."

"So the accident was in August?"

"Yep. The first game of the season."

I swallowed. It was painful, but I couldn't deny how alive I felt today. "So I missed Thanksgiving and Christmas." He nodded. "I'm sure that must've been hard on...those two." I ticked my chin toward the woman still asleep in the chair.

"It was hard, but they were here." He pointed to the windowsill.

There were five or six small wrapped boxes there with red ribbons and Santa-in-a-sleigh wrapping paper. I just stared at it. He set his cup aside and leaned his hand on the railing of my bed. I saw a glimpse of a tattoo peek out of the rolled-up sleeves of his button up. I looked up at him. He pulled his sleeve back down and put his fingers to his lips in a 'Shh' motion while he smiled. I found myself smiling, too.

Then I looked back to the presents. "I feel guilty," I whispered. "I don't even really know why, but I do."

"You shouldn't," he assured. "They don't blame you. They just missed you."

"What if I can't be who they want me to be?"

"Then they'll just have to learn to live with that."

I jerked my eyes to his. "You mean...I don't have to be the girl who does cheerleading and likes pink?"

He laughed in a little choke. "No, I don't think so. It's understandable that you'd be different. Besides, I don't really see you as the cheerleading type."

"You and me both."

He laughed again and ruffled his hair a little as he leaned up. "You're pretty funny, Emma."

"I wonder if I was always funny," I mused.

He looked at me closely. "It doesn't matter who you were or what you've done in the past. The only thing that matters is who you are right now."

I sat stunned before finally spouting, "Are we talking about me or you?"

His lips twitched with a smile. "So not only funny, but smart, too."

"I hope you're right," I sighed.

"I usually am," he teased and winked as he turned. I found myself smiling after him. He was such a nice guy. I felt no pressure from him and that was welcomed.

He went to the window and opened the blinds. He was whistling something. Some old song that I knew I must have known, but the pinpoint escaped me. The sun came in, warm and yellow. It felt so good on my skin that I found myself leaning my head back and soaking it in.

I heard someone coughing and opened my eyes to find the woman waking up and Mason smiling at her. "Mason," she crooned. "Oh, how are you?"

"I'm great." He handed her the extra cup he'd brought in. "I brought you the usual. Black as night with two sugars."

She smiled in gratitude and I watched. She hadn't noticed me yet. She was a gorgeous lady. Her cheekbones were high and her form slight. Her light blond hair was pulled back into a ponytail that showed a slim neck that I envied even in my state. I wondered if I had inherited that neck. I couldn't even remember what I looked like even from the mirror the other day. I remembered that I kept it and turned to find it right where I'd left it on the bedside table. I picked it up and slowly turned it over to reveal myself in the shiny oval.

She was there, all blond haired and thin. Me.

I gulped and turned my head side to side. I lifted my hair on one side to see my ears. They were rounded, no points at all. Diamond stud earrings lined the lobe. I counted six and balked at that. I then looked at my nose. It was short and cute, I guess. It fit my face, but my eyes were big. They fluttered with long lashes and the color was a dark brown. My lips were normal looking. My eyebrows looked cared for, no strays in sight. I had no blemishes either and no problems that I could see at all.

I looked up to find them both watching me patiently. "You've been here every day, haven't you." I didn't ask her as a question, because I just knew.

"Of course," she answered and smiled sheepishly.

"You...plucked my eyebrows."

She laughed and Mason smiled. "I did. I didn't want you to wake up one day and find yourself..."

"A hairy beast?" I supplied.

She giggled and fiddled with her necklace. It was very endearing. "Yes, exactly."

"Thank you," I said carefully.

She caught her breath and pressed her lips together in an attempt to stop the tears. "Of course, honey."

I licked my lips and looked down at the mirror in my lap. I lifted it again in my shaky grip and looked at my neck. It was slim and defined. I *had* inherited it from my mother. I set the mirror aside and almost groaned at the ache in my arm. I could barely hold a mirror up by myself. The next few months were not going to be fun, but I was ready.

I looked up to Mason's watchful eyes. "I'm ready."

He smiled the biggest smile I'd seen on his face so far. "Good. We'll get started this afternoon then. Let them get all their tests over with first."

"Tests?"

"To make sure that you're all right physically. It's just a formality. I have complete faith in you."

I nodded. He really did and it was a little weird. He seemed to be so at ease with me and my parents. He had seen me every day and them as well, apparently, but I didn't know any of them. I wanted to though and I planned to embrace this 'therapy'.

I found myself nodding at my internal decision. Then the door opened to reveal a new face in the form of a young woman. She smiled at me and then at Mason, then at me and back at Mason. "Mason," she acknowledged, sultry and intimate.

Ooohh. This must be Mrs. Mason.

He cleared his throat in an odd way. "Adeline."

She smiled back at me. "Emma, Emma, Emma. So you've decided to come back to the land of the living and see us, huh?" she said sweetly, like I was a toddler.

I nodded. I didn't know what else to do. She continued.

"So, I'm going to start you on your therapy right away."

I looked at Mason. "I thought you were my therapist?"

"I am," he confirmed. "Physical and occupational. Adeline is your mental health counselor." I felt the blood drain from my face and he rushed on. "It's just a formality, Emma. It doesn't mean anything. Every person who has been through this has to be put the wringer."

"Yeah, of course," Adeline agreed too sweetly. When I looked up, her face had changed. She wasn't nearly as warm as before. In fact, it was as if someone had taken the hot knob and given it a quick wrench to cold. I wondered at the turnaround, but forged on.

"What kind of therapy are you talking about?"

"The kind where we make sure that everything is okay in that pretty little head of yours, sweetie." I frowned at that, but she kept going. "So, for today, work with Mason. I'll see you tomorrow for our first session."

With that, she smiled and exited the room.

I stared after her suddenly exhausted, just as the man who was supposed to be my father bounded in. "Is she…awake?" He smiled. "She is," he answered for himself.

"Hey," I supplied softly. That must have been more than he hoped for because his grin was wide.

"Well, hey. How are you feeling today?"

"I'm all right. How are you?"

He laughed and came to my bedside. "I'm pretty good now." He exhaled a bit, his shoulders visibly lifting, and I realized that I had been upsetting them. I hadn't been meaning to, but if they were my parents, and clearly they were, then they would be worried when their daughter stopped eating and became catatonic right after waking from a coma. I felt guilty again and looked down at my lap.

"Well," Mason started and came to pat my…dad… on the back, "I'm going to let you guys visit. Emma, we'll start this evening, all right?"

I nodded. He leaned down and didn't stop. Like he leaned down into my personal space. Our faces were only a couple inches apart as he fiddled with some imaginary wires that needed fixing by my arm. His eyes were absolutely hazel. No way to be mistaken for green or brown, they were mixed perfectly to be both. His hair was a light brown that he had pushed back to look professional. He whispered, "It's not your fault." Our eyes locked. "It's not."

"It kind of is," I whispered back.

"No," he whispered harder. "They just need time, Emma. So do you."

I stared at him as he leaned away and smiled at my parents. "I'll come back later for our session."

"All right, Mason, thank you," my mother said before coming to kiss my father's cheek. "Did you get your proposition done?"

"Finally, yes," he said relieved. "Mitch is coming home tonight."

"Oh, good," she crooned. "Felicia said she was flying in tomorrow. Perfect timing."

"Who are they?" I asked. They both looked at me as though I'd asked something really stupid. Or crazy. Or both.

"They're your brother and sister," he supplied and gulped. "They wanted to come sooner, but we told them to hold off. In fact, lots of people have been wanting to come see you."

I licked my lips. "Like who?"

"Your friends, our family, your..." He looked at the woman with a look of irritation, but I could tell it wasn't directed at her. "Never mind. Just lots of people who miss you."

"Mitch and..." I stumbled.

"Felicia," she supplied sadly. She looked as though she might cry. I said the names over and over in my mind to remember them the next time.

"Felicia," I finished. "Where are they?"

"College," the man said. "You're the baby of the family."

"And I'm a high school senior this year?"

"Yes..." she trailed off awkwardly. I guess I'd miss half the year by now. I couldn't technically call myself a senior anymore, could I?

"OK," I said and tried to absorb that. "I'm sorry." They seemed unsettled by my sudden apology, so I hurriedly said, "I didn't mean to worry you, I just needed a little space...in my head. I'm ready now, to start trying to get better."

"Honey," he approached gently, "we aren't trying to pressure you." He may not have been *trying* to, but I felt pressure all right. "We just want you to be...you again."

I decided to be honest. "I don't know if that will ever happen. Right now, my focus is walking and brushing my teeth. I want to focus on one thing at a time, so can we just focus on my physical recovery? Then I'll start trying to work on remembering."

They nodded like they were the children and I was the parent. I almost sighed, but held it in. They needed to adjust, just like me. Just like Mason had said.

"So, what's the deal with Mason? You seem to know him well."

"We brought you here a couple weeks after the accident. We wanted round-the-clock care and support, something the hospital couldn't offer.

Mason was here from day one. He's been helping you ever since. He's been so great." She smiled affectionately. "I figured he'd get tired of us coming here every day, but he always greeted us warmly."

I nodded. "And the boss doctor guy?"

My dad's lips pursed. "He's not the easiest man to get along with, but this was the only facility that we could drive to every day and we didn't want to risk sending you further away."

I nodded again and licked my lips. I felt tired beyond belief, but wasn't it rude to go to sleep when they'd just gotten there, and all the grief I'd put them through this past week? My mom must've known, because before I knew what was going on, she was kissing my father goodbye and he was waving and telling me he'd be back later.

She on the other hand started her primping session.

With me.

She told me to lie down and relax, go to sleep, whatever, but she didn't let anyone bathe me but her this whole time. She had even shaved my legs for me every day and painted my toenails and fingernails, clipped my nails, and brushed out my hair. I didn't know whether to be extremely grateful, especially knowing that Mason had been touching those legs, or extremely grossed out. But she was my mom, so it shouldn't matter, right?

I did what she asked and laid my head to the pillow. To my awkward satisfaction she went to the bathroom, got what she needed, and began her ministrations. I actually fell asleep as she took the soapy cloth and ran it over my legs and feet. It was nice and soothing.

I didn't fight it when sleep knocked on the door. I just let it in.

Useless Fact Number Three

Mosquitoes smell with their feet.

I woke up to movement. I opened my eyes once more to find my bed being leaned down to lie flat. Mason smiled down at me. "Finally," he complained. "I was about to get the hose."

I squinted at him. "Are you joking?"

"I am totally joking." He grinned wider. "You're gonna stay funny for me, right? I'm all about the sarcasm."

"I'll try my hardest," I said as sarcastically as I could manage.

"Yes!" he said and pumped his fist. "Finally! Someone who can keep up with my witty repertoire."

"I've got six months' worth stock piled," I pointed to my head, "right here."

He laughed harder and then leaned down to pick my head up by my neck. "OK, seriously now, I'm going to remove the pillow," and he did so, "because I find it's best to do the exercises when you're flat on your back." He looked behind him and I noticed a man there for the first time. "This is Mr. Garner. He's the physical therapist I work under." He leaned in and whispered, "But honestly, I do all the work." I found myself smiling. "They came and did the blood test while you were sleeping, so we're ready to get started."

I looked up at him. In the movement of the air around me, I realized that I smelled different. I turned my head to sniff my shirt and found it clean with a hint of peppermint. I squinted. Did I even like peppermint? And I

19

realized I had lipgloss on. Upon tasting it, I found it was cherry. I did like that, I could tell, because my tongue sneaked out to taste it again. I moved my gaze back to Mason.

"Are you done?" he teased.

I flushed. "Sorry. My mom gave me a...sponge bath, I guess."

"She does that every day before our session."

"She does?"

"Yeah," he sighed. "No better people than those two, let me tell you. They may be strangers to you, but I guarantee you, you have their unconditional love, no matter what."

"You're so..." I could think of nothing, so I stuck to sarcasm, "wise, Yoda."

He smirked. And I'd be lying if I said it didn't make my heart, which was just as much a stranger in my chest as anything else, beat a little faster.

"Mason," Mr. Garner said, looking up from his clipboard, "I've got to finish all this paperwork for the audit. Are you fine here alone?"

"Sure. Of course."

"Great." Mr. Garner looked at me. He was in his thirties, and tall and lanky. His head was quite large, which led me to hope his brain was large, too, if he was deciding my fate. "I'm so, so sorry. It was nice to meet you, but honestly, you'll see way more of Mason than me anyway. I run the entire therapy department and Mason is the best I've got so, you're in good hands."

I tried not to gulp at that statement. "No worries. Nice to meet you."

"And you, Miss Walker. Mason."

"Mr. G," Mason regarded and nodded at him before looking back at me. "All right, you, let's get to it, shall we?"

"What do I have to do?"

"At this point in the game?" He shrugged and lifted my foot in his hands. "Nothing. Little by little we'll start to add some strength exercises, but for now, I just want you to get a feel for your muscles."

He moved my foot up and down, side to side, then bent my knee in and out. At first, I watched in fascination, waiting for some miracle to burst through my skin and make me whole again. But when he switched legs, I knew that wasn't going to happen. So I lay back and was caught by something on the ceiling. "What's that?"

He glanced up to where I was looking. "Oh, that's your dragonflies. Your dad and I put those up."

"Why?"

"They were in your bedroom, so he said. He told me you loved them and if you woke up in the middle of the night, he wanted you to feel safe, like you were at home and it had all just been a bad dream."

I stared up at the dragonflies that I hadn't seen before. They glowed, I could tell. They had little sparkles on their wings. Me, a nineteen-year old girl, had dragonfly stickers on her ceiling? And my father — the man I didn't even know — had been so thoughtful and insightful to bring those up here for me…so I'd think it had all been a bad dream if I woke up in the middle of the night from my coma.

I felt the first tear slide down the side of my face and into my hairline. I didn't close my eyes, though. I just stared at the dragonflies; beautiful and silly, lovely, pointless and thoughtful.

I realized Mason had stopped moving my legs at some point. He watched my face and when I looked at him, he didn't smile. I looked back at the dragonflies and took a deep breath. "I'm scared. What if I don't ever remember? What if the girl he brought dragonflies to doesn't exist anymore?"

I heard his sympathetic sigh. He wiped a tear away with his finger before leaning down and taking a hard seat into the chair next to my bed. "Emma…I know you don't feel like it right now, but you're so lucky. Your parents love the crap outta you."

I chuckled and turned to find him smirking once more. "I can see that."

"Don't worry about tomorrow so much."

"Ok, Mr. Miyagi, what's next?"

He grinned. "Well, smarty pants. Wax on, wax off." He lifted my arm and moved it up and down, side to side, and around, bending it at the elbow. I just closed my eyes and let him finish everything he needed to do. I played rag doll very well apparently.

When he said he was done, he went to get my parents, who were waiting in the waiting room. I felt worse. Gah, it was like they *never* went home.

They came in and he was in the process of telling them all about my schedule for doing more progressive treatment when the door to my room opened. I looked over to find a guy there. He smiled at me so sweetly and looked so relieved— I thought for sure this must be my brother, Mitchell.

So I said so. "Mitchell?" Look at me trying to be quick and smart. But no, it wasn't Mitchell.

"No," he said and looked at my parents with anger. "You didn't even tell her I was coming by today?"

"I hadn't had the chance yet," my father argued. "Besides, I already told you that I didn't think it was a good idea."

"Bullsh-" he stopped and sighed. "Nonsense, Mr. Walker." He smiled at me and I glanced at the flowers in his hands. "I know you hate flowers, but..." He came to the bedside and leaned in...

I jerked my face to the side to avoid his lips. I felt my brow bunch in confusion, but he was even more confused. "It's true?"

"What is?" I asked and then huffed a little. "Will you please back up a bit?"

He leaned back, hurt all over his face. "You really don't remember me?"

"I don't remember anyone," I countered. "It might help if you told me *who* you were."

He set the flowers on the bed and crossed his arms in a pouty motion. "I'm Andrew. You used to call me Andy, everybody does. I'm your... I *was* your boyfriend."

I looked at his face. He was thick in the way that football players and wrestlers were. In fact, he was even wearing a letter jacket. His hair was blonder than mine and his brown eyes begged me to remember him. I got nothing.

"My boyfriend," I tested the words and swallowed that down. "Look, I'm sorry." I didn't know what else to say.

"Really, Emma?" he asked, almost angrily. "You don't remember me? You don't remember anything about us or your life or your friends? You don't...remember what happened the night of your accident?" I felt my eyebrows rise as he just waited. "Really?"

"Really," Mason answered. He had a scowl on his face and I wondered about it. "What part was it that you didn't get?"

"And who are you?"

"Her therapist."

"So you're not her doctor," Andrew...Andy said in a growly way. "So why don't you just get out of here and let me have some catch-up time with my girl."

"No," I found myself saying. The thought of them all leaving me alone with this guy that I didn't know was the most terrifying thing since I'd woken up.

"What do you mean 'no'?" He sulked and glared at me. "You really don't remember anything?" he asked again and seemed to be holding his breath. "Have your parents been talking to you about me?"

"What? No."

"Really?" he drawled in disbelief. "Then why are you being so cold to me, huh? You're glaring ice cubes."

"I don't know who you are!" I said loudly. "I don't remember anything!"

"I just didn't believe it," he mused and shook his head like he was disappointed. It was starting to be a running theme with the men in this room. "How could you forget everything that was *us*?"

Dad scoffed angrily. "You forgot pretty fast yourself, pal."

The uneasy silence that followed was telling. "What?" I questioned.

"I…" Andrew started. "I didn't think you were gonna wake up."

"What does that mean?"

"I started seeing someone else," he confessed, but continued quickly. Too quickly. "But I'm here now. I broke up with her as soon as I heard the news. On the TV, I might add, not from your parents, who *should* have called me. It's over now. We can pick up right where we left off," he said sweetly.

He acted like he was handing me a pretty little package instead of a heaping mess of sloppy seconds. I spoke soft and slow. "Look, like I said, I don't even remember you. I'm taking things slow, OK?"

"I understand, babykins."

I grimaced. "Babykins?" I muttered.

"That's your nickname, babe. I always called you that, especially when you…" The smile he tacked onto the little nickname had me wishing I'd never asked.

I threw up in my mouth a little bit and decided to switch gears. "Right now, I just want to focus on getting better. I can't worry about trying to remember everyone."

I thought he'd be deflated, but instead he grinned in challenge. "Oh, you'll remember me."

My dad leaned forward to…what? I didn't know, but Mason stopped him with a strong hand to his chest and nodded his head toward the door.

"I think visiting hours are just about done. Why don't you go on home and give them a few minutes." It wasn't a request.

"Listen, pal-"

"Mason will do. Or therapist if you need to get fancy."

I wanted to laugh, but didn't.

"Whatever, glorified orderly. I can see myself out, thanks."

"You do that," Mason said carefully, but hard and demanding.

Andrew looked back at me. "I'll be back tomorrow, babe, OK?" He smiled and bit the side of his lip as he leaned in to touch my chin. "I *really* missed you."

I didn't know what to say. His touch was warm and he looked so happy to see me. I hated to make him feel badly like I had been doing to my parents, so I just smiled a little. "OK."

"OK. Awesome," he whispered and grinned. He walked backward and pointed. "Tomorrow."

I nodded and when he shut the door, I immediately turned to the woman who was supposed to be my mother. "Was that really my boyfriend?"

Her eyebrows lifted. "He was," she answered, "though we...never really liked him." She smiled wryly. "You have been a cheerleader since you were seven years old, and Andy has been right there with you in football. You've been together since..." she waved her hand in the air, "I can't even remember how far back. He's just not the most honest guy. He's not the guy I would have picked for my daughter, but we tried to give you space and let you choose and make your own decisions."

I had a thought. "Am I... *Was* I shallow?"

"Shallow?" Rhett asked. "No, honey. You were just...preoccupied, as are all teenagers."

"If that guy has been my boyfriend for as long as you say...and I let him call me babykins..." Rhett and Isabella laughed, but Mason and I didn't. To me, it was anything but funny. "I just feel like... I don't know," I sighed in frustration. I did know one thing though. "Can I have a tutor?"

They both blinked. "Well..."

"I don't want to keep falling further behind," I explained. "If I'm going to be stuck here for a while, at least I can be productive while I'm doing it."

Rhett swallowed and stuck his hands into his grey suit jacket pockets. "You *want* to do school? You've always done anything and everything to get out of it. Puppy-dog eyes, lying about being sick, begging...literal begging."

I wanted to sigh. The discrepancies kept piling up against me. "I'd like to still graduate this year if we can find a way to make that happen," I amended. "I know it's a long shot, but I'd really rather not have to add another year of school on if it can be avoided."

Isabella nodded, but looked at me in disbelief.

Everyone said their goodbyes and I lay there looking at those dragonflies as they glowed softly in the dark. My chest ached with all the pressure that I felt. My life piled onto me and my breaths were almost nonexistent. I needed to find the balance. I had to.

"It's all about the balance, Emma," Adeline was saying. I hadn't seen anyone that morning. Mason had not been by, nor my parents, which was a first for me to be left to my own devices all day. But I did find a book left beside my bed. It was a worn and beaten book that had seen better days. I spent all morning pouring over it, not even knowing who'd left it there. It was a book of useless facts; things that were true, but you would never actually have an opportunity where you would benefit from knowing it. I loved it immediately. Completely useless information that couldn't be turned against you. You weren't tested on it, and it didn't make you look smarter for knowing it or not knowing it. And they were funny. I didn't know if I liked to read or not, but I was in deep with this book.

I had reluctantly set it aside, only a couple of pages in, when Adeline, the mental health therapist, paid me a visit as she promised. She started her session, overbearingly standing at the bedside. She never stopped moving her pen, and her eyes never really focused on me, and now she was coaching me on the importance of balance.

"I want balance," I insisted. "I just don't know how to do that, I guess."

"Well, I think you should whole-heartedly embrace the old you."

I jolted. "What?"

That had been the last thing I would have expected.

"Yes," she said shrilly. "Embrace it! Your parents, your friends, your bedroom, all of it. Even if it feels strange, you should just go with it. I think this is the best course of action to see about getting some of your memories back."

"Even my boyfriend?"

She smiled. "Especially him. See, he's going to be an emotional connection that's not like anyone else's. Lots of times, the ones that we love are the ones who can bring us back, so to speak."

"But what if I didn't love him?" I couldn't imagine it.

"Just try," she said wryly. "Just try to be the girl that everyone wants you to be."

I gulped at the advice. That was the absolute last thing I wanted to do, but I still found myself nodding. She said she was finished for the day and that she'd see me in a few days for another session.

I lifted the book from the table and turned to the page I had stuck a napkin in to mark my place. *A dragonfly beats its wings at thirty beats per second.* I glanced up to look at my white dragonflies.

Unfathomable.

Useless Fact Number Four
Only one third of the people that can twitch their ears
can do it one at a time.

"Either that book is evil or the ceiling is." I turned to look at Mason at the door. He was in grey sweatpants and a long-sleeve t-shirt today.

"No, just...nothing. You didn't come by this morning," I heard myself say. I held in my blush by some miracle. My mouth just seemed to say these things. Why was he obligated to come and see me? Because his eyes were hazel enough to make me forget that I was a freak show, and he never made me feel like the girl who woke up from the coma?

He looked a little taken aback. Great. Add insult to injury. "Uh...I didn't think you'd even notice. Sorry, I had a couple of other patients this morning."

"No, it's fine." I stuttered on. "I...don't know why I said that. I've just seen you every day....so..."

The smile that he fought was an elated one. Why did he seem so happy about that? I bit my lip hard so as not to smile back. "Well...I'll remember that. Let's get started. Today I want to do some exercises with you."

"Is that why you're in sweats?"

He laughed and motioned to his pants. "You don't like my sweats?"

"They're fine," I said softly. I was having a hard time looking him in the eye today. I felt strange after the talk with Adeline. She wanted me to be the girl I used to be, the one with a boyfriend. I licked my lips nervously. I didn't even know how to act anymore. When I looked up, he was watching me curiously and silently. "So how many tattoos do you have?"

He smiled wryly at the subject change. "More than I should to keep this job. I, uh...do some tattooing on the side."

I felt my eyebrows rise. "You're a therapist slash tattoo artist?"

He chuckled in a hesitant way. "Yeah. Long story."

I wondered—did I have any tattoos that I didn't know about? I had twelve earring holes that I had found. Who knew what I'd done to myself in my teenage rebellion.

"So," he clapped and smiled, "you can sit up today. We're just going to work on your arms, all right?"

I nodded and waited for instruction. I watched as he went to the table, taking his MP3 player from his pocket. He set it up with a little square speaker and soon, *Keep Your Head Up* by Andy Grammer started playing through the room.

I knew who that was! I smiled hugely. He turned to find me that way and stopped with a slow smile. "What's that for?"

"Nothing," I told him and tried to rein in my grin. "It's just...knowing that song made me suddenly giddy."

"Understandable. It's funny how the mind chooses what it wants to remember." He let the rail down on my bed and grinned at me as he bobbed his head to the music. "Ready, little puppet?" I nodded and let him take my right arm. "All right, take this first." He put a little rubber ball in my hand. "Squeeze that in your palm in a slow, but steady rhythm. Follow the beat."

I tried to do what he said. Not only could I barely squeeze the ball in my hand, but it actually hurt to try. I hissed and gave him a look. "I know," he said sympathetically. "This part sucks. In fact, the next few weeks are going to suck, but if you want to get back to normal, you've got to push through this part. I do things a little unconventionally, but if you trust me, we'll get you back to it in no time."

I squeezed harder and pretended that the pain was what I wanted.

Next, we worked on my arms. He had me lift them straight out in front of me and hold them there. He helped me lift my arms above my head and pass the ball back and forth between my hands. Then he had me push my palm against his. That hurt worse than anything else we'd done.

I sucked air through my teeth and closed my eyes, but didn't stop pushing back. First, we were palm to palm, and then he changed it to lacing our fingers and holding our arms out straight, but bent at the elbow. He gripped my other shoulder to steady me as I pushed. I still had my eyes squeezed shut. When my arm stopped straining and began to shake and wobble, I stopped pressing and rested, surprised by how labored my breaths were.

With my hand still in his, I opened my eyes and tried to catch my breath, but lost it again to find him so close to me. He was sitting on the edge of my bed, his grip on my arm the same as before. I couldn't look away. The way he watched me was so protective; I didn't really understand it.

I licked my lips nervously and when his eyes watched the movement, I knew something was different than it had been before, but when his eyes met mine once more, I saw something else.

Regret.

He slowly pulled back and swallowed loudly, removing his fingers slowly from mine. "Tomorrow, we'll focus on the legs. We'll see how you're doing with that and where we need to work most."

I nodded and looked at my lap. I felt so self-conscious. Would the old me have jumped in his lap and kissed him? Or slapped him because I apparently…had a boyfriend? I had no idea how to react. If I were being honest, Mason was on some pedestal that I never meant to put him on.

"Emma?" he whispered. When I didn't answer, I felt his fingers under my chin, lifting my head to force me to look at him. I stared silently. "Emma…you are a really great girl, but I…"

Girl…

I sighed and closed my eyes for a pause. I knew what else was coming, so I forged on to stop him. "I understand."

"Do you?" he asked softly, not even a hint of snide.

I nodded. "I'm too young, and I come with lots of baggage, right? I get it."

He sat back, taking his hands with him. "That's not what I meant-"

"Emma?" I heard from the door. Mason growled under his breath and stood. Andrew, oblivious to Mason, was all smiles and came forward. He bent and kissed my cheek before I even knew what was happening. "Hey, babykins."

"Hey," I scowled and sighed my words softly.

"Where are your parents?"

"I don't know actually. They haven't been here all day."

Adeline poked her head in the door. "Mason, sweetie, can I see you for a minute?" She smiled intimately.

I couldn't help the glance I threw at him. He and Adeline were involved. He had been about to tell me that I was a stupid kid and even more stupid for looking at him like I had a smidge of a chance with him. I just woke up from a coma! I shook my head at myself and marveled at my naïveté.

"They're getting your sister from the airport," Mason supplied and grabbed his MP3 player. He looked back at me and I could see irritation there. I wondered if it was directed at me. "They'll be here any minute," he said and gave Andrew a look, but he spoke to me. "Are you OK in here alone with him?"

"Hey!" Andrew complained.

I just nodded. He sighed and went out to Adeline, who waited and watched from the door. I wondered if the old me would be as embarrassed as I was right then.

As soon as the door was closed, Andrew was a completely different person. He grinned and leaned down to kiss my lips. I was so startled that I didn't stop him. His lips were soft, too soft, and he smelled like the cologne he was wearing. I pushed him back a little. Oh, no...the first kiss I could remember, stolen. "Oh, come on, babe. No one's in here to see."

"I don't-"

"You can cut the act, now," he said through a smirk. "It's just me."

"What act?"

"You told your parents you couldn't remember anything so you didn't have to go to school? Genius, babe! Genius!"

"Andrew," I said slowly. "I'm not acting. I don't remember anything."

"How can that be?" He crossed his arms and looked down at me like I was a sullen child. "Babe, look. I know you've got the whole gimmick going, but this is ridiculous. You can trust me. Unless you're angry at me for something. Or scared."

"Andrew," I said slowly, "I don't know you. I don't remember anything about you or us or anyone else. I am not lying or playing around or trying to trick anyone. Someone ran me over with their car," he flinched, but I kept going, "and left me there to die. Why would I ever lie about something that was so close to taking my life away?" I felt my breath hitch. "No, scratch that, they actually *did* take my life away. The only life I knew. Now I'm stuck in a body I don't know with people around me I've never seen before."

I felt out of breath from my speech. I gripped my forehead in my fingers. I could feel my pulse beating under my fingertips. I felt strange.

He was stunned, I could tell, but he came forward and leaned down to see my eyes. "Are you OK, babe? You look green. Do I need to get your man-nurse?"

"No," I said in irritation. "He's not a man-nurse. Mason is my therapist and he's helping me so I can be normal again."

"You are normal," he said with a condescending laugh.

It hit me. This was the chance to send this guy that I no longer had the capacity to care for packing. "Andrew, I'm not normal. Do you understand the extent of my...damage?" I said bitterly.

"You..." he floundered. It made me angrier. "You don't remember anything. I get it-"

"You don't get anything!" I yelled. "I can't walk! I can barely feed myself. I can't hold my hand up for more than seconds at the time. I can't even go to the bathroom by myself, Andrew. I am *not* normal."

He grimaced and even glanced toward the bathroom, but I saw his resolve. There was something there in his face that I just knew wasn't going to be giving up anytime soon. To my surprise, he got down on his knees by my bed and held my hand gently. He looked me straight in the eye and muttered some of the sweetest words I would imagine had ever come from his mouth. "Emma, I know that I've been... I haven't been here. I haven't been what I should have been for you. When I heard what happened to you..." His words choked off as he held back a sob. I stared at him. He was actually fighting tears. "I came to see you every day when it happened, but then they moved you here and wouldn't let me see you except on weekends. They told me you were going to die, that hospice was for people that were going to...die, Emma. I was missing so much school and..." He shook his head. "Anyway, my parents said I needed to find an outlet. So...I started dating as a way to take my mind off." I raised my eyebrow. "I know," he placated. "I know. That's stupid and selfish and childish. And I know it sounds lame, I do, but I loved you, Emma. You don't remember that. I get it now, but I love you just the same. I want to be with you. I want to help you through this. All of it, no matter how embarrassing you think it is or whatever." His thumb rubbed over my knuckle. "I'm not leaving you again. I won't make the same mistake twice. I love you, babe. I always have and I'll make you love me again, too."

I didn't know what to tell him. I wasn't really interested in loving him. I mean, I didn't know him, but Adeline had said I should embrace anything that was a direct line to the *old me*. She seemed to think this guy was a key to my memories. And there he was, pouring his ever-loving guts out all over my hospital bed. It felt wrong to accept this, but it felt even more wrong to spit in his face when he was so open and raw before me. "OK," I whispered.

"OK?" he said with hope.

"OK. Let's try and see how things go."

He smiled. It looked real and nothing like the cocky grin he'd been wearing before. He leaned forward a little and let his fingers touch my chin. "I know you want to take things slow, I get that, but I've missed you so much." He whispered, "Would it be all right if I kissed you?"

I felt my lips part with a rejection, but forced a stop on that. One kiss to appease him while I got used to the idea. I nodded small and looked up at him. He continued to smile as he stood from his kneel and leaned down. He paused before touching my lips to stare into my eyes. I wanted to feel something familiar as I stared back into them. I wanted it like I wanted to walk and run and dance again, but nothing happened.

He let his lips touch mine gently as his hand came to hold my jaw.

Like I mattered.

Like I was important.

Like he really did want to help me.

His lips pressed harder and his hand moved a little in a caress. I sighed as I let my resolve go. I was going to try. My therapist wanted me to, my parents also, and Andrew. Mason…he was seeing my therapist and had made it clear I was a 'great girl'. What was holding me back? So I threaded my fingers through his and let my lips part just a bit in silent invitation. He took it and gripped my fingers tighter as he slipped his tongue through my lips, just barely. Then he pulled back and leaned his forehead against mine. He sighed, "God…I missed you, Emmie."

"I know." I patted his cheek. "Taking things slow, right?"

"Sure," he answered and sat back in the chair, but scooted it all the way to the bed edge. "You say when, where, and how much, OK?"

"Thank you, Andrew."

"Andy," he corrected. He seemed irritated, like he'd had to correct me too many times already. "You always called me Andy."

"Andy," I said softly. It sounded like a kid's name when I said it like that. "I'll try to remember that."

"And you'll try to remember me, too, right?" He smiled. "In no time, we'll be just like we used to be."

"What if I'm not? What if I never remember?"

"Then, like I said, I'll just get you to love me again. Won't be too hard," he said and winked with his joke. I found myself laughing a little.

"OK. If you say so."

"So, how about I meet you here every day after school and I'll bring your school work. I heard your parents went to the school asking about a tutor for you. I can help. Then I'll take you for a walk. Or a..." he glanced at my legs, "a roll?"

I laughed. "I've never even been out of the bed yet, let alone used a wheelchair."

"I'll help you," he promised. "I'm not going anywhere."

He kissed my fingers, and Mason took that opportunity to come in. Of course. I felt a rip of guilt go through me at the look of anger that flashed across Mason's face, but why? He was probably just angry because he knew Andrew...err Andy...was going to be sticking around. And, granted, he hadn't been even an honorable mention for boyfriend-of-the-year, but he was here now. And he was trying. I felt that I owed it to not only him, but myself, to explore that, even if just for a little while. I owed it to myself to see if I could remember this boy who said he loved me.

Though *he* had moved on to someone else and *I* found my own eyes drifting up to meet the hazel one's who held the fate of my mobility in his strong, capable hands.

Useless Fact Number Five

A pregnant goldfish is called a twit.

The next day, my family came—the whole wide family. My brother and sister, who were as pristine as my parents, were awkward. I tried to talk to them, but they seemed like they didn't know what to say even when I started the conversation.

Rhett and Isabella tried their hardest to perk things up by having them tell me all about college life and what I had to look forward to next year. My sister was majoring in business, but she planned to keep working in the bank where she was a teller once she graduated. Her fiancé was apparently very rich and she said she had no need to do anything else since he would take care of her.

Honestly, studying and working your butt off for a degree that you weren't even going to use…just to say you went? Not for me. College didn't seem at all like something I wanted to partake in.

But they all seemed happy that I was awake, tension or no tension. Finally, I just couldn't take it any longer. I needed to make them see that just because I broke once, didn't mean I was going to break again.

"You don't have to walk on eggshells," I yelled in the middle of yet another awkward silence. "I'm not going to fall back onto the bed into another coma. I'm fine. I…just don't know who you are."

I laughed a little. It was silly and ridiculous. Mitchell laughed a little, too. I gave him a grateful smile. He was probably the one I got along with more than anyone else in my family. The sister seemed a little too uptight for my taste, but maybe the old me was fine with that.

"Emmie," she started and bunched her brow. "You're just so different and it's a little unnerving."

"How am I different?" I said and sat up as much as I could to hear her better. I was suddenly fascinated by what she was about to say.

"Well, you're…" she shrugged. "I mean the old you would have yelled at us the minute we walked in here for not bringing you something." I scowled at that, but still swallowed that down and listened. "And you wouldn't be watching Judge Judy." She flung her hand at the impossibly small television on the wall. "You don't care about people's problems. You'd be watching MTV because that's *all* you watch when you're home."

I blinked. "What else?"

"What?"

"I don't know who that is you're talking about, and good or bad, I want to get to know her. What else would the old me have done?"

She looked to her dad — my dad —for the OK to proceed. He nodded and sighed as he sat on the end of my bed and patted my blanketed leg with a weak smile as she continued.

"The old you wouldn't be caught dead in the clothes Mom put you in." She looked to Isabella. "No offense, Mom."

She smiled. "None taken. Go on."

"The old you wouldn't have your hair down like that, it would be in a high ponytail like always. Or have accepted these flowers from Andrew," she looked at the card and smirked, "because you always say a guy that brings you flowers must not be able to afford anything good."

On it went. She laid out my transgressions like an itchy blanket at my feet and all I wanted to do was throw it off and tear out of the room, but I was immobilized. Not only by this useless body that betrayed me, but also the overwhelming shock and chagrin that was currently wracking my body.

The girl they were talking about couldn't possibly be me.

After a while, I shifted down into the bleach scented sheets and pretended to still listen, but I was really in a world all my own. I stared up at the dragonflies and tried to imagine this vain girl that still loved stickers of a fragile little flying insect. I tried to imagine someone who would snub a gift someone brought her while fawning over a fashionable ponytail.

Later on, after they left and a supper I barely touched of pot roast and rolls, I opened the book back up that plagued my mind with my little obsession for it. *An ostrich's eye is bigger than its brain.* Great. I wondered if that rule applied to me as well.

I shut the book, and, just as I was putting it on the table, I saw Mason's head retreating. "Hey," I called, welcoming the distraction.

He came in, but didn't look happy about it. "Hey. Sorry, I wasn't trying to disturb you."

"You didn't. You couldn't," I found myself saying. I bit the inside of my cheek in chagrin.

"Well..." He shoved his hands into his pockets and shrugged his shoulders, looking really uncomfortable. "I just wanted to check on you before I left for the night. I know your family being here was a big deal for you."

I glanced out the window to find it dark. "You're here late, aren't you?"

He nodded, his eyes narrowing in thought. "Yeah."

"Are you OK?" I asked.

He finally looked up at me. "Yeah. Why?"

"You're acting strange."

"I'm not," he insisted. "I'm fine." He looked around the room. "I better go."

"Were you just going to leave without saying anything?" He squinted in question, but I knew he knew what I meant. "When you were checking on me?"

He half smiled as he said softly, "Yes, I was. I just wanted to check on you, not bother you or...start some long, late-night conversation."

"Oh," was all I could say.

I gulped and pressed the button on my bed that controlled the light to turn it off. I heard his sigh and when he started to say something, I said, "Goodnight, Mason."

"I didn't mean that I didn't want to talk to you, Emma. It's just so very...complicated."

"What's *it*? What is there to be complicated about?"

He sighed again. "Emma," he said pleadingly.

"All I did was ask you if you were OK." I shut my eyes and felt my throat ache a little at holding in tears. I was about to cry for this man that I barely knew, and I didn't even know why. "It's fine. It's not a big thing."

"It *is* a big thing," he argued. "You just can't understand why yet."

"What does that mean?"

If he sighed one more time... "I just wanted to make sure you were good for the night, that's all." I heard him shuffle to the door. "I hope your visit with your family was good."

"It wasn't," I said truthfully. "They don't want the girl in this bed, and I don't want a room full of strangers."

"Em," he whispered. My body tightened with some response at this nickname he'd given me. Pleasure, I thought. I shook it away.

"I'm fine."

"Emma-"

"Goodnight, Mason."

The door squeaked as he toyed with it in his indecision. Finally he said, "Goodnight, Emma."

And then I was alone once more.

"The key is not letting up. Just use a constant force and push for as long as you can, all right?"

I nodded up at Mason. It had been almost two weeks since Andy had made his grand reveal of his feelings and his plans for me. He came every day, just like he said. And every day was a repeat of the first; he came and tried to talk me into how awesome he was and how I'd love him again in no time. He said he would take me on a walk, but had yet to do so, and then he'd try to force his tongue into my uncooperative mouth, and I'd try to sit there and pretend that I was enjoying it and it wasn't so bad.

But it was. It just was.

He was so adamant about things, that it seemed he was there more out of obligation than love. And he'd told me his parents didn't approve of his still seeing me. That it was 'creepy' he came to see me when I didn't remember him. Even though I should have been insulted, I wasn't. I was beginning to be a little creeped out, too.

And Mason, he was the same, only not. He was polite and his jokes seemed normal, but it was different than it had been before. And I noticed that during our sessions, he never looked at me for more than a couple seconds at a time. Like right now. I just tried to ignore it. He thought I had some school-girl crush on him, which wasn't far from the truth, and he wasn't interested and felt weird about my feelings. So, I played the passive, unemotional girl around him.

But it was hard to be too worried about that, though I had a good idea of why he was acting so strangely, because…I was walking again. Barely, but walking.

I used my arms on the parallel bar things that were holding me up and scooted my legs the tiny inches that I could muster. I could now wear clothes instead of a hospital gown. My mom was putting me in pink and purple velour track suits every day. It made these workouts better and less degrading. Progress was achingly slow, but I'd take it. And it just happened to be during one of these sessions that the radio rang out with a song. A song that sparked some kind of violent reaction in me, in my mind. It was *Yeah, Yeah, Yeah* by New Politics. I let go of the bars and gripped my head as if to shield myself. I felt my knees slam into the floor pads before my torso followed. Mason bent and caught me just before my head slammed, too. "Whoa. What happened?"

I pushed his arm off, not wanting the comfort right then. The feeling I got from that song was indescribable and it crawled over my skin. I heard his sigh as he sat down beside me on the mat. "I know it's hard-"

"It's not hard," I insisted. "Walking is all I can think about anymore. That song…the radio started playing that song…"

A phone rang and he pulled his cell out. He glanced at the missed call and sighed again before saying, "The song?" He looked back at me and saw me. *Really* saw me. "You are white as snow, Emma." He moved forward on the mat and though I flinched back, he didn't accept my silent barrier. He touched my face gently and made me look at him. "What's wrong?" I stayed silent, unable to find an answer. "Tell me what's wrong."

"That song just gives me the willies," I explained.

He tried to hold in the smile. "The willies?"

"The heebee-jeebies," I explained further.

He did laugh then. "A heebeewhat?"

"Nothing." I pushed his arm and he felt like stone under my palm. I shook my head at my own strength. I was so weak.

"That big word you just spouted was not nothing. Are you trying to show me up with your smarts?" He smirked in a way that could have been construed as a half-smile.

"I'm not smarter than you," I said. I managed to turn a bit to face him. "You're a therapist. I'm just a high school kid."

I made sure to emphasize 'kid' for him. I saw his face change. He opened his mouth to say something, but I stopped that real quick like. "Help me up, please? I want to keep going."

With pursed, unhappy lips he heeded my request, knowing I was drawing a line on where the conversation was to halt. The rest of our session, as he helped me and instructed me, he was contemplative. I tried to block him out. For me, walking was bigger than any boy could ever be.

When Andy — yes, I started calling him Andy — came by that day, he could tell something was off. I lied and told him I was fine, but I really wasn't. I seemed to be coming to a crossroads. A stay or go situation. A left or right predicament. I needed to get out of this place and start trying to figure out what I wanted most. To try to be some girl I didn't know, or try to be happy and live out my life as the girl I was now.

I had no idea the answer to the problem yet.

I was surprised when the door opened and it was Mason, not Andy. He smiled and it was the first time I'd seen that real smile in weeks. "What?" I asked. "Why are you so smiley?"

"Let's go, Emma. Up and at 'em." He took my hand and I gawked at him. He had barely spoken to me, let alone touched me, unless it had to do with therapy, and now he was pulling me up and steadying me with his hands on my arms.

"Where are we going?" I asked breathlessly. He didn't seem to notice.

"The yard. I want to take you for a walk, if that's OK with you."

A walk. Like, with my legs and stuff. I smiled in spite of being weird with Mason. "Please."

He held my arm tightly, but gently, in his and walked beside me down the hall slowly. He completely had my trust. If I fell, I knew he'd catch me. "Andy was supposed to take me," I finally said to fill the silence.

"I know," he admitted, but didn't look my way. "Your mom told me that you'd said that a couple times, but *Andy* always heads out, so…you're stuck with me."

Stuck. I shook my head at the absurdity.

"Thank you. I feel like I have a list in my head of things that will make me feel normal again. Taking a walk outside is one of them."

"I'll have to hear this list sometime," he said and tightened his grip when the stairs came into view. "Just keep a tight grip on my hand, OK?"

I nodded and we managed the stairs. My neighbor, who was in the room next door to me, was being pushed in her *stroller* as she liked to call it. I waved to her and she scowled back, but finally waved. She was ornery with a capital O, and with a name like Mrs. Robinson, I could only imagine why.

"You and Mrs. Robinson getting along?" he asked. I looked up and saw the smirk in his profile.

"As a matter of fact, we are," I retorted.

He laughed. It was rich, delicious, and spellbinding. I felt guilty because one laugh from this guy was more fun and happiness for me than two weeks with Andy had been.

I groaned and was happy when Mason didn't comment on it. I glanced around the yard at the pristine landscaping and benches lining the pathway. It was as if Mason read my mind and eased me into one before sitting next to me. I hated to admit how tired I was, but it was there—a constant reminder that I wasn't whole, that I wasn't capable.

"Don't do that," he said softly and touched my hand. "Don't beat yourself up. It takes a long time to build your strength back up. You're doing amazing."

"But it feels like something so simple should be easier."

His hand was still there on mine. When he paused and let his thumb sweep across my knuckles, I barely contained myself. "You're doing amazing," he repeated.

I suddenly felt a need to confront him. He was so hot and cold, and it just didn't make any sense to me. "How's Adeline?"

His brow rose. "Adeline?"

I nodded. "Yeah."

"Uh…I guess she's fine. Why? Did something happen at your session with her today?"

I licked my dry lips. So it was going to be this way, huh? "No, she's fine. She's very adamant that I get back to being the old me."

He tilted his head in confusion. "What does that mean?"

"She said I should embrace my old life…and everyone in it."

He got my meaning right away and shook his head. He looked angry and I didn't really know why. "She said that?" I nodded. "Did she specifically say to start seeing that guy again?"

Why would he say it like that? "Yeah. She said since I loved him before, he was a lifeline for me that I should embrace if I wanted a chance at remembering anything."

He scoffed and shook his head angrily. "Wow, Adeline, low blow," he muttered under his breath.

"What?"

"So that's why you've been so into him lately," he said in realization.

"I'm not into him," I heard myself say. I hung my head a little, playing with the strings of my eggplant sweatpants. "I feel so bad about it. He seems to be so interested and…invested in me. I've been trying, but I just don't really like him at all."

He seemed relieved. I stared up at him in confusion as he said, "So if you don't like him, then it's safe to assume that you don't love him, either."

"No," I said quickly. "Honestly, I can't imagine how I ever did. All he ever talks about is us getting back to the way we were. Ruling the school and making out all the time. Doesn't he know that high school is almost over?"

He chuckled deep in his chest. I closed my eyes for a few seconds, letting it absorb into me. "I'm sure someone like him isn't concerned with much."

"I used to be just like that," I whispered. "I was this vapid, stupid girl."

"People change," he reasoned firmly.

"He stole my first kiss. I mean," I twisted my fingers in the air in frustration, "I know it wasn't my first kiss, technically, but I don't remember any of the other ones. He just swooped in and stole it. And I let him."

I glanced at Mason. He was looking at me with sympathy, but also something else. Something I wasn't sure even he knew what it meant. "None of those things matter until it's the one you're meant to be with. Then all those kisses, all those things that happened with someone else, become insignificant and practically vanishes." I wasn't even breathing as I listened, hanging on his words like they were a cliff and my fingernails were the only thing keeping me there. He leaned in further. "My momma used to say that a girl had to find her prince after wading through the frogs." He smiled. I smiled, too, drowning in the sweetness of him calling her 'momma' and wondering what happened to her.

"I like that," I told him.

"She was a smart lady."

"What happened to her? If I can ask. I'm sorry if-"

"No," he said and shook his head. "No, it's fine. She was in an accident a few years ago."

"I'm sorry. That…sucks."

"She was awesome."

I squinted in sympathy. "I hate that for you. And I hate this for me."

"Bad things happen to good people, Emma," he said pointedly. I shrugged. He leaned forward and touched my cheek with his big, warm palm. "It doesn't mean that no one's looking out for us. It means that we're being prepared for something bigger and better."

"You think this was supposed to happen to me? And to your mom?" I asked incredulously. How could he think that?

He paused. "It's not that I think it was supposed to happen; you just can't dwell and regret the things that *do* happen. You've got to keep moving forward, keep pushing through everything that's thrown at you." He leaned back, wiping his palms on his pants before standing. "If you don't, you'll be standing in the same spot forever while the world keeps living around you."

I waited for more, but he stopped there and held his hand out to me. "Ready to go back inside?"

"And suffer through another night of boredom and bad reality TV? Why, of course."

He laughed. "That's the spirit. Come on."

He helped me stand, but my legs seemed to have grown too tired. The short rest gave them a false sense of readiness, and when I stood, I fell, clinging to Mason. He caught me easily and his breath coasted across my face. I looked up at him since he was looking so intently down at me. He seemed even more confused and dazed than I did. When I felt his fingers sweep across my cheek, I knew he could have asked me to do anything right then and I would have jumped at the chance.

But he didn't ask anything, he just stared in fascination as his fingers inched their way back to my hair. "You have to be the softest woman alive," he whispered in distraction.

He said woman. Not girl. Woman.

"I highly doubt that," I answered.

He smiled at that and cupped my cheek. "I think you don't give yourself enough credit. I hear comas are *great* for the skin."

I burst with a laugh. My laughter almost scared me since it was the first time I'd heard it. It sounded like someone else was laughing through me, but it felt great regardless.

A cleared throat interrupted our…whatever it was. "Mason. What is it that you're doing?"

We turned to find the man who ran the place. Mason automatically stiffened, his whole demeanor changing and shifting. He gave me a pleading look, but I wasn't sure what it was for until he pulled away. "Let's get you back to your room, Emma. Night, Dr. Wrigley."

He didn't give me the option as he placed my arm over his and guided me away. I didn't speak until we reached my room again, long, silent minutes later. "What was that about?"

"You're a patient, Emma," he said as if that explained it all, and he placed me in the bed gently.

"What does that mean?"

"I need this job," he replied quickly and moved about the room, straightening the blinds and then dumping the old cups into the trash.

"What did we do wrong?"

I wanted him to say it.

"Emma…" he said and I could tell he was exasperated.

"What did *I* do wrong?"

He stopped, but wouldn't look at me. "You didn't do anything. I'm the stupid one."

"Why?"

"Don't you have a boyfriend?" he asked harshly. He didn't wait for me to answer. "So why does it matter, Emma? You're just trying to get out of here, right? Go back to being the old you?"

I nodded like he wanted. "Yes."

"Then you don't need me complicating things."

I gritted my teeth. "I wish you'd speak English, just once."

"I'm speaking English, Emma; you're just choosing not to listen. You know exactly what I'm saying." He sat on the edge of my bed and touched my knee. "I'm sorry. I got carried away before. You're my patient and I'm your therapist. I work here and you will be walking soon and right out that door. And you have a boyfriend. Did we cover it all?"

"And you're with Adeline. You forgot that part."

He seemed confused and opened his mouth to speak, but stopped. He seemed to have some small revelation and swallowed before saying, "OK. So everything's covered. Let's just get you better, OK?"

He was drawing the line in the sand, though it had been him out there with his hands trailing my skin. Like I was different, special, like he needed to do it more than anything else. I felt so confused in that blindsided kind of way. "OK," I said softly.

"Don't be upset with me. I'm sorry if I overstepped. I'm sorry if I…gave you the wrong impression." He smiled. It was fake and didn't reach his eyes in the slightest. "I'll see you tomorrow for your session and we'll work extra hard to get you going, all right?"

So, he was back to patronizing me. That tone, so formal and placating. I just nodded and looked at the sheets. They may as well have been my prison bars.

He shuffled out and stopped at the door. He looked back and licked his lips. "What's best for everyone is you getting better. That's why I'm here."

I didn't answer. None was needed.

He closed the door gently and after staring after him, confused and angry and completely alone in my own little world, I fought stupid tears.

I took out the book once more. *Snails can sleep for three years without eating.*

Snail comas. Welcome to my world.

Useless Fact Number Six

Every time you sneeze, brain cells die.

The next time Andy came to see me, I told him that I needed to take a break from him. That I appreciated his help and visits, but I wanted to really buckle down and focus on my therapy so that I could get out sooner and get back to reality. Get back to *him*. The fact that last part wasn't true didn't matter. It placated him enough to where he seemed just as anxious for me to work hard as I was. He said it was good that I had decided this because he needed the afternoons for baseball practice at school instead of coming to see me.

He hadn't known how to bring it up to me, he said. How convenient.

This wasn't about Mason though. I told myself that, basically believed it, but it was more about me. I had to start taking my fate into *my own* hands.

The next few weeks brought plenty of action and events. I focused harder on the therapy and tried to focus less on Mason. He seemed to be doing the same. My crabby old neighbor and Mrs. Betty, one of the nurses, played cards with me sometimes. I knew it was for boredom, but had seen Mrs. Betty watching my hands and Mrs. Robinson's. I knew it was also a therapy thing and my hands holding the cards ached and burned while we did it.

I had renewed vigor, which led to stamina, which led to more workouts, which led to exhaustion, which led to tons of sleep, which led to healing, which led to me walking.

All.

By.

Myself.

This simple task, this simple thing that we all take for granted, that's so cute and monumental when a baby takes his first steps...but these first steps were so much more than that. Though I cried like a baby, I wasn't one. And though my mother cooed and fawned over me (because I had invited them *that* day to come because I just knew that day was going to be *the* day) I wasn't a toddler. I was me. I was finally getting a little piece of myself back. And though I tried so hard not to, my eyes drifted to the one person in the room that I knew would understand all this better than anyone else.

Mason's eyes were already on me from across the parallel walking bars. This time, I didn't shy away from his gaze. I knew that our terms were shaky, but so was I, and I needed the stability of my lifeline. As our gazes collided, I expected a smile and happiness, but I didn't expect the level of pride and utter joy to be so prominent. The man was bursting at the seams with it. It filled his face and the smile he wore was the beautiful one that made me feel like everything was going to be OK.

His lips parted and even in the loud room, I could still hear his breath. He said quietly, "You did it, Em." He moved forward and touched my arm. It was the first time he had touched me in weeks that had nothing to do with therapy. "I'm so proud of you."

As his fingers circled my elbow, and I tried not to shiver in his grasp, I asked softly, knowing the answer, "You didn't believe that I was going to walk again someday?"

"Of course I did." He smiled wider. "But today was the first time that *you've* ever believed it."

He was right. Having faith and having hope were not the same thing, and I was just now understanding that.

"Thank you for having faith in me. I wanted to, but I…"

"I know." His fingers that had calluses from working hard moved against my cheek like I more than mattered. "It's hard. I know."

Out of the corner of my eye I saw the bugged-eyed look on my mother at seeing Mason's affection to me, but it was the fact that he was actually *showing me affection* that had me stunned and careless if she saw or not. Mr. Garner had also looked up from his clipboard, but Mason was all that mattered.

"It's just going to get harder, isn't it?"

"Afraid so." His smile was easy. He moved closer and stood right in front of me, putting his hands on the sides of my waist. He squeezed his hands a little into my skin. "I've got you."

I relinquished my death-grip on the bar and gripped his upper arms instead. When my nose bumped into his chest, I almost laughed, but as I looked up I saw how close his face was. It was the closest his lips had ever been to mine. He didn't move away, just watched me. After the moment grew, an awkward little smile began to tug at his mouth. I followed suit and soon, we were both grinning.

I moved closer and we did a tandem-step routine all the way to my wheelchair. I hated the thing, but after workouts it was necessary because I was all tapped out. Isabella, or uh, my mother, said she would see me the next day. She had some dinner meetings with my father's work and needed to go, but said she'd be back. She leaned down, and though she seemed weird about it, she kissed my cheek and said how proud she was of me.

After she was gone, Mason began to wheel me back to my room. I felt his lips press on my ear. "How about I go get you a real dinner? No prison food for you tonight."

I managed not to shiver, just barely. "Doesn't really matter. Eating alone…it doesn't matter what you're eating."

"You won't be eating alone tonight."

I pushed my door open with my foot and held on to him as he lifted me easily to put me back in the bed. "You're staying with me for dinner?"

"Sure. If that's OK with you." He folded the chair and put it off to the side. He came back to the bed and sat, putting his hand on my knee over the covers. His fingers moved in a swirl and he smiled. "Would that be OK?"

"Of course. I just don't…"

He scratched his arm, pushing his sleeve up, causing his tattoo to show. He seemed nervous. "It's different being with you for therapy and being with you because I've missed you. I miss the smile that you seem to have only when I'm around and not being a jackass."

Should I ask him and risk ruining this moment? "What changed? I thought you said you needed this job."

"I do," he agreed, "but you worked your butt off. You took a step, so…so will I."

I felt myself smile just a bit. "You don't have to do that."

He looked at the blanket and licked his lips. "I want to," he said softly and looked up at me. "Gah, Emma…I want to so badly."

I didn't know what to say, but it didn't matter. He stood and took my hand in his.

"I'll be back." He kissed my palm and there was no way to stop the gasp that came from my lips. And there was no way the small noise, groan, whatever, that came from his throat was imagined either. "I'll be back really soon. And then we'll…talk."

I nodded. He rubbed his head and chuckled as he made his way out.

I waited. After twenty minutes, I turned on the TV and after an hour, I started to feel stupid. Mrs. Betty usually brought me dinner at night and came by for the second time, asking me again if I wanted some dinner. "It's just that this is my last round, so there won't be anything for you after this. I'd hate for you to go to bed hungry because you're waiting for him."

"But he said he'd be right back," I sulked.

"He probably had an emergency. Mason has lots of emergencies."

What did that mean? She lifted a brow that said *Take the food, silly.* "All right. Do you have any sandwiches?"

"I got the best darn grape-chicken sandwich this side of the Mason-Dixon." She handed it to me. I looked at it skeptically, all wrapped in cellophane and not what I wanted to eat tonight.

"Thanks," I murmured. "Though technically, I have no idea what it tastes like anyway." I pointed to my head in jest. "I'm amnesiafied. Remember, Mrs. Betty."

She smiled and went on. "I'm sure he had a good reason. Mason's not the kind of guy who leaves a girl hanging. He's one of the most responsible boys I know."

"He is not a boy," I said wryly, and she smirked at me from the doorway.

"Well, I guess not." She smiled in a knowing way. "I've leave you to your gourmet meal."

"Ha, ha."

She waved and went out. I stared at the sandwich, my appetite nonexistent. I set it on the bedside table and almost picked up the book…but decided against it. Instead, sulking was the order of business and I got right to it. I rolled my head to the side and stared at the Christmas presents still wrapped in the windowsill. I couldn't bring myself to open them. They were for *her* after all. They were for that girl I used to be, and I wasn't interested in seeing what they would have gotten her.

I closed my eyes and wondered what would have made Mason change his mind like that. I was confused in the worst way, because not only did I not understand what had happened, I couldn't even make it into the bathroom to sulk like a girl properly.

So I settled for a mild pity party and tried to sleep. Soon, I did.

"Emma, time for your meds."

I squinted and turned from the annoying noise. "What?"

"It's time for your meds," she said more forcefully. It was the morning nurse. Why they insisted on coming and giving me meds at seven at the butt-crack-of-dawn was beyond me. I downed the pills and smiled angrily at her. She turned, unfazed, and left, letting the door shut with a small slam.

It was then I noticed Mason. He was sitting in the armchair asleep, one leg over his knee and his head leaned back. He was even snoring just a tad, and it kinda pissed me off how adorable it was. I wanted to be mad at him. He had blown me off and I wasn't going to accept his cute little snore as an apology. Even though it was obvious he had slept there uncomfortably and had come back. But why? What had happened last night? I was beginning to think Mrs. Betty was right. It must have been some emergency. I tried to think of any other family members he talked about, but had only heard of his mother, who died in an accident.

I leaned my head against the pillow and watched him. He had watched me when I had my freak-out and it was time to return the favor. He swallowed and I watched his throat work. I was shocked at how much I liked that. Then he moved a little, tilting his head. He seemed to be dreaming.

On his lap was another book. The title read *Even More Useless Facts.* He was the one who gave me the first book? I was so confused. First he ditched me after making a point to tell me he wanted more, and now he's bringing me more books?

I decided not to wake him, though I couldn't deny that my traitorous body was happy that he was here. I just couldn't let him see how much I wanted him there when he clearly was even more confused than I was. I wanted him to make the decision for himself to want to be here, not just be here because that was what he thought I wanted from him.

While he slept, Isabella brought in a box of things for me. She kept looking back at Mason curiously, and then at me with a small, guilt-inducing expression. As if I were doing something wrong. I didn't understand why.

Did she not want Mason here when he was clearly there for other reasons than business ones? But I thought she loved Mason.

"And here's your cell. It's been turned off all this time so there's no telling what's on here, but I charged it before I came. Maybe it will be good to see your friends' names and what they had to say to you."

I raised an eyebrow at her. She just smiled as I put the phone to the side. That was something I'd have to do later when I was alone. Next she handed me a purse. It had a 'D&B' on the side. I wondered what that stood for because it wasn't my initials. After unzipping, I peeked inside, almost scared of what I'd find. Sitting on top was a small pouch that had a ton of make-up in it, lipgloss of every color. I uncapped one and it smelled like coconut. I put a little on and tasted it with my tongue. It was sweet.

"You have a thing for lipgloss," she said sweetly as she put an errant strand of hair back behind my ear. "That's why I always made sure to put it on you here."

I remembered. "Thanks. I can see why I'd like it."

"I need to discuss some things with the warden," she said and winked at her joke. "I'll be back in a bit, OK? Your father will be here after work."

I nodded. When she closed the door, Mason jolted awake. He looked around and when he saw me watching him, he smiled sadly. "I bet you're wondering why I'm sleeping here, huh?"

I shook my head. He wasn't weaseling any smiles out me. I wasn't going to let him off the hook for this so easily. Or so I thought.

He swiftly came, setting the book on my table, and sat on the sheets next to me. His weight pulled the sheets tight, making me roll a bit toward him as I sat there. "I am so sorry, Emma. I had an emergency and couldn't get away in time. When I finally made it here, you were asleep. I'm so sorry."

"It's fine," I dismissed. I looked down at my sheets. They seemed to be a constant source of visual stimulation for me. I just had this vibe from him that he was holding something back. Maybe he thought hurting my feeling would halt my progress in therapy, but I felt his fingers under my chin and when I looked up, he was so close that his breath skated across my cheek.

"No, it's not fine. I'm the worst kind of scum. I'm fish-tank algae. I'm horse-hoof matter. I'm-"

I laughed in spite of it. "OK, I get it. It's fine."

"It's not," he argued again, serious, "but I don't know what I can do to make it up to you. I have a lot of family emergencies unfortunately, and I can't sit here and say that it won't happen again. It might." I nodded at his honesty. "But I'll try my hardest, and beg you to understand that I wasn't here because I didn't want to be. I did, very much."

I wanted to ask what emergencies there were, but he hadn't divulged anything as of yet, and I didn't want to make him. Again, I wanted him to *want* to share these things with me. "I'll take that."

He smiled that Mason smile that set me on fire all over, and then he put one hand on the other side on the hospital bed and the other lifted toward my face. I waited...bated breath, gulping, sweaty palms, the works. His face got so close before he stopped. I thought he had decided against whatever he was doing he waited so long. I began to pull back in disappointment, but he reached behind my neck gently and pulled me to him. The barest of touches was the best way to describe our first kiss. It wasn't really a kiss at all. His bottom lip barely brushed my top one. When he leaned back and opened his eyes, he must've seen the confusion and frustration in my face. He chuckled. "I just had to taste that coconut..." he licked his lips, "but I don't want to kiss you when you've been angry at me and I messed up our date." He said 'date'. Like...a date. "I want to kiss you when, if we go another second without it, one of us will combust."

My breaths were raging. I tried to calm myself. "I..." I failed.

"I want to give you back your first kiss, the one that jerk stole from you. And I want it to be something that even a coma can't make you forget."

I gave him the smile he wanted. Even though I couldn't remember my life, I was positive no one had ever said anything like that to me before. He reached his arms around my waist and I found my face pressed into a warm neck that smelled amazing. His collar pulled down further and I saw another tattoo peeking out. I reached my fingers up and traced it. He shivered and I found myself laughing. He pulled back, laughing, too, and touched my chin. "I'm seriously ticklish. Like, it's a problem."

"I'll remember that," I said coyly.

"Don't tell anyone." He smiled and leaned up to kiss my forehead. "I've got to make my rounds, but Springer's on at noon. Lunch date? We can make fun of all the baby-daddies."

I laughed loudly. "Please."

"OK," he said softly. "It's a date."

"It's a date."

He kissed my forehead once more, lingering with his eyes closed. Mom came in just as he was leaning away. The pinched look on her face made me want to ask her why she all of a sudden didn't like Mason.

He smiled wryly and gave a small wave as he made his way to the door. "Bye, Isabella."

"Mason." Her tone was clipped to say it mildly. He looked back a fraction of a second before closing the door.

"What's the matter?" I asked, because I couldn't *not* ask. "What's wrong with you and Mason?"

"What's *up* with you and Mason?" she countered.

I felt my lips part in surprise. "What? He's a nice guy."

"He's your therapist and he's too old for you," she said softly.

"He's only a couple years older. That's nothing." I squinted in confusion. "What's this about?"

She pursed her perfectly lipsticked lips. "Emma, you may not remember it all right now, but you had a very detailed plan laid out for yourself. You had the college in place, applications sent in and accepted, cheerleading scholarships, the perfect pretty and petite roommate chosen, and though you were dating Andrew, you planned to…dump him before leaving so that you could focus on everything that needed to be done for your future." My face had to be displaying not only my shock at her words, but my disgust. Did she not see that what she just said was one of the shallowest things I'd ever heard?

"OK…"

"Just because you don't remember now doesn't mean that you should blow all your plans. When you remember, you won't like it that you blew your chances and wasted so much valuable time."

I paled. Wasted time?

She saw and backtracked. "Oh, gosh…Emma. I'm so sorry. I didn't mean it that way." To her credit, she did look so very sorry. "Please, honey…"

"It's OK." I swallowed. "But even if I do remember everything…I'm not sure I even want to be the person I was before."

She looked pale before, now she looked positively like she was about to hit the hospice linoleum. She pushed her hair back, her eyes drifting to the spot above my bed and not on me. Not my eyes. "We'll talk about this with your father. I have errands to run for the church since the secretary had her baby and I'm filling in, so Mrs. Betty can give you your sponge bath, if that's OK?"

"Sure."

She finally looked at me. "I love you, honey. I know that you don't know that yet, but it's still true." She kissed my hair and left without looking back.

I sat soaking in a puddle of doubt. I thought that my decision to focus on therapy hardcore and then figure everything else out later was a great one, but now I was learning it may not have been something that's conducive for family closeness. Was I more interested in figuring out who I was, or trying to please my parents and figure out who I used to be?

Mason did come in later at lunch to watch Springer, but he sat in the chair and though we laughed together, I could tell that a heaviness had settled over him since he'd left my room that morning. When it was over, he said he had rounds to do and that he'd see me at my session later that afternoon. I thought maybe he was just tired, but when session time rolled around and he decided that instead of real therapy I was back to squeezing the therapy balls…with him leaning on the back wall looking dejected, I knew something was up.

It made me feel like I was living that saying, two steps forward, three steps back. My progress with my therapy was slow but steady. My progress with Mason was confusing and pretty much nonexistent, because it wasn't really progress if the person couldn't even look you in the eye, and his heart was practically laying on his shoes it was so heavy.

I wanted to ask him what happened, but I had a feeling — a really, sinking feeling — that his answer would make me feel worse and make him feel guilty. So I settled on stewing in self-pity that night. I wanted him to *want* to explain things if he was having a problem with us, but I assumed it had something to do with Isabella…my mom…and the look she gave him. In fact, I would have bet on it.

Useless Fact Number Seven

The first couple to be shown in bed together on television was
Fred & Wilma Flintstone.

The days passed in a hectic blur. Mrs. Betty was fast becoming my best friend, whether she realized it or not, and my parents were still the same old, same old. Of course, my mother was a little more chipper these days because Mason had backed off considerably. I had whiplash from the boy, but seeing as how I knew his reasoning for backing off, it was hard to blame him. He was one of the good ones, and the good ones wanted to be respectful and do the right thing and…all that stuff. Even though they seemed like they were helping you, it was still breaking your heart.

I tried to cut him some slack, and we found a good work pace and a sense of normalcy to our relationship that consisted of sarcasm, Springer jokes, and working our butts off to get me out of there. Mason's renewed vigor to the task only led me to believe that he hoped things would change once I got out—once I was not his patient, once I was not off limits. It wasn't exactly wishful thinking. It's like when you go to the zoo and you see the panthers. They prowl and stare at you from across the fence, sniffing and eying you. Make no mistake, that panther wants you for supper, and if that fence wasn't there, you would be. But he *knows* the fence is there. So he settles on prowling and longing looks. Mason was the panther and this place was the fence. He'd practically said as much. His longing looks when he thought I wasn't looking were obvious. He probably caught me in my own daydreaming about him, dreaming of the day when the gate opened and the panther was set loose to devour me.

It made my skin flush just thinking about it. But, in a way, it had helped tremendously. We focused on therapy instead of anything else, and it had paid off. This was my last week here. I could walk on my own, though not for very long and I was still pretty shaky, and I was brushing my own teeth. And the bathroom no longer required an audience. You just have no idea the amount of dignity and confidence I'd acquired since Mason had decided to back off. It was the strangest thing how things seemed to just work out sometimes.

But with only days left until I was set free, I was being put through the wringer with tests and final evaluations. With Epsom salt baths every night, and massage, and even some acupuncture they tried on me, I felt better and better every day. I was so tired, but it was a *good* tired. I felt accomplished. Adeline was still Adeline, prissy, snide, and just doing her job. I told her what I thought she wanted to hear basically, and I knew that could hinder my 'progress', but I'd never felt this alive since I woke up. I would do anything to get out of there.

One of my therapies was to write. Letters, whatever I wanted, but making my hands work the way they should again was important. It was one more thing that I felt like a child about. My handwriting was atrocious to say the least. A kindergartener would laugh and tell me to try again. So that's what I did. I used Mason as my motivation, weirdly. I wrote the same line over and over again until it was legible, and then it was almost normal looking. It was something funny in the book he'd gotten for me and I figured it might be something worth knowing. I felt compelled to give it to him, for him to see that I was making leaps and bounds and strides to get the heck outta Dodge.

The fact that I kissed the line I'd written with my pink cherry lipgloss wasn't important.

The next thing I started writing was a list. It was an *I want to be normal again* list and the very first line read, *Walk*. So I crossed that out. The next thing on the list was, *Get out of the facility.*

So today, as Mrs. Betty walked me to therapy because Mason was running late, I was giddy on a new level. I had stopped using the wheelchair, even though they thought I should. I just felt any extra exercise, though it made things harder for me, was better. Since I'd sent Andy away, my mom had started to tutor me. Well…she brought my schoolwork every day and I pretty much caught up by myself. Because, just like the therapy, I wasn't backing down. This was my life we were talking about. Was I going to go through an extra year of high school just because things were hard? Just because doing so much work for a few weeks wasn't fun? Just because it put Isabella in my room more often?

Absolutely not. I was determined to walk, check. Get caught up in school, check. Get out of here and go home, check. And now, decide which girl I wanted to be. I hadn't done that yet, but I was on my way. Once I got back in school and into all those things I'd done before, I could make an objective decision, right? For now, I was just excited to see Mason.

We tiptoed around each other in awkwardness most of the time, but I still enjoyed his company more than I should have.

"What am I going to do without my favorite patient, huh?" Mrs. Betty asked. She gave me a cheeky look. "You're just going to run off and leave me here all alone?"

"Absolutely."

She laughed. "Well, all right then."

"I will miss you terribly though." She smiled at that and I pulled her to a stop and hugged her. She was a bigger lady, but as short as me, and she felt so much like a mother. "I really will miss you."

"A pretty thing like you will have tons of friends waiting for her back at school," she assured.

"But I don't know those people, and they are going to want me to be Emmie."

"You be Emma," she said harder and pulled back to look at me. "You be you, honey. They will either like it or they won't, but at least you'll know that you were yourself."

"Thank you. I know that you don't have to do all the things you do for me."

"I get paid to wash your sheets and bring you supper." She smiled wider. "But I'm privileged to know you and be able to see you walk right out of this hell hole." She laced her arm through mine and pulled me along with her. "You're going to be great. I have no doubts that this world better watch out, 'cause Emma Walker is coming back to town!"

I laughed just as we reached the therapy room. "Now you're just fluffing my ego."

Mason leaned against the doorjamb. "Now Mrs. Betty, you causing trouble for my Emma?"

Mrs. Betty and I both jerked our faces to look at him. He realized what he'd said and licked his lips, a little smile of chagrin there, as he looked away and cleared his throat.

I looked back at Mrs. Betty and she was grinning. "Mmhmm," was all she said before winking and walking away. I fought to hold in my laughter and my grin.

"Ready, Em?" he asked from behind me. I turned to find him smiling, apparently deciding not to try to hide from what he'd said. His hand was outstretched to me. I put my hand in his without a second's thought. It was warm and calloused from work, but also soft. Maybe it was just my imagination.

I pulled the note I'd written out on some hospital letterhead and forked it over. "I wrote you something…very interesting that I found in your book."

He opened it and his smile grew quickly before a full on belly laugh emerged. I stood in awe at that sound. "Wow." He shook his head, reading it again. "That's kind of awesome. Thank you."

I smiled and bit my lip. "You're welcome. Beware of turtles."

He laughed again and stuck the note in his front shirt pocket, buttoning it, locking the note inside. I had expected him to throw it away.

"You look really good today," I stated factually. And he did. He wasn't wearing sweats. He was in dark jeans that were baggier than normal and a black button-up. His hair was shaggier, too. Not so coifed as usual. "You going somewhere today?"

"Just here," he commented and swept his thumb over my knuckles. "You're almost out of here," he said casually, but it was anything but casual.

I smiled. "Can I get an Amen?"

He laughed hard and pulled me to a stop in the middle of the room. "Amen," he whispered as he stared into my eyes, his longing and whatever else you wanted to label it shined out at me. "You know…every room in this place is just dark and tainted, and yours is the only light and life here. This job is going to suck without waiting to see you every day."

"Then you'll just have to come see me," I said coyly. "Though I'm sure I'll be busy with…school." I grimaced. "Maybe something happened while I was in the coma. I feel like a thirty-year old trapped in a teenager's body."

He smiled knowingly. "You couldn't pay me to go back to high school, or God forbid, go to the prom I skipped." He visibly shivered.

"I want to go, but just to get it over with." I shook my head, very much conscious that he was still holding my hand. "All those people waiting for me to come back to them…my friends, my family, Andy. I feel like trying so hard these last few weeks of school will help my parents to deal with me, and it'll help me decide who I want to be."

He twisted his lips. "And decide who you want to be with, right?"

I ticked my head to the side. "I wasn't the one who couldn't decide," I said softly.

"There was no Adeline. You know that, right?" I nodded. I knew he had just let me believe that so I could make up my own mind. "Are you saying that Andy won't have a part of your life once you go back to school?"

He'd been so careful not to breach the line he'd drawn, and now he was practically scratching that line out with his foot.

"I don't know. I honestly don't know what's going to happen, but will I be in love with Andy? Will I pretend to be his girlfriend and live happily ever after with him? No."

He gulped a little, staring at my neck. "I know I've confused the heck out of you." I gave him a 'duh' look. He smiled a little. "Emma, you'll never know how much I've hated doing that to you."

"I know why you did it."

He jolted in surprise. "You do?"

I nodded. "My mom. She told you that she didn't want you to see me, right? And you thought you were making it hard for me to make a real choice about who I wanted to be. You thought that I had to embrace my life and explore everything that was the old me so that when I actually make my decision, I'll know that it was my own mind and not anyone's influence about who and what my life will be."

His mouth was open in shock. "Yes."

"It's OK," I soothed and even found myself moving forward and cupping his scruffy chin with my hand. His course hair scratched my palm and I could only imagine what that would feel like against my neck. I took a deep breath. "You did me a favor. A painful favor," I clarified, "but a favor nonetheless. When I woke up, you were there. I had this strange connection to you that I didn't understand, and still don't." He gulped again and looked like he wanted to say something, but I continued on. "And I latched onto you so quickly because of it. But I needed to focus on getting better. Not anyone else, not worrying about anything but my goal. And I've done it. I can walk, I can go to school, all caught up and ready to graduate, and I can leave this place because of you. Sometimes, knowing when to let go is just as important as knowing when to hold tight."

He licked his lip. "I thought you were excited about leaving because you couldn't wait to get away from me." I felt my eyes go wide. How could he think that? He answered me. "You were upset before when I said we couldn't be…together. And after that, your mom talked to me," he confirmed my suspicion and nodded, "and told me that she didn't want me to be a distraction for you. That I was stealing your focus and stealing your choices by not letting you live your old life a little first. That I was too old for you and would never be good for you. I felt like...you didn't know or remember anyone else and I was stealing you. It felt like stealing to just snatch you up when you hadn't experienced anything yet, but...you seemed so OK with it. I thought my ship had sailed. I thought you'd moved on and was working so hard to get out of here so you could go back to your old life and forget all about me." He smiled wryly.

"No," I told him and shook my head. "No, I just agreed that for me to start my life, I had to get out of here. So thank you," I whispered. I let my thumb rub his chin. "You worked just as hard as I did and I would not be getting my life back had you not been there for me." I couldn't hold it in anymore, but it was the first time happy tears had come, ever that I could remember. "Thank you."

He wiped a tear from my chin and shook his head. "All I want is for you to be happy. I knew this place wasn't going to do that for you. You needed to go home. You did it all by yourself, Em. It was your strength, not mine."

I shook my head. "It was yours, too."

I wrapped my arms around his neck. When his arms went around my back and settled, warm and steady on my ribs as he held me to him, I sighed with pleasure. The man had no idea what he'd done for me. I found myself searching for his skin. When my nose touched his neck, I let my lips rest against him and breathed him in. He shuddered and moved his own lips to my cheek, nuzzling my hair out of the way to find my skin. But he didn't stop there. He kissed the side of my neck and sucked a little, making me flush all over. The little noise that escaped my lips had him pressing harder before pulling back. My arms already ached from holding on for so long, but I pushed that away as he leaned back and our noses brushed when he settled me back to the floor. "Your mom wants me to leave you alone," he confessed. I balked. Leave me alone? What, like he was a predator or something?

"I know," he soothed and tunneled his hand through my hair. "But I feel inclined to respect her wishes."

"Mason," I protested.

"For now. They love you. You have your mom, Em, and..." He seemed really sad and understanding smacked into me. His mom... I had my mom and he missed his own fiercely. He thought that by being with me, he was putting a rift between my mom and me. "It's not fair to you. It's not fair to make you choose between them and me so soon when you haven't even really gotten to know them yet. You'll choose me," he whispered and let his thumb rub across my earlobe, "and I'll feel guilty because it wasn't a fair fight. You need to get to know them, Emma. You need to get back to the place where you love them again, and though you may never remember the way you used to be with them, I have no doubt that you'll figure out a way that works with them one day. And when you do, when you figure everything out and decide with no regrets who you want to be, if you still want me, I'll be right here waiting for you."

"So..." I wanted to cry again, even though every word he uttered made scary sense, it still hurt to imagine a life without Mason in it in some form. "I can't see you at all?"

"You'll still need to come in once a week for therapy." He licked his lips. "I can give your chart to someone else if you'd be more comfortable."

"No," I said quickly. "No. I don't want anyone else."

He knew my words held more than one meaning.

"It won't be forever. I'd just...I'd give anything for five minutes with my mom, the way she used to be. The way she seemed to have Yoda-like answers for everything."

I smiled and laughed a little, though another tear slid down my cheek. "I understand."

"I just can't take your mom from you. Hopefully, she'll get over whatever aversion she has for me."

"She didn't tell you?"

He shook his head. "Just that she didn't want us to be involved and that you had big plans for yourself that didn't include someone like me. Someone that wasn't...good enough."

"My mother said that?" I breathed an angry breath.

"She's your mom, Emma. She's just trying to protect you. My mom was like that, too, but worse. She was like a pit-bull." He laughed at some memory and it made more tears surface. He seemed surprised. "Why are you crying?"

"Because I hate that your mom was taken from you when you obviously loved her so much. I hate that for you."

He rubbed one of the tears with his finger. "These are for me? Emma, you're making this so much harder."

"What?"

He smiled sadly. "Being the good guy."

I smiled back. "You are a good guy," I insisted. "As much as I hate it, you're right. Just like therapy, I need to focus on my life and try to get all the pieces in place. But I won't want anyone else," I said slowly and fiercely.

"Then I'll be right here waiting."

Useless Fact Number Eight

It's possible to lead a cow upstairs, but not downstairs.

"Mrs. Betty, thank you so much for all your help." Rhett kissed her cheek and took my suitcase from her. "Emma talks about you every single visit."

"Well, I'm gonna miss her." She looked at me and I swore I even saw her fighting a little tear. "You be a good girl, now. Come see me when you come for therapy. I'll make you a chicken-grape salad sandwich."

"Deal," I said and choked on my own tears. I was so happy to be going home, wherever that was, but this woman who had taken care of me for so long and never judged, just listened? I was going to miss her. I hugged her and her vice-grip said it all. "Bye."

"Bye, Emma girl."

I got into the back seat of a white Land Rover. The leather seats looked brand new and never used. They were cold, and it was cold outside.

Then I realized I had no idea what state I even lived in. It had never come up. As my parents pulled away from the hospice, I didn't even look back, but I asked, "Um…where are we?"

Isabella turned halfway. "We're going home, honey."

"No, I mean…where are we? What state do we live in?"

Rhett's eyes jumped to mine in the rearview mirror before focusing back on the road. He sighed loudly. "We're in Colorado, sweetheart. Why, are you cold?"

"A little. I just didn't realize is all."

"We should have said," Isabella apologized. "I can't believe we didn't think to."

"It's OK. I think, compared to everything else, the state I live in is a mole hill, not a mountain."

She giggled. "That's something you would have said. I mean…you. You know what I mean."

"I know," I said, understanding her giddiness, but not sharing it. It was obvious those two were still pretty set on me being Emmie. I looked out my window as the heat blasted my face from Rhett turning it up for me. There wasn't snow, but it was cold and everything was dead looking with just a hint of spring beginning to peek out of things. New life was starting all around me, getting a fresh, new start.

Just like me.

I opened my purse and fumbled around for a lipgloss. My cell slipped between my fingers and I remembered that she had given it to me that day in my room and never turned it on. I pressed the button until it sang its start-up song and then slipped it into my purse again.

It wasn't long before they pulled into a gated community. The gateman waved them in and smiled extra bright as he bent down and waved to me. I waved in kind, but took a deep breath as I tried to prepare myself for the onslaught of people knowing me, but I would be surrounded by strangers. Suddenly, I felt sick to my stomach and my chest seemed too tight. It didn't want to hold my breaths for very long. I tried not to gasp loudly.

"This is our neighborhood," Isabella explained. "Mostly older people, not too many of them had children. But there are a couple of kids that you go to school with that live here, too. Kali will be so happy that you're home."

"Who's Kali?"

"Oh, she's your best friend," she replied a little shrilly. "She used to be at our house almost every day, before…"

"I have a best friend that lives in the same neighborhood as me, who used to be at our house every day…and she didn't come see me in the hospital?"

She exchanged a look with my father. "She and your other friends said you wouldn't want them to come. That you'd be angry if they saw you that way."

"Even after you told them that I couldn't remember?" I asked skeptically.

She shrugged. "You have a certain way with your friends. You were kind of the…queen bee, I guess."

What the hell? What did that mean? I let it go. I had a sinking feeling that every ounce of joy I had about coming home was about to be demolished quickly with all the expectation and disappointment.

Rhett pulled into a driveway and I was scared to lean down and look through the windshield to see it. This was it. This was the first step to my old life. I leaned down and managed to hold in my gasp at the huge three-story white house sitting at the end of the driveway. There was a huge paved, circle driveway out front with two other cars there already. Expensive cars.

"Who's here?" I asked, not ready to see anyone else yet. I needed to get my bearings a bit.

Isabella looked at me sharply. "What do you mean?"

"Whose cars are those?"

She looked relieved. "Oh. That's mine and yours."

I knew right away which one was mine. "You bought me a convertible?"

"It's what you wanted," Rhett reasoned and laughed. "You were so adamant about that car for your sixteenth birthday."

I stared at the little black Mini Cooper convertible with red leather. The way these two talked, I was spoiled. But they found it amusing…endearing. I swallowed that down. OK, one thing at a time. I took a deep breath and opened my door. That prompted them to do the same, as they were waiting for me.

I looked up at the big house and was saddened by the fact that all I could think about what how much I couldn't wait for my therapy session with Mason tomorrow. He came by early, so my parents wouldn't see him, and said his goodbyes, but it wasn't really goodbye, it was see you later. Namely, see you tomorrow. And then he had hugged me and told me he hoped it was everything I wanted, but if it wasn't, to just have faith that it was all going to work out. Then he had kissed my cheek and left in the nick of time before my parents arrived.

"Come on, sweetie." I looked at Isabella. "Let's go in. I'll show you your room."

Rhett was already inside with the bags, so I accepted Isabella's help that she obviously wanted to give, and let her wrap her arm around me like I couldn't make it up the stairs leading to the door without it. When she opened the door, there was a man there. He startled me, and apologized. "Sorry, Miss."

"This is Hanson. He's our butler," she said dismissively. I looked back at him as she towed me away and he shut the door, not showing an ounce of emotion. "And this is the housekeeper, Maya." She waved her hand at her, but kept going. I looked back at Maya the same way I had Hanson, but she, too, was a picturesque statue of poise.

"And this," she preluded before opening a huge double door, "is the library. But honestly, this is more my favorite room than yours."

I felt my jaw open wide with wonder. The shelves lined the walls completely, floor to ceiling. The shelves were so tall, there was a ladder on a track to reach the top shelves. There were several large lounge chairs and pillows in the center. I ached to go in and sit for hours. "It's…epic."

She giggled. "Oh, you don't have to pretend you like it. I know reading's not your thing."

I let her pull me away. She showed me the kitchen and dining room that looked more like a restaurant than a home. She showed me the living room, the den, the sitting room, the drawing room, the cocktail room… At that point I was exhausted from all the rooms that held no function but…just sitting there. I asked where my room was, and she smiled and took me upstairs.

I tried to hide how winded I was from step after step after step. My legs even wobbled a little.

She waited, looking at me with a little smile with her hand on the knob. I could tell she was apparently proud of this room and was trying to build the suspense. I tried to act excited. When she opened the door slowly, I felt my eyes bug…in a bad way.

It looked like Barney ate too much eggplant and then threw up in my room.

The walls, floors, pillows, bed, chandelier, and lamps were all purple. She seemed to be waiting for a reaction so I turned and smiled. Or at least I tried. "Wow. Purple, huh?" She smiled and nodded. "She liked purple an awful lot, didn't she?"

When she didn't answer, I turned back to her. She was pale in a scared way. "You OK?"

"*You* liked purple. Not her, you."

"Oh…" Crap. "I'm sorry. I meant me. I liked purple an awful lot. I thought my favorite color was pastel pink?"

She smiled a little bit. "It is, but purple was your second favorite. You even threw a fit about the convertible because your dad got red leather when you wanted purple."

I scoffed. "Wouldn't I have just been grateful to have the car at all?"

She laughed uneasily. "Well, honey, you're very particular. You like things the way you like them. There's nothing wrong with being certain of what you want."

"Well, no, but…you make me sound so ungrateful. It's a freaking car that I didn't pay a dime for. I should have just been happy to be getting a car, not focused on the color of the leather."

That sounded like a new level of ridiculous.

"Your daddy wanted you to be happy," she said, a bit more loudly. She was offended that was I was insulting…myself. The old me. My head was spinning.

"OK. Sorry."

"You don't have to be sorry. But we love you. Don't talk about yourself like you're an ungrateful, spoiled brat when you don't even really know yourself yet. It's like you're gossiping or something."

I stared. Gossiping about myself?

She moved on. "Your bathroom is in here." She pointed, but didn't go in. "And your closet is here." She giggled at some memory. "You could spend hours in here." She eyed me over objectively. "But…" she said carefully, and toyed with the pearls around her neck, "I'm afraid not much is going to fit you in this closet. We'll have to go shopping as soon as possible."

"Yeah," I drawled and looked down at myself to the jeans and sweater she'd brought to the hospital. "I imagine this skeleton could use a few pounds, huh?" She pursed her lips. "I mean…I guess being in a coma and not eating as much, I probably look different than I did."

She went into the closet and came back with a pair of jeans. She turned me to the full-length mirror next to my armoire and held the jeans up to my waist. They were too small. *Too freaking small.*

"Are you seriously telling me I *gained* weight while in a coma and recovering?"

"You were very conscious of your weight," she said in a manner that said she was speaking carefully. "You exercised daily, on top of your cheerleading schedule, and you put yourself on a very strict diet. It was another reason I was glad that your friends didn't come to the hospital to see you. They would have been…harsh on you. Your appearance was very important to you."

"What exactly was my diet? Water and carrots?"

She pursed her lips again. "Remember what I said about judging yourself."

"How does one gain weight when they aren't eating anything? I was in a coma! I was literally eating nothing and I gained weight. Which can only mean that I had a serious problem before I went into that coma."

"They put food into a tube for you, Emma. You had to be eating something to survive."

"Yeah. What they put into my tube was more calories than I was eating here," I said. I had to make her see. The daughter they had, the girl that I used to be, didn't walk on water like they wanted me to believe.

"Whatever, Emmie. It's done," she stated in exasperation. "We'll go shopping soon, when you feel up to it. In the meantime, you can order some clothes online if you like. You have credit cards in the purse I brought you. It's in your luggage."

"Thanks," I muttered.

"I'd really like it if you bought some clothes and anything else you want. This is your room, your life, and your credit cards that your father got you. It's yours, Emma," she pressed. "You don't have to feel guilty, or like you don't have the right or don't belong. You do. We'll all get used to things together. It may take a while, but we're family. Thick or thin, hell or high water, fire or brimstone. Deal?"

I found myself feeling soft toward her. She was trying so hard.

"OK." I took a deep, deep breath. "OK. I'm sorry."

She came and took my face in her hands. She smelled like expensive vanilla. "Honey, I love you any way that I can get you. I'm just trying to help you by showing you the person you used to be, all right? We're a very open family here. We always talked about everything." She chuckled. "You used to come home from cheerleading practice and complain to Felicia and me about boys and school and just everything. So you can come to me about anything. Anything at all."

"I'd like that," I said. "Honestly, it's hard to imagine having a mom that you talk to about everything."

She smiled wryly. "And sometimes, I wanted to strangle you, but you were always honest, I'll give you that. The time you came to me after you and Andrew had sex the first time, ugh…"

My world fell to the floor. I wasn't a virgin? Now that I thought about everything they had told me about myself, and the way Andy was with me, it wasn't a surprise, but to know that I wasn't a virgin…and couldn't even remember it…

She was oblivious to my turmoil as she kissed my forehead and said she'd let me get settled, she'd buzz me when it was time for dinner. I didn't know what that meant, but it didn't matter.

Andrew not only stole my first kiss, but now he stole my virginity as well. OK, so maybe I was being a little harsh. I probably threw it at him from the way he talked, but not being able to remember something like that…

I felt robbed.

So I dove in, deciding to distract myself by exploring my room. I couldn't think of a better way to get to know myself anyway than to find out all the nooks and crannies of the girl who used to live here.

I started with the closet. All the clothes were impossibly small. I probably gained two sizes since I'd worn anything in this closet. The extremely sad thing? I had been thinking before that I needed to gain a couple pounds to be healthier.

I pulled one shirt after another out and stared at them. It looked like a toddler's closet. The shirts were so small and skimpy. And the shorts were the same. Jean shorts underwear. That was exactly what it looked like. My mother was fine with me leaving the house that way? And school? What did I wear to school?

I found myself pulling everything out, item by item. Skirts that were *so* not skirts and everything else. I threw them into the empty hamper and stared at the empty closet. Not one thing…not one that I could or *would* wear. I finally searched high and low and found a pair of cheer sweatpants and a t-shirt. I folded the clothes I had removed, not sure of what to do with them. I placed them on the dresser neatly and tried to pretend that I wasn't a stranger there.

I looked around the room. A little table was full of make-up and jewelry. Two prom tickets and pictures lined the mirror's edge. It took me a second to find myself in them. There were several cheer photos, some random, some posed. There were a couple of my sister and me, and a whole slew of Andy. The ones of us, we didn't look happy, we looked privileged. We didn't look like we were in love, we looked like we loved being on top of the world. I always positioned myself in front of him, and his arms were always wrapped around me from behind or around my shoulders. It wasn't intimate, which surprised me.

I looked so aloof and uncaring, like this was all just part of the job or plan. I squinted and tried to make some sense of it. Then I heard a dinging sound. I looked around and followed the sound all the way to my suitcase. I opened my purse and fished my phone out. I had a text message. I smiled when I opened it.

Mason.

I know u probably don't miss me yet, but I miss u. I hope going home was good for you...but I have a feeling that it wasn't. Just remember that I'm here whenever u want to talk. - Yoda

I laughed and found myself fighting against clutching the phone to my sad little chest. How was it that my own family could be so clueless about me, but Mason could send one text that said it all?

I texted back.

Stalker! How did you get this # ;) Thank whoever it was. And ur right. Coming home wasn't fun, but I'm...adjusting. & I do miss u. - The other me

I sent it and heard another noise. It was a buzzing coming from the wall. I followed it to the speaker box and pressed the button that said TALK. "Hello?"

It was Isabella. "Come down for supper, honey."

What could I say? "OK."

I had a freaking call box in my bedroom. It was going to take some serious getting used to. I put the phone aside and peeked my head out into the hall. Surely it wouldn't be too hard finding my way to the dining room, right?

After about five minutes of searching, I finally found it. When I showed up, my parents were there at the head of the huge table, but it looked as though they were going out to a fancy restaurant. I followed their eyes down to my sweatpants and back up. "I didn't realize I needed to dress up for dinner."

"You don't *have* to," Isabella reasoned, "we just always...have."

"I'll remember that." I went to the chair she pointed to and sat down as quietly as I could. The place was not only immaculate, but it was irritatingly quiet. I felt like my breaths were the loudest thing in the room, and they had waited on me to get there to start eating.

Even the gentle clanking of Isabella's spoon on her soup bowl wasn't as loud as my breathing. I felt beyond awkward. She ate in silence and my father was just as quiet before he began the inquisition: How did I like my room? How was I holding up? Did I do some online shopping yet?

"All fine," I said, encompassing the whole shebang. "So, um, when do I start school?"

"Don't you want to hold off for a bit?" he asked. "I thought maybe I could take some time off of work and we could maybe go on vacation."

"Oh, yes!" Isabella cried in happiness. "Let's go to Fiji again!"

Fiji?

"Uh...but I need to make sure that I keep caught up with school. I want to graduate, no matter what."

"But you love Fiji...you may not remember, but you do."

"I'm not doubting my love for Fiji. I'm sure it's just fine." I tried to rein in my irritated tone. They were treating me as though I were ungrateful because I wanted to go to school instead of vacation. Go figure. "I just got home. I just want to start to feel normal in my surroundings again before we go on vacation to get away from it all. Plus, I have therapy every week."

Isabella's eyes settled on mine at that. She seemed to be searching for something. I tried not to supply what she was looking for. "That's fine," she eventually said. "I already called the school and said you would be making your way back at some point soon, so they know to expect you whenever."

"Thank you."

"Don't worry about it." She smiled. "So the sooner you go shopping for some clothes, the sooner you can go back to school."

"Let's go tomorrow," I replied quickly.

Rhett chuckled and exchanged a knowing look with Isabella. "There's our girl."

Little did he know that shopping held nothing for me, but it was the only way I was going to get back to school and out of this house.

Useless Fact Number Nine

When possums are 'playing possum', they aren't actually playing.
They literally pass out from sheer terror.

The next day, we went shopping. Isabella disapproved of every outfit choice, so we settled on a happy medium. She'd go do her own shopping and I'd meet her at the food court in an hour. So that's what we did.

We lugged the bags home, ate some dinner, and I had my session with Mason. She drove me there and even sat in the therapy room for our session, which she'd never done before, so I didn't really get to speak to Mason at all. But we got some more progress as I lifted and did twenty reps with a three pound barbell. It doesn't sound like a huge feat, but for me, it may as well have been the Grand Canyon of feats. Mason grinned with his back to Isabella and was so proud. It made me feel amazing. But though Isabella was happy for me, she couldn't quite grasp the importance of it.

Mason told me to take a long, warm Epsom-salt bath, and that's what I did. I was still sore, but it was amazing how loose I felt afterwards.

That night, I tried to sleep through the anticipation and anxiety of going to school the next day. It was a Friday, no less. So one day of school and then a weekend, so the next Monday was practically going to be just like the first day with that much time to dwell.

The little glowing dragonflies on my ceiling were my only source of comfort. Not only did it remind me of the love my father had for me even when I didn't remember it, but it also reminded me of the hospital, which reminded me of Mason.

As I was falling asleep, I got another text from him.

Tomorrow's the big day, school girl. Go learn something. ;)

I grinned.

That is the plan. Thank you.

Goodnight, Em.

Night, Yoda.

It was amazing how easy it was to fall asleep after that.

"But you always wear your hair up, Emma. I'm just trying to help you."

My exasperated mother didn't understand that I wasn't trying to pretend I was the same old me that I used to be. I wasn't trying to put on a show and play like I was fine or remembering or willing to be the old me so easily. Which was of course what she wanted.

"I hate ponytails. I don't even know why I used to like them."

"I just think it'll be easier for you to get along with your friends and all if you just be the girl that they remember."

I shook my head and caved. "Fine."

She smiled in triumph and set right out to rectify the hair. She gently brushed it out and set it up high. All I could think of was swinging my head and it flopping back and forth like Malibu Barbie.

"See. Now when you turn your head, it swings out to the side. So cute like that."

I rolled my eyes where she couldn't see me. "OK. I'm ready. Let's go, please."

She nodded and kissed my father goodbye. He stood at the counter, watching me go like I was leaving for kindergarten with a furrowed brow. "It'll be fine," I assured him. "I have my cell. It's just school."

"But are you sure you're ready to go back?"

"I am. I'm ready to start living again."

He nodded slowly and leaned in to kiss my forehead. "Have a good day, Emmie."

"Thanks. You, too."

Once we made it outside, I knew exactly what had happened when I saw Andy leaning against his Beamer in the driveway.

"You called him?" I accused.

"Someone had to take you to school."

"I thought that someone was going to be you."

"I thought you'd feel more comfortable with Andy taking you. He can guide you, get you back in with your old friends, and show you the ins and outs again. Plus…he is your boyfriend."

I could have laughed. So, if she had to choose between Mason or Andy, she chose him, huh? I scoffed and made my way to him. "Hey, babe." He grinned. "You look…great. Different, but great."

I was comfortable, that's what I was. I had decided to wear jeans and a couple of layered tank tops, but my hair *was* in this ridiculous ponytail, now wasn't it? "Ready to go?"

"Hey," he protested and laughed. "No loving for the guy who's been waiting patiently for you to come back?"

I sighed and let him engulf me in his arms. He smelled too good to be going to high school. He leaned back and took my lips before I could see what was happening. I pushed him slightly. "Andy."

"Sorry. I've missed you, babykins. Can't blame a guy for that, right?"

Actually, I could.

He opened the driver side door and hopped in. He jerked his head, telling me to get in. I raised my eyebrow at that, but did what he asked. The ride to school was too short. I had no time to mentally prepare myself before he was pulling in and getting a perfect spot up front, as if it had been saved for him, though his name was nowhere to be seen on it.

"You nervous?" he asked and took a small comb out, fixing his spike in the rearview mirror.

"A little," I answered truthfully.

"Don't be." He tossed the comb into the backseat and turned to me with a smile as he slid his arm along the back of my seat. "We have almost every class together. And the crew knows that you're coming back today. They're expecting us. Besides," he leaned in and kissed my cheek, "the girl I knew was fearless and feisty. Don't let them get to you. If someone says anything, and I highly doubt they will, I'd bust their teeth in. OK?"

"I'll be fine." I started to open my door, but he stopped me by grabbing my arm. "What?"

"Just wait a second," he said easily. "I really missed you."

"You keep saying that," I said wryly.

"It's true. Kiss me, babe."

He yanked me to him with a hand on the back of my neck. He almost touched my lips before I pushed his chest and cleared my throat. "Andy, please stop, OK? I'm still trying to figure some things out. I know my mom called you, but I'm just not sure…what I want right now, OK? Friends?"

"As long as we're together, it doesn't matter. I can wait," he said sweetly. "Come on, beautiful."

I got out and felt the burn of everyone's eyes on me all at once. It was actually welcomed when Andy glared at everyone and threw his arm over my shoulder. I'd have given anything to have Mason there with me instead, but I guess my mom was right. Andy knew the school and our friends and everything, and it was apparent that he had pull with the kids when he glared and they turned away quickly.

He pushed the double doors to the school and this was it. Banners telling seniors to buy their prom tickets soon lined the walls. Signs saying that sign-ups for summer school were coming to a close and you better get to it if you didn't want to repeat the year again. Grey lockers lined the walls with people standing all around them, getting things out, chatting, and putting on make-up.

I gulped when I saw Andy leading us to a gaggle of girls and guys who all seemed to be the *pretty* people. They all stopped and stared. In fact, the entire hall stopped and stared. I hated to feel so weak, but I still found myself cringing into Andy's side. He tightened his grip on my shoulder and I felt him jerk as he yelled, "Got a problem?"

People slowly turned back to their own groups and I actually felt pretty darn grateful to him, but then I was faced with the people who were supposed to be my friends. Three of the girls came forward while the other hung back. They practically tackled me, taking me from Andy, and all three hugged me at the same time. Over the shoulder of one of the girls, I saw Andy smirk before shaking his head at them and making his way to the group. He bumped fists with a couple of the guys and stood back, watching me.

"Emmie!" one of the girls said. "We've missed you so much."

"Yeah," another one said. "My goodness. Everyone's been talking nonstop about you coming back to school! You are so *it* again. It's so sickening." She smirked. "You don't even have to try!"

They giggled, but I was so confused that I just stood there.

"Emmie, you ok? You look pale. Or…maybe it's just your lack of make-up." She grimaced. "Did you not have time to get ready this morning?" She eyed me up and down. Her grimace grew.

"I, uh... Who are you?"

She scoffed. "Really?"

The redhead came to my rescue. "We knew she had amnesia. Don't get your Victoria Secrets in a twist, Cookie."

Cookie? The redhead looked back at me with sympathy. "I'm Kali." I remember her name from my mother earlier. "And this is Cookie and Tonya."

I licked my lips. "Hi."

Cookie shook her head. "It's just too weird."

"Cookie," Kali hissed.

"It is! She's so…docile!"

"I'm sorry," I said. "I'm still adjusting. I really just want to get through the rest of the year and graduate."

"Andy told us you were doing your schoolwork in the hospital." She scoffed. "You had a perfectly good excuse to get out of schoolwork and you *asked* them to bring it to you?"

I bristled a little. "I was already six months behind, remember? I want to graduate and not be stuck here another year."

She grimaced. "Oh, yeah. You're right. Can you imagine being stuck here next year with juniors?" She made a gagging noise.

I tried not to roll my eyes. Then Andy came back to us and wrapped his arms around me from behind. I pulled his hands away and gave him a look. He winked. *Winked.*

Suddenly, I felt him tense up and followed his gaze to a girl. She looked stricken, but the second her eyes met mine, she turned away guiltily and practically ran the other way. I looked at Andy with question, but I understood everything with his silence. This was the girl he'd been dating. This was the girl he'd dumped for me. I felt awful because she felt so guilty. How would she have known I would wake up?

"Seriously, skank. She had him first," Cookie sneered at the girl who was already gone and chuckled. Andy just worked his jaw.

They all seemed nice enough, be it a *ton* shallow. Andy took my hand to take me to the office. Mason flashed through my head and I took my hand from his quickly. He looked horribly dejected. "Friends, remember?"

He nodded, but didn't look happy about it. When we reached the office, he let me go in and said he'd see me later. I knew I'd upset him, but having Mason's trust was more important to me. I turned to the secretary at the desk and went to tell her my name and why I was there, but she beat me to it. "Emma Walker! Oh, so glad that you're back. How are you?" she said and dragged it out for emphasis.

"I'm...OK."

She smiled wryly. "You don't remember me, do you?"

Wow, really? "No ma'am."

"I'm Mrs. Schuller!" she said excitedly. "Come on. Let's get you to your first class."

I followed her to a classroom and she opened the door, peeking her head inside.

"They're ready for you," she announced and slung the door open. When I made my way inside with nothing but my purse, I jumped in surprise when they all started to clap. I tried to smile and show them I was grateful, but I felt so raw. I didn't know one single person there except for Andy, who was sitting in the back. He smiled as he watched me cringe and make my way to the empty seat next to him.

The first half of the day passed in a blur. Andy took me to all of our classes and I tried to pay attention, but it was pretty impossible when people stared everywhere I went. After lunch, Andy showed me where my locker was and gave me my combination. I didn't ask how he knew it, I was just grateful to have it.

But looking inside definitely gave me an inside peek of the girl I used to be. It was filled with make-up, a couple of school books, a Cliff's Note on The Scarlett Letter, a huge mirror tacked to the door, tons of cutesy notes and kiss-lips on paper, and a few class notes...but they had other people's names on them, not mine.

When I turned to go, I ran smack into a blonde girl with red streaks in her hair. "Oh, gosh. I'm sorry."

She sighed and picked up her book from the floor. "It's fine." She eyed me objectively as she righted herself. She looked to be waiting for something. "You don't remember me?"

I waited. She knew the answer already. Andy was impatient though. "Babe, come on."

"Yeah, *babe,*" she sneered. "The royal court is waiting for you."

I squinted in confusion, but Andy took my arm. "Come on. It's lunch. Everyone's waiting. Plus…we don't associate with them."

"Them?"

"People who aren't us," he replied, as if that explained it all.

I felt my mouth fall open with shock. Did he really just say that with a straight face? He towed me to the cafeteria. And I say towed because that's exactly what happened. It was just like the pictures in my house of us. It was a picture or façade of togetherness and love, but it was more like we were posing. When we walked in, it didn't escape my notice how his arm conveniently stopped tugging me and wrapped itself around my waist instead. He leaned in and whispered in my ear, "It's all right, babe. Don't freak out. The old you ruled this school. Show them that you're still that girl."

But I was not that girl anymore.

Then he kissed my cheek and grinned like he said something sweet…or dirty, maybe. I let him. I put myself on co-pilot and Andy was apparently driving. He steered me through the throngs of staring eyes and sat us at a table with all the people from this morning. I sat and the redhead, Kali, slid me a diet soda across the table. "Here, babe," she said sweetly. "Now," she sat up on her elbows, giving the guys behind her a perfect view of her backside in that too-short skirt, "tell us all about sleeping for six months. What was it like?"

A guy beside her laughed and said, "Man, six months of sleep sounds like a dream come true for me. No school, no parents? Just dreaming of Kali in that skirt." He leaned back and bit his lip as he took a good view. She smacked his shoulder playfully and giggled, but they sat and waited for my answer.

Andy squeezed my leg under the table, making me jump a little. He leaned in. "You rule the school, remember? Buck up, babe."

I felt a scoffing breath escape my lips before I turned back to the group. They all waited so patiently and I wondered for just a second what it was like to be the old me. To have the attention and obvious allegiance of all these people. The old me probably soaked this up like a biscuit to gravy. She probably instigated their giggles and egged them on to make jokes and do all sorts of things. I swallowed and tried to be that girl. I tried to give them what they wanted.

"It sucked." They all laughed and looked at me affectionately, as if I'd said the punch-line instead of the opening statement. "Apparently they didn't put diet soda in my IV."

They laughed again. I felt this empowering bubble grow in my gut, but instead of it feeling awesome and…powerful, I felt wretched. I felt like the shepherd of a flock of sheep. The old me probably ate that up. It made me sick.

"Oh, sweetie," Kali said softly. "It's OK. It's understandable." I was shocked by her sweet words, but then…"We'll get you back to a size zero in no time! I'll order you a bigger size for your cheerleading outfit 'til then."

"Thanks," I muttered under my breath. She backtracked.

"Not that you're fat, honey." She looked to the other girls for help. "Right? You're still so fabulous."

"Yeah, so fabulous," Cookie said excitedly.

Kali kept going. "I mean…maybe I'll come over and help you get your wardrobe back together, OK? Your mom must've thrown your good clothes out. Poor thing." She made pout lips in my honor.

I just smiled and nodded.

"So," a guy in the back started. "You don't remember me? At all?"

I shook my head. "No. I don't remember anything from my life at all."

He grinned sadly in jest. "So that time we spent Seven Minutes in Heaven in Kali's closet in sixth grade—you've forgotten all about that? Really?"

"Shut it, Mark," Andy growled playfully. "That's probably why she went into a coma; to make sure she wiped *that* from her memory."

"Whatever!" Mark protested and pounded his chest. "I give the best tongue at this table. Ask anyone."

They spent the rest of the half hour just like that. The questions were stupid and the answers I gave were stupider, but they laughed and laughed. Maybe they were just trying extra hard to make me feel welcome by being so accommodating, but I somehow doubted it.

We left and Andy took me to math class. They didn't clap this time, but they all stared once again. And so the day went. He took me home and said he'd pick me up the next day. I didn't want him to, but agreed.

I was starving when I got home, so I searched the kitchen for a snack. A woman came in and said she'd make me whatever I wanted, but I told her it was OK. I could make my own. She seemed miffed and put out, but I didn't understand why.

Isabella bugged the crap out of me with all her questions about it. She was excited as the Chihuahua I didn't even know that we had. How I had missed that, I didn't know, but today, the little snippy beast followed me everywhere. Isabella said it was my dog, but he didn't seem to like me much. Maybe he could tell that I was different.

It sounded like he was telling the stranger to get out of his house.

Rhett was in meetings until late, but when he came in, he knocked on my door and asked me questions that were similar to the ones Isabella had. I hope I passed their tests as I tried to act excited and be upbeat. I texted Mason and told him everything was great. I hated lying, but didn't know what else to do.

The next day was a repeat of the first, except I tried extra hard on my wardrobe. I let Isabella help me a little, and she relished in it. Once I had some make-up in place, a high ponytail with swing factor, a scarf of hers wrapped around my neck with a pink tank top on, and the hoop earrings she'd slung in my ears, I was ready to go. Andy nodded his head in approval when I reached his car.

"Man, you look gorgeous. Just like you used to."

I tried not to sigh.

School was the same, like it was on repeat. Everyone stared, my friends acted like I walked on water, and I tried to smile and fake it. It must've worked. They asked me a million questions at lunch and I assumed that must've been normal with the old me. I must've been the attention holder, because they seemed almost at a loss for another question to ask when I wasn't speaking. It was beyond weird and sheep-like. I hated every freaking second.

This time at my locker, I found a note inside that said, "The baa baa have found their leader again."

Sheep. Exactly what I had been thinking. But Andy wasn't amused and said he knew whose handwriting it was. At lunch that day, I found out what happened to you when you crossed my so-called friends.

Kali was missing, but not for long. After we sat and lunch was underway, over the loud speaker we heard, *"Misty Potter, please come to the office. Your mom is here with a clean pair of underwear."*

I was horrified. They all sat and laughed. In fact, the entire lunchroom cackled and hooted. I searched for Misty, the red-streaked girl. When I saw her, it was all I could do not to run and tell her I had nothing to do with this. She was attempting to leave the cafeteria, but the football players were jostling her around and whooping. Finally she broke free, without a backward glance at anyone, and ran into the hall.

They'd done this for me. My *friends*. They probably thought I was proud of them for such a display of loyalty to me. That the old me would have ordered such an attack. I wanted to vomit.

I sat back in my chair. No one noticed that I wasn't partaking in the festivities with them. They were all too absorbed in one statement that seemed to be on repeat. "Did you see her face?"

Yes, I saw her face. It would haunt me.

Useless Fact Number Ten

Barbie's full name is Barbara Millicent Roberts

After school, Andy didn't drive me home. Apparently, I had cheerleading practice and my new, bigger sized uniform was here and should work just fine, they said. I shook with regret and disgust as I looked at myself in the full-length mirror. Who was this girl?

Kali came up behind me and put her chin on my shoulder. "Oh, honey. You'll be back to your old size in no time. Don't worry." Then she smacked my backside and yelled, "Let's go, skank! You've got a lot of catching up to do!"

She giggled as she left.

I felt...dirty for some reason as I made my way to the practice field. I wanted to go home, and bathe and wash away whatever this grimy feeling was.

"All right, beyatches! Listen up!" Kali yelled. "We've got our Emmie back." They all clapped and cheered. "But, as you can *see*," they giggled at my expense, "we've all got our work cut out for us whipping her back into shape. So, in Emmie's honor, everyone take a lap!"

They gasped and groaned. "Not fair!" one girl yelled.

"Run, skanks, run!" Kali yelled and laughed as they took off.

"You're not running?" I asked.

She smirked. "I took over as captain when you...took a nap." She smiled, but there was so much behind that smile. "Get going, Walker. Run that ass back down to manageable size."

I stared at her. I had an inkling to strip down right here, get the offending outfit off, throw it in her face, and tell her to kiss my fat, manageable assets. But I just stared instead, in silent contest. I needed to let her see that I wasn't about to be stomped on just because I couldn't remember the pecking order.

Eventually, like when you stared down a dog to see who'll look away first, she caved. "Dang, Emma, lighten up. I'm just joking. But you really do need to run. You've got to get your body back up to par for working out every day and going to competition again. Come on, I'll run with you."

What a change. I almost laughed, but instead, I ran with her. I didn't say a word, just listened to her chatter on about some boy she had been sleeping with from another school. After a short while, when I was about to pass out from exhaustion and had to stop, I ignored her thinly veiled insults about being so out of shape.

Not only had the coma taken my memory, but it had taken my ability to outrun her. And right then, that pissed me off more than anything.

That night, I was too exhausted to do anything. I barely made it into the house before crashing in the bed, not showered and not caring. My stomach growled, but I couldn't move a muscle. I didn't even get to text Mason because I fell asleep and stayed there until morning.

In the morning, I followed the same routine as the day before, and let Isabella doll me up. Andy growled his happiness about how gorgeous I was, and I endured another day of my friends and their disdain for anyone that wasn't in our circle.

But math class changed everything for me.

You know when you have an epiphany? If you've ever had one, you'll know that it hits you at a moment you might not expect. The smallest thing can set it off, but it will change your life. It will ruin everything you've worked to build and it will not think twice. And when it comes, there's no stopping it.

I sat in the back and tried not to think about much. It was closer to the end of the day. Honestly, I felt more than tired. My legs felt like Jell-O, my brain was mush from all the fake smiling and pretending that I was OK, and my right arm hurt from taking so many notes. It was amazing the simple things we take for granted. I'd have to rest for a minute while note taking and then hurry to catch back up.

Andy leaned over. "Babe, we'll just get notes from someone later. Don't worry about it."

"Get notes from someone?" I thought back to the notes in my locker. "Like make someone give me their notes?"

"Yeah. I told you, everyone loves you. You're the *it* girl." I made a face. He made his own face. Resolve. He forged on, harder to make his point. "Guys want to bang you, and girls want to be you." I made a gross face and he held his hand up. "I'm just saying. Stop acting like a…nerd or boob or something. They'll give you some slack for a few days, but you've got to start acting like the old you. The old you takes what she wants, doesn't work for anything, doesn't care what people say, and is gorgeous and on her game every damned day. Stop being *this*, and start being the girl that I want to be with."

I soaked that in. I leaned back in my seat and felt his eyes on me. He was just like my parents. They didn't have any interest in letting me work things out; they just wanted *that* girl back. Andy wasn't going to let me be me. He expected me to pretend that I was that girl, even if I wasn't.

I raised my hand.

"Yes, Mrs. Walker?"

"Can I go to the restroom, please?"

She looked at me carefully. "I guess so. Take the pass."

I stood and looked at her blankly. Oh, gah…she was going to make me say it. "Where's the pass?"

Every face turned to mine. She ticked her head to the side in question. I realized then that she was testing me. She didn't believe that I didn't remember? She finally moved her head to the right. "It's by the door. The little baseball bat keychain."

"Thanks," I muttered and grabbed it quickly before bolting. I practically ran until I saw the girls' bathroom sign. I pushed my way through and that was the invitation my tears had been waiting for. I slid down the wall with my back to the gross and grimy floor, but I just didn't care. Oh, how my chest hurt with the ache of holding in those sobs. And now they burst through me and all I could do was hang on to the ground for dear life and hope I survived.

I realized then what this was. I'd never mourned my life. I never understood until that very moment…that Emmie, that girl that everyone wanted me to be, was dead. She was gone. I may not have known her, but I mourned her. I was sorry that she died and I took her place. I pulled my knees up to my chest and cried and cried, and sobbed, and ached, and mourned, and rocked.

The coma was a liar. It gave everyone this false sense of security that she'd come back, but she was gone and I was here. And I wasn't her. No one here, or my parents, or anyone, got to mourn Emmie. They all assumed she'd come back one day or die on that bed the way they remembered her. But I took her place and I didn't belong.

This wasn't my body or my face or my life.

I cried for all of the people who wouldn't understand that Emmie was gone and didn't realize they needed to stop waiting for her to wake up. That this was my body now and they needed to bury Emmie and move on. And then I cried because I knew they'd never do that. They'd never understand that she was gone. They would all wait for her to come back one day, for me to miraculously remember everything and go back to being her. But even if that did happen, if I did remember, I couldn't go back to the way things were.

I was different and I think Emmie would be different because of me.

I sat at a loss of what to do with myself. Everyone was so eager for me to get back to normal, but I may have moved too soon. Maybe I wasn't ready to face her life. I thought it would help me make my decision, to come here and be with all of her friends, but it just made me doubt her.

And then it hit me. I just made my decision, didn't I? Emmie was gone. I couldn't take her place. I had to be me.

I felt a weight lift from my shoulders. I was going to be a disappointment and people weren't going to like me, but I had to be myself. I could no longer put on the façade that I was Emmie Walker, head cheerleader, girlfriend of Andy, and queen to the royal court.

I was Emma Walker, girl with a life to figure out, girl that was falling head over feet for her tattooed therapist, and who loved useless facts and glow-in-the-dark dragonflies.

I stayed there all the rest of that period and the next. I heard the bell ring, but stayed. I felt an odd calm in that moment and I wasn't ready to let it go yet. So it shouldn't have surprised me when the door opened and a group of girls poured in. It was the girls' bathroom after all.

"What's the matter with you?" one of them asked, making them all turn to find me, tear-streaked and sitting on the dirty floor. I could tell by her tone and their looks that they had no love for the old me.

"Just thinking," I answered softly.

She scoffed in a laugh. "Yeah…" She checked her lipstick in the mirror. She was a normal looking girl, but a little on the heavier side according to my *friends*. I could only imagine that I'd picked on this girl at one time or another. "Trying something new, huh?"

"I don't remember you," I told her. "Any of you. I'm sorry if I ever did anything to you, but I'm not the same girl anymore."

She scoffed again. "Miss Emma Walker is apologizing to me…while bawling her eyes out on the bathroom floor." She laughed. "Wow." She looked back at me and smiled. "Karma's a beyatch, ain't it?"

Then she led the way for all the girls to walk out. The girl who I had bumped into, Misty with the red streaks, was there, too. A sympathetic look crossed her face for just a second before it fled and she followed them out the door.

Yeah. I had to agree with her. Karma had no love for me.

I made myself get up. I washed my face and hands, looked at myself in the mirror, and knew the one thing I wanted to do more than anything else in that moment. I pulled my cell out and called the hospice hospital and asked to talk to Mrs. Betty. When I asked her where Mason lived, she hesitated. I wondered about that, but begged her for it. She caved and I stuffed the phone back into my pocket. Even though I knew I couldn't hide my puffy eyes from everyone, I left the bathroom and went right out of the school. It was time to leave anyway, apparently, as the parking lot was unloading.

Andy saw me and seemed relieved, but I turned the other way to avoid him. When I looked back to see if he was following, I saw the understanding on his face. He knew I was done. He got into his car and slammed the door.

I didn't know if Mason was home yet, but I'd wait if he wasn't. It wasn't too far away and I needed to see him like I needed to breathe.

A few minutes later, a car rolled up slowly beside me. The engine revved a bit and I felt a shudder roll over me. It was like a flashback, but…not. It was like that day when Mason's ringtone jolted through me in such a vile way. That's what this did to me. I caught myself on my hands in the grass beside the sidewalk. Andy slammed on the breaks and was there before I could think. "Are you OK? Emma?"

He took my face in his hands and that seemed to bring me back down. "I just had a…" I shook my head. "Nothing. I'm fine."

"Emma…" He released my face and sat on the sidewalk beside me with a hard thump. "Please don't do this. I'm sorry about what I said to you."

"Andy…look at me." He did, reluctantly. "I'm not her-"

"Not listening to this." He stood. "Come on. I'll give you a ride home."

"I'm not going home."

He seethed. "Fine." He eventually gritted out. He reached into his open window and grabbed something. "Here. I got your purse for you from math."

"Thanks," I whispered.

"I'll pick you up tomorrow, Emmie, give you a little time to think. But this isn't over. I've got a lot to make up for with you and you're not going to just run away from me."

With that, he got in his car and left. I was so confused, but stood and slung the purse over my shoulder to rest across my chest. I looked in the way of Mason's street. Even if he wasn't ready to be with me, or he thought I wasn't ready, I needed him tonight.

So my steps quickened until a couple streets over when his house came into view. With my breathing out of control, I rested my arm on his mailbox and tried to catch my breath. His mailbox said, "You're at the Wright house." I laughed at that and made my way up the driveway.

It was a small, beaten little house. And the car in the driveway was as close to a beater as I'd ever seen. Or remembered.

I stepped on his porch and it didn't matter what his house looked like. I missed him and couldn't wait to grab him. I knocked softly at first, then a little harder when no one came.

And then there he was. I smiled wide and it took me a second to notice the look on his face didn't match mine. He quickly came outside and shut the door behind him. "What are you doing here, Emma?"

I was stunned for just a second at his reaction before I could speak. "I wanted to see you. Needed…to see you."

"You can't just come by like this. How did you even get my address?"

"I called Mrs. Betty," I blurted before I realized that maybe I shouldn't have told him who told me. "I begged her."

He shoved his hands in his pockets. "Why? You could have just texted me."

I tried once more. Maybe he was just surprised to see me. Maybe he didn't want me to see his house. "Can I come in for a minute? I want to talk."

"No," he said quickly and looked at the door before back to me. "No, I'm...busy."

Oh, no... I looked at the door and the puzzle pieces got closer together. "Is someone here?"

He licked his lips. "Emma."

"Is someone here with you?" I said a little louder. It was then that I heard the noise from inside. I looked at him pleadingly, once more, to tell me that he was alone. That I hadn't placed all my faith into this man and had been so, so wrong.

"Emma..." He looked away guiltily and I turned to go. "Emma!"

I didn't stop. Though I was dead tired, and my head practically dragged behind me, I walked all the way home. When I reached my house, I didn't go inside. I sat on the bench under the archway to the garden and somehow cried even more after the day I'd had. I thought my tears were empty, but they came powerfully. I sat on that bench, and even when the darkness came, I stayed.

I guess I was putting too much pressure on Mason, right? We weren't a couple. I was just a stupid kid and he was a man with a house and...needs. Gah, that was so stupid. He was the one who said he'd wait! He was the one who said he wanted me and was willing to let me figure things out. I didn't realize that meant that he was going to be dating or whatever he was doing in the meantime.

I heard the engine, but I assumed it was Rhett when it pulled in. It wasn't. I looked up to find the beater sitting there and Mason stepping out. He looked up at my house much like I had a few days ago when I arrived. Like it was a monster that real people didn't live in. Like it was over the top and gaudy. Like it was...unreal.

He finally saw me and stopped. His face carried a range of emotions. Regret...longing, resolve. I stayed still as he shoved his hands into his pockets and came my way. The street lamps were the only thing that lit his path, but I could still the small movements his lips made as they twitched.

He sunk to his knees at my feet and put his hands on my knees. "Emma...I didn't want you to find out this way."

I pushed his hands off and stood, but he grabbed my hands to stop me. "Wait. Just hear me out. It's not what you think."

"What else could it be?" I looked back at him. "Besides, you're not mine, right? I can't tell you not to be with someone else." I was proud of myself that I managed to say it without bursting into tears.

"Come with me. Please?"

"Where?"

"I want to show you something," he confessed, but it didn't sound like he really wanted to.

I steeled myself. "I'm not sure that I want to see it."

"Please," he begged, still on his knees.

I couldn't say no to him this way. "OK," I whispered.

He kept my hand as he stood and towed me to his car. He held the door open for me and it squeaked with the motion. "Sorry, it's not a Lexus," he sneered as he looked at the house.

"I'm not a Lexus kinda girl," I answered and climbed inside.

He came around and put the car in drive. The drive was so much shorter than it was walking it. He opened my door for me again and held my hand all the way to the door. I wish I could have enjoyed it.

He stopped at the front door and waited, as if preparing himself. I softened at the look of agony on his face. "I don't know what you have to tell me, but I can see that you don't want to." I looked at the floor of the porch. "I know that I don't have any claim to you, but I thought-"

He cut me off as he lifted my chin and kissed the corner of my mouth. I no longer breathed as he said, "Stop it. This isn't about you and me. That's a given." I felt my heart skid. "This is about...facing demons." His breath shuddered. "And it's time that you met mine."

I didn't know what to say to that, so I stayed quiet. He blew a big breath before opening the door and closing it behind us. He took his jacket off and hung it on the wall tree, doing the same to mine. Then he looked at me as he called out, "Mamma?"

Useless Fact Number Eleven

*In an average lifespan, the human heart circulates
55 million gallons of blood.*

Mamma? As in his mother who had died in an accident?

"Mamma, I'm home," he called again and went around the corner, taking me with him. In the back of the den was a woman, very thin and pale, who sat in a wheelchair. She looked up and held a frightened look on her face. Then she looked closer at Mason and sighed in relief before saying, "Mason, what happened to you, son. Your hair…"

He rubbed it self-consciously before squatting down in front of her. "I know, Mamma. Look," he looked back at me, "I brought someone I want you to meet."

She smiled at me. "Are you a senior, too?"

I squinted in confusion, but answered. "Yes, ma'am."

"This is Emma," he said softly and gave me a shy smile that had me melting at its honesty. "I wanted her to meet you, Mamma."

"She must be a special one," she said and eyed me. "You never bring girls home."

I felt a weight lift from that statement.

"My Mason is Salutation this year. Did you know that?" she said proudly. Mason looked at her sadly with a look I hadn't processed yet.

"No, ma'am."

"Well, come have a seat. Mason, get her a drink or something. I taught you better manners than that."

He chuckled and stood, calling over his shoulder as he went to the kitchen, "Yes, ma'am."

I sat next to her on the couch beside her wheelchair. The place was clean and clutter free, but small. There was a table near the fireplace that was lined with medical supplies and the place smelled like bleach and other things. It reminded me of my room at the hospital. I looked back to her. "I love the fireplace. I'm always so cold," I said. "It would be nice to have one."

"It's not much, but it's home. And my other son, Milo, will be here soon, too."

Mason has a brother, too?

"Mamma," Mason said, handing her a cup with a lid and me a glass of tea. "Milo's not coming home, remember?"

"What do you mean?" she asked haughtily.

He looked at me, as if this meant something, and then back to her. "Mamma, there was an accident, remember? You were injured and were in a coma for a month? You lost your memory. Milo moved out."

"I was…" She looked around the room and back at Mason. "I was in accident," she said, tears already pooling. "What happened?"

"It's OK, Mamma. It was a long time ago. I'm going to take Emma for a walk, OK?"

"OK," she said carefully and looked around confused. He handed her the remote.

"Here. *The Price is Right* is on."

"Oh, how I love that show." He flicked it on for her and put the remote on the chair arm. He grabbed my hand and towed my stricken self out of the room. An older woman came in from the other room. She wore scrubs and Mason said we'd be outside for a while.

I heard his mamma yell, "What happened to Bob Barker?" as we shut the door.

He slipped my coat back on me and took us across the backyard to a picnic table. He shifted down to lay lengthwise on it and beckoned me to him. I lay next to him and wrapped the coat around myself tighter. I waited. I knew I was about to learn something epic and life changing from Mason Wright.

After a long while, he began. "When I was in high school, I was a little bit of a troublemaker. Nothing bad. I did well in school, but we partied on the weekends a lot. One weekend, I left my phone at home. Usually, when I got too wasted to drive, I'd get a ride or I'd call Mamma, she'd come get me and yell at me." He laughed sadly. "But that night, I was really drunk and stayed out later than I usually did. My friend offered me a ride, but I declined because he was just as drunk I was. I tried to get him to stop, but he got mad and pushed me down before speeding away. So I decided to walk. On the way home, I heard the sirens. I knew something bad had happened." He stopped, his body jolted a little at his memory. I turned to him a little and took his hand in mine. I laid it across my ribs and cradled it with my other one. He continued on. "When I came up on the scene, I saw my friend's car. I knew he was drunk and should have tried to stop him harder. I ran to his car and he there, on the ground where they laid him out. He was dead."

"Oh, Mason," I whispered.

"But the worst part?" He said and sneered at himself. "I didn't even realize for a few minutes that the other car involved, the other car that my friend had hit? It was my mom."

"Oh, Mason," I pleaded harder, begging him in a whisper to tell me it wasn't true. "Mason, no."

"He died driving drunk, and she was in a coma for a month because she saw my cell phone on the mantel. She was worried I couldn't call her to come get me and that I might try to drive home drunk. So she was coming to get me from that party."

I let the tears come then, unable to dam them back any longer. He turned to look at me and moved his unoccupied hand to wipe under my eye. "When she woke up after that month, she could remember things from her life, but could retain no new memories. Every day since then, over four years ago, when she wakes up in the morning, she believes I'm still nineteen. She doesn't know that she can't remember. She doesn't remember that my little brother Milo left after that, and moved in with a friend because he hates me and blames me for what happened." I bit my lip to stop the sob. "And when we go back inside to say goodbye, she won't remember that she met you, and she won't remember that I told her about the accident."

I lifted one hand to his cheek and just stared at him. Finally, I said, "So you basically have to tell her what happened, every single day. You have to remind her about the accident."

"And she notices that I look older. But what will happen when I look *really* older? What about when she does? What about her freaking out because she can't figure out why, for her, I'm nineteen one minute and then thirty-five the next?"

"I had no idea," I whispered. "Is that why you started working in physical therapy?"

He nodded. "It was my fault. She was coming so I wouldn't drive drunk and was almost killed by a drunk driver instead. I had to make amends as much as I could. So I took local classes. Didn't go away to college like I had planned, and I have no life. She is my life," he said with a smile.

I ached for the man. I would have given anything to take that all away from him. "It wasn't your fault."

"Don't," he recoiled. "Don't try to make me feel better. That's not why I told you. I brought you out here so you'd see what my life was like. This was another reason that I wanted you to figure things out for yourself before getting too attached to me."

"You think I'd want nothing to do with you because of your mom?"

He swallowed, his eyes full of hope. "Do you? This is my life, Em. I want to make sure you understand that. I work so that I can hire a nurse and pay the bills, but that's it. I'm broke. I'll always be here with her because I can't leave her."

"That makes you honorable and amazing, not someone I'd want nothing to do with," I countered.

"No, it doesn't, Em," he shouted and stood from the table. He paced in the grass and gripped his hair. "I didn't tell you all of that so you'd kiss me and make it all better, OK?"

"I know. I'm not trying to do that. I just-"

"Can't do this," he growled. "I cannot sit here and listen to you make out like what I did was perfectly fine."

"I'm not-"

"Come on," he ordered and gripped my hand. He gently pulled me up, despite his obvious anger, and he towed me to the back door.

"I don't want to go home yet," I protested.

"I need you to," he said and softened at my obvious look of distress. "Emma, I've got so many things going on in my head right now. Please."

"Fine," I whispered and pushed the door open. I waved to his mom, who looked confused. "Bye, Mrs. Wright."

"Bye, Mariah."

I looked at Mason. Mariah? He squinted at her in confusion. "Who's Mariah, Mom?"

"She is, silly. Now, shh. *Price is Right* is on."

We left, with me more confused and upset than I was when I got there. He drove me home and I didn't wait for him to say anything. I just got out slowly and walked up the path. He didn't say anything, and he didn't leave. I finally heard him pull away when I shut the front door. Isabella was there, and she wasn't happy. "Do you have any idea what time it is?"

"Sorry. I'm going to bed."

"That's a good idea," she bit out. "Next time, text me or something. You always texted me when you were going to be late."

"That's great," I mumbled. "An order of guilt with a side of disappointment, please."

"What?" she hissed.

"Nothing. Goodnight."

I threw myself into my bed and texted the contact that said Andy in my phone that I wasn't going to school the next day, so don't bother coming in the morning. But he did come. I told Isabella I wasn't going to school. I needed a break. Instead, I thought about all the things Mason had revealed last night. I looked up the accident on the internet and read the newspaper article.

After sitting there all day, wondering what I'd said to Mason to make him so upset, I'd had enough of stewing there.

I got up and knew I hadn't been cleared to drive yet. Apparently, I had to be cleared from therapy before I was allowed to again. So I got dressed in jeans and a normal t-shirt. I threw on a jacket and gloves, and practically ran to get out of the house. All this walking I was doing had to be good exercise for building up stamina, right?

So I walked. I found myself heading past the school and closer to Mason's. I didn't know why I was doing that. This early in the afternoon, he was still at work, I was sure. But my feet kept pushing me there, and soon, I was knocking on the door.

The nurse must have remembered me, because she smiled and swept her arm for me to come in. I awkwardly peeked in to see his mom in her same seat. The wheelchair was covered by the blanket and she seemed oblivious to it. "Hi, Mrs. Wright."

She looked at me. "Mariah."

"Uh…" Why did she keep calling me that? "It's Emma, actually."

She pursed her lips. "Emma, right, right. Are you selling cookies or something?"

"No, ma'am," I chuckled. "I'm a friend of Mason's. I just thought I'd…come sit with you for a while."

"Well, come on. *The Price is Right* is almost over."

I sat on the couch next to her and wondered what I was really doing there as I slid my coat off. I saw the same woman who had been on the show yesterday. I knew it was her because she was wearing a shirt that she made saying, 'Kiss Me, Carey.' So…this was a rerun that they had recorded. I wondered how many times she'd seen this episode.

This woman, who held Mason's heart so completely, that he'd given his life up for…

After *The Price is Right*, I asked what she wanted to do then. She shrugged before looking at a book on the mantle. "Oh. I can get caught up on my book. Do you mind reading to me? My eyes aren't what they used to be."

I nodded and picked the book up. It was bookmarked and I would bet that she had been reading the same chapter for over four years now, not realizing she'd read it hundreds of times. It broke my heart into a million pieces for her. I discreetly wiped my eyes and sat on the couch. The book was worn and aged badly. The pages barely held up as I opened the book. I read out loud. After reading a whole two chapters, with her gasping and biting her nails at the drama going on in those pages, I heard a car pull up.

Oh, no. I wanted to be gone by the time he got home.

"Mrs. Wright, I've got to get going." I put the book down quickly and tried hurriedly to put my coat on. "I'll come back and see you again soon, OK?"

"All right, sugar, please do. I... Mason!" she said happily. I turned to find him, slack jawed and in awe at seeing me there.

I turned to her again. "See you later, all right. Promise."

"Bye, Mariah!"

I didn't dwell on the fact that she was still calling me that, I just bolted around Mason as quickly as I could. I was still trying to yank my arm through my coat sleeve in his driveway when he came out. "Emma!"

I kept walking. I couldn't handle another lecture about why he was so guilty, and more than that, I couldn't handle him telling me to leave again. I just couldn't.

I heard his footsteps as he ran only a second before he grabbed my arm gently and turned me to him. "What are you doing here?"

This was exactly how it started yesterday, and it ended so well for me, now didn't it? "I'm sorry. I thought I'd be gone before you got here."

I tried to leave again, but he held tight. "But why did you come then if not to see me?"

"I came to see your mom." His brow bunched in confusion. "I feel...close to her." I cleared my throat. "Her life was taken from her, too. I know she can't remember the accident, or the fact that she has amnesia. I almost envy her that." I licked my lips. My reasoning wasn't coming out right. "I just wanted her to know that someone else was thinking about her. That she wasn't...alone."

"You came to see my mother...not me?"

I nodded. "Yeah. Sorry. Like I said, I thought I'd be gone before you got back. I wasn't trying to overstep. I know you don't..." I chuckled without humor, "want me here."

He came slowly and when his palm touched my cheek, lighting ran across my skin. "I was just coming to see you. Just stopped at the house to check on Momma first."

"What?" I said in surprise. "Why?"

"To beg for your forgiveness," he said softly, "for being such an ass. I can't forgive myself for what I did to my mother. That's my problem, not yours. I shouldn't have taken it out on you."

I shook my head. "Mason..."

"You came here today, even after what I did to you yesterday, to show my mother that she wasn't alone. You still came to show her kindness when I did nothing to deserve it."

"Mason, you took care of me for months, just like you're taking care of her. Everyone makes mistakes."

"Emma," he begged. "Please don't."

"So..." I began and couldn't stop the tear that slid down my cheek. "I learned all about the person I used to be this week. All the things I did, all the people I hurt. So you're saying that mistakes shouldn't have any forgiveness? Does that mean that I should never forgive myself for all the horrible things I did to people?"

"It's not the same," he growled in agony.

"Your mother was coming to save you because she loves you, because she wanted you to be safe."

"And now she's paying the price for me!" he yelled and pulled at his hair. "She shouldn't have to pay for my mistakes, not just once, but over and over again."

"I bet if you asked her if she'd do it again, she'd say yes in a heartbeat. Mason, you weren't drunk driving. You were doing the right thing by not getting into anyone's car that had been drinking and making the long walk home. You left your cell phone. That's the only thing you did." I felt the tears, but I couldn't stop. "You were a kid trying to do the right thing! How can you blame yourself for that!"

"I should have made him stop!" He shook his head furiously. "I should have stopped my friend somehow. Not only did I lose my mom that day, but I lost my friend and my brother." He looked into my eyes and they were as glassy as mine with unshed tears. "I lost everyone and everything that day. There's no one left to blame, Emma. There's no one left."

He turned and walked to his car. I didn't know what to do to make him all right except let him go. He obviously had been struggling for so long. As I watched him crank the car and drive away, I was once again left wondering if I was doing the right thing. Was this the real me? Was this where I was supposed to be?

I sat down on his porch step. I know he wanted to run away. He hadn't had anyone on his side for years, but he had been on *my* side. He helped me walk, for goodness sake! He stood up for me when no one else would. I couldn't leave him now. I couldn't walk home, be angry, and just forget how he'd told me about his world falling to pieces.

It was about a half hour before I saw him pulling in. He stopped the car and seemed more than stunned that I was still sitting there on his porch steps. He got out and walked slowly to the front of the car. "You're still here."

I nodded and gave him a look that I hoped said it all. "And I'm not going anywhere."

I saw his face crumple. I stood and he made quick strides to swoop me up. He buried his face in my hair and held me off the ground; the weight and pull of his arms made me feel absolutely alive. I felt him shaking, his chest wracked as he finally surrendered to himself. I held him tight and tried to fill him with every ounce of love and courage I possessed. I kissed his hair. I kissed his neck and his ear.

We stayed like that for hours it felt like, wrapped up together in his front yard. I was emotionally exhausted from the past few days, but I couldn't even imagine what Mason was going through.

When he settled and was just holding me, I decided we needed a change of scenery. "Will you show me your tattoo shop?"

He moved back a bit and looked at me from under his lashes. He shook his head. "Even after *that*, you still want to be here?"

"I'm not going anywhere," I repeated. I would say it as many times as it took to sink in.

"I see that," he said in awe. "God...I'm so sorry, Emma."

"Don't apologize."

"I wasn't trying to be mean or... I just couldn't take it. I felt like I was going to explode if I didn't get away."

I nodded. "I felt like that yesterday at school. And I left."

"You did?" he asked, full of concern. Then it dawned on him. "Oh, no. You were coming here to tell me about it, weren't you?" He covered his face. "And then I sent you home like a complete...jackass."

"It's OK." I smiled. "I'll tell you about it later. Will you show me your shop?"

"Anything." He took my face in his hands. "I am sorry."

"I know." I turned and kissed his palm. "I know."

He looked like he wanted to kiss me, but I didn't want it this way. He'd promised me a kiss that was going to last with me forever and never be able to forget, and that was the kiss I wanted. I took his hand and urged him to lead the way.

He pulled his keys out and unlocked the door to a small room on the side of the house. A world of opportunities opened when he swung that door open. I smiled and turned to him. "You said you still do tattoos sometimes, right?"

"Yeah, on the weekends, mostly." He saw my face. "What?"

I didn't even have to think. "Will you tattoo me?"

He laughed. "Yeah, right."

"I'm dead serious."

He realized that. He shut the door and rubbed the tattoo on his arm as if accessing a memory. "Why, Em? Why do you want one?"

"Because number one," I pulled my *To be normal* list from my pocket, took a pen from his work table, and wrote 'Get a tattoo' for number three. I turned it in the air to show him. He read it all and I saw his shoulders sink a little in concession.

"You made a list to be normal again?"

"Yes, and I'm going to fill it with all sorts of things that normal people do that can remember their lives and want to have memories of things like that."

"And you think a tattoo is what normal people get?" he said incredulously, but his mouth was beginning to show signs of a smile.

I continued with a grin. "Yes. And it would really piss off my parents, but I'm legal," he laughed, "but most important, I want to mark myself, like a timeline." I tucked my hair behind my ear and licked my lips. "I doubt the old me would have gotten a tattoo. I want to do something that will remind me every single day that I am not her. I want to get a tattoo in her…memory." I tried not to cry and cleared my throat. "Something for me to remember that the girl I once was doesn't have to the girl that I am. All the things I've done," I gave him a pointed look, "don't have to define me."

He nodded slowly. "You're sure? You know this isn't a Henna shop, right?" He had a teasing smile.

"I want it as permanent as can be."

"What do you want?"

"A dragonfly." I pulled my jacket off and laid it over the chair. I turned, lifted my shirt, and pointed to the back of my hip under my jeans. "Right here."

He licked his bottom lip and looked at the skin there for a long minute before gazing back at my eyes. "Are you sure? It'll hurt there."

"It'll hurt everywhere."

"Touché." He took his jacket off, too, and the button-up shirt that covered his black wife-beater. All of his tattoos were on display then and I couldn't help but move forward and let my fingers dance across them to explore. He shivered and chuckled. "Ticklish, remember?"

"Yeah," I said softly. "I remember." I ran my finger across a black cross on his left shoulder blade. "I really like this one."

"Thanks. It's my friend's…memorial."

"It's really beautiful." I examined his shop closer and looked at the chair with interest. "You still do a lot?"

"About one or two a weekend. Usually just friends, or friends of friends." He leaned his hip against the counter edge that held all the tools. He watched my every move and it made me feel more beautiful than I ever had before. Even with Andy saying the word, Mason's honest gaze was so much more potent. It went right to my gut.

"OK, what do we need to do?"

"If you're sure," he tested again and looked at me closely, "I'll draw something up and we'll get a print on your skin. Then I'll...get to it."

"OK, but I don't want to see what you draw."

"What?" He stopped.

"I want it to be a surprise."

"Emma," he protested. "Come on. You can't ask me to do that."

"Why not?" I asked softly. I went to him slowly, loving the way his throat worked through a gulp. I let my hand grip the front of his shirt. "I trust you."

He sighed. "What the hell did I do to deserve it?"

"You brought me back to life. You made me able to live again. I'd still be in that hospice bed if you hadn't pushed me and gave me the want to get better. You know it's true. Mr. Garner was always too busy. He would never have put the time in for me that you did. You took care of me."

"Anyone would have."

I shook my head. "And you never pressured me to be anyone but myself. You didn't even know me before, but you still wanted me to be me. Plus...it's not like I'm asking you to put a Mike Tyson on my face. No one will see it on my hip but me...and you."

His eyes closed for a second and a flash went across his face before it was gone. "OK. I'll draw something up."

"Are these yours?" I asked and flipped through a huge album of pictures of tattoos on all sorts of people, on all sorts of body parts.

"Yep. That's my résumé." He chuckled as he got some weird paper and tools out.

"Can I look at it?" I said, setting it on the counter and leaning on my elbows.

"Of course, baby."

I bit my lip at that and he locked eyes with me. He smirked at being caught saying such a thing and then turned around with a smile to start his drawing. The smile stayed permanently on my face as I looked through the artwork Mason had created. And it *was* art.

The way he put all those colors together that I wouldn't have known would even look good. The way he drew something in a way I would have never thought to do. Though I was so grateful that Mason was there when I opened my eyes in the hospital, his talents were definitely here. I wondered why he worked at the hospice at all when he could do this full time.

"How come there are only guys in this book?"

He looked back for a second. "I've never tattooed a girl before."

"Really?" I said with maybe too much satisfaction. He smiled in his profile as he worked.

After about a half hour, he said he was done. He left the drawing on the table and got some things ready. Then he beckoned me to the chair, which he laid all the way down flat. I was so nervous, in a good way. I absolutely couldn't wait to see what my skin was going to have when he was done.

"All right, uh…" He eyed me strangely, his eyes jumping from my jeans to my face. "The pants have got to go, at least down to your knees."

"It's fine." I kicked my shoes off and unbuttoned my jeans. The carpet was thick and cool under my socked feet. Mason's heavy eyes watched me the entire time. I slid the pants from one leg, then the other and laid them across the counter. And I was immensely thankful that my underwear were cute today. "Lay down here?"

He nodded. "On your stomach. I'm going to rub some cold antiseptic on you first."

I got situated and waited for him. When he came back, he rolled a small stool next to the chair and sat down. "I've got to pull these down on the side just a bit, OK?" His fingers hooked in my underwear, and I nodded. He tugged the side down and tucked a small cloth under the waistband to keep anything from getting on them.

I leaned my head on my arms, but looked back over my shoulder once more before letting him have complete control. He had gloves on and a small cloth that held the stinky, brown antiseptic in his hand. He held my eyes as he bent down and kissed my hip where he was about to put his artwork. I sucked in a breath. "Ready?" he whispered.

I nodded and turned to lay my chin on my arms again. I felt the bite of cold from the antiseptic, then him wiping it away, laying the paper over my skin and peeling it off. Then the whir of the needle began. One hand rested over my skin around the area and the other held the machine. "Here we go. Last chance to back out."

He waited, but when I didn't say anything, he began. The sting was considerable, but not unbearable. I could tell that he was being as gentle as possible. Don't ask me how. And every time he hit a particularly sensitive spot, and I hissed through my teeth, he hissed through his in sympathy.

I bit my lip so long and hard that it was practically numb by the time he was done an hour later. All my muscles ached from being tense for so long, but when he said he was done, I was more than happy to get up and move around. He helped me up and said, "I'll let you look at it in the mirror, but then we've got to tape it up, OK? It'll have to be bandaged for a while."

"OK," I said eagerly. I couldn't wait to see what he'd done. I knew I was going to love it. I was just curious as to the degree of love. Would I jump him right here and force him to hand over the mind-blowing kiss he'd promised? Or was I going to burst into tears because it was so beautiful?

There was a full-length mirror on the door and he stood me in front of it. I probably should have been embarrassed to be in my underwear, but I wasn't. This was *Mason*. He was in a box on the shelf all by himself. He was the one person I could be myself, utterly and completely, with.

"Let's take a look at it, shall we?" he taunted and smiled as he turned me around.

My eyes glued themselves to the beautiful white and ethereal green dragonfly. It looked like it was…glowing on my skin. Just like the ones on my ceiling did. I found myself crying on the spot. So between jumping him and bursting into tears, I was apparently going for option two.

"Oh, no. Emma…" He turned me to look at him and I fought him to turn back. I couldn't stop looking at it, but he took that as anger. "Dang, I'm so sorry. I should have known not to do it when you've been upset."

"I love it," I said through my tears and laughed. "I love it so much."

"Really?"

"Yes, really," I promised and turned a bit more. "It's like you read my mind."

"See, this is why I don't tattoo girls. I've never had a dude break out in tears before." I punched his gut lightly, making him laugh. He sobered as he said, "But they didn't look as beautiful as you do right now either."

He was looking at the tattoo, but when our eyes met, I waited for the fire alarm to sound. But it didn't. Mason did, however, give me my answer. He was going to kiss me, and it was going to be *the* kiss. His hands went around my hips, careful of the tattoo, and he pulled me to him. I stared up at him. He so wasn't who I thought he was. He turned out to be so much more.

"I made my decision," I told him in a whisper.

"I can see that." His voice was huskier than I'd ever heard it.

"My family can accept me, or they can't."

He nodded and rubbed his nose against mine, holding the closeness. "I've made a decision, too."

"And?" I waited, my bare feet on my tiptoes and my pounding heart in my throat.

"I'm done waiting."

He pressed his lips to mine and I held so still. When I felt the pressure there, his lips pushing against mine, I felt my legs threaten to buckle. The softness of his lips felt like taking a first breath, like opening your eyes and seeing the sun for the first time. I realized then that I had experienced all of those things with Mason, so it was fitting that he continued to give me my firsts in this new life. Soon the pressure increased even more and I knew he was asking me to open for him. That was it for me. I did as he asked, and when his tongue eased past my teeth and came to dance with mine, it was already better than anything Andy had ever dreamt about, let alone done to me. And my next thought was, Andy who?

He was such a gentleman. I was sure a guy like him that hadn't dated in such a long time, who had a willing, half-naked girl in his arms, had plenty of things that we could do on the brain. But this kiss, though mind-blowing in every sense of the word, was still setting a pace that said, *One thing at a time.*

His hand moved from my hip slightly, placing it snugly into the small of my back and pressing me to him. The other came up to hold my face like I was precious, like I was the only thing that mattered in this world for the time being. His lips pulled and drew little noises from my throat that surprised me. I pushed both arms around his back. He was hard all over, always hidden by the shirts he had to wear for work, but now, with barely anything but scraps between us, I felt it all.

His muscles moved under my palms and I found my fingers digging into his back to anchor me. The surprised groan that rattled through him and into my mouth had me sighing and sagging against him. He held me up to him easily and continued to ravage me. I loved how his tongue tasted. And I loved how that scratchy chin of his rasped against my cheek. It really *was* like I'd never been kissed before. He was so, so right about that. Nothing else before this mattered. And a hundred comas? I'd *never* forget this.

Then he changed pace, and instead of using his tongue, he sucked on my lips, one by one, like each was equally important. So I sucked back. While he firmly had my top lip, I gripped his bottom. He groaned louder at that, and I loved it so much that I didn't want him to ever stop making that noise. So I pushed my tongue past his lips like he'd done to me and pressed myself as close as I could get to him.

The hand on my cheek moved to the back of my head, tunneling through my hair and tugging just a little to give him control. And just like that, I was back to being the one unable to control the noise coming from me, and hanging on for my life.

He pulled back slightly. His ragged breaths loud. "Are you OK?"

"Yes, why?" I said too quickly. "Why are you stopping?"

He laughed a little. "You're shaking like a leaf, Em."

It was then that I realized how cold I was. And my muscles were giving out, too. My legs were trembling with the effort to stay on my tiptoes after all that walking. I looked at them like the traitors they were.

"Here." He reached for his coat and threw it around my shoulders. "I'm sorry. I should have thought about you getting cold without…your clothes on." He set me on the couch gently, mindful of the tattoo, wrapped in his jacket that smelled like him, and then sat beside me, pulling my legs into his lap. He massaged my calves. I wanted to moan at that, too, but held myself in check. "The muscles take a while to get used to strain and use."

He dug his thumb into the inside leg muscle and I did moan, unable to keep it in. He smiled smugly and kept doing it. "Sorry about this, too. I could have made sure we were sitting first before…that."

"I wouldn't change a second of…that." I smiled at him when his own smug smile turned shy. So honest. You could always see what was right on his face as the truth. "Thank you."

"For what?" he asked softly.

"For keeping your word."

He leaned forward and let his fingers rake through my hair, his thumb tracing my earlobe. "You're more than welcome, Emma."

"And thanks for the tattoo, also." I smirked at his silent chuckle.

"You're more than welcome," he repeated. "Anytime. Though," his thumb rubbed across my ankle bone, "inking this pretty white skin makes me feel like a villain."

I giggled slightly. "Are you going to start tattooing girls all the time now? Did I start a trend?"

"No," he said softly. "You will always be my one and only girl." We stared at each other. "You want to come back over tomorrow? I'll check your ink and we can eat some dinner if you want. You can tell me everything that's been going on with you."

"Yeah. I'd like that."

"It's getting late. Are your parents going to wonder where you are?"

"Probably," I answered truthfully. "I'm trying with them, but maybe I need to try harder. They both are still so closed-minded about it all."

"I figured. Especially Isabella." He shook his head. "She was so good with you before, but she's...just a little different now." He rubbed his head and looked at the clock. "You have a session tomorrow, too, but we can just do it here if you want, that way they don't have to drive you anywhere and you can...stay for a while. If you want."

"I want." He stopped massaging and let his hand rest on my knee. He was looking at the floor.

"I'm sorry about...earlier." He cleared his throat. "I just, uh... I don't normally burst into tears in front of people. That's never happened. Not even at my friend's funeral. I just...couldn't cry. One more reason I felt so guilty."

I twisted my fingers together. "It may sound weird, but I'm glad you did with me." His look was comically confused. "I just mean that you trust me. That was why I let you do the tattoo without me seeing the design first." His face softened. "You trusted me with this huge thing and I had nothing to give you back, so..."

"Em...you have no idea what you've given me." He sighed. "When I pulled into the yard after leaving, and you were still here, I could have run away with you right then."

I laughed. "I may take you up on that one day." He smiled and continued to caress my skin. "You've got so much pressure on you," I stated. I didn't want to bring everything back up, but I just wanted him to know that his struggles were noted. He shrugged a little. "So much pressure and so much responsibility."

He touched my chin. "Don't worry about me. I've got broad shoulders."

He leaned over my knee and gave each of my lips attention before he pulled back. "I'll take you home, OK? And tomorrow, I'll be home at four. Text me when you want to come over and I'll come get you, whenever you want."

"I will. I want to be here."

He ran the pad of his thumb over my lips. "Thank you, Em."

Useless Fact Number Twelve

The right lung takes in more air than the left.

I had somehow managed to skip school again that day, but I knew it would be my last offense without consequences. I texted Mason and said I was coming, but was still surprised when I reached the end of the gate. He was there, grinning and opening the door for me. I laughed as I got in. I winced as I plopped down and rubbed my hip. He wasn't lying about it being sore.

When we got to his house, I went in and said hello to his mom. I watched in sympathy as he once again explained to her why he looked different, and why she couldn't remember. We spoke a little, mostly about *The Price is Right*, and when I said my goodbyes, she once again called me Mariah.

"That's so weird why she calls you that. We don't even know anyone named Mariah," he said, and opened the door to the shop for me. When we came inside, there was a man inside, sitting in the chair.

"Mason! What up, man?"

"Rob?" Mason put his hand around my waist and moved me to sit on the stool. "What are you doing? Long time, no see."

"I came to get fresh ink," he said slowly and eyed me closely, "but I can see…that you're busy."

"A little bit, yeah," Mason said with a smirk.

"Well, I won't keep you." He stood, but gave Mason a look. "But…"

"Oh, no," Mason groaned. "Milo? What happened?"

"His boys are doing a rager tonight. Thought you should know."

Mason cursed and punched his fist into the counter top. "All right. Thanks, man."

"Later."

He left and I sat wondering what was going on. "Mason?"

"It's my brother Milo," he explained through a sigh. "They organize these parties and get busted. I've bailed him out twice already. One more strike and he's going to juvi."

"Oh...sorry."

"I just don't know what to do anymore." He plopped down on the couch. "He doesn't even want my help, but I can't just...abandon him. He left because of me, because he blamed me."

I replied slowly, "Mason, you can't take responsibility for his actions and choices."

"But he *said* he blamed me."

"But you're not making the decision for him to throw a party for a bunch of underage kids, Mason."

He huffed. "I know, but I can't give up on him."

"So let's go get him."

He jerked his gaze to mine. "What?"

"Do you know where he is?" He nodded. "Let's go get him. Come on." I held my hand out to him. He took it slowly and stood up in front of me.

"Let's change your bandage first." His voice had suddenly gone husky. He moved toward me, never taking his eyes off mine, and tilted my chin up to meet his mouth. I felt myself sway toward him, but he held me firmly. Too soon, he released me and told me to turn around. I did as he asked and he pulled my jeans down just enough to replace the bandage.

His hands were gentle and he pulled the tape off slowly and easily. When he was done, he once again kissed my skin above the bandage. He gripped my hand as he pulled me outside.

Then we were in his car and heading across town. "You don't have to go with me. I can take you home."

It was already getting dark, but it didn't matter. I wanted to do this with him. "I'm with you."

He reached over and took my hand in his, letting them rest in my lap. "Thank you."

"Where's your Dad?"

He made a disapproving noise in the back of his throat. "He's a real bastard with bastard filling. He used to beat my mom when I was a kid, but he finally left us when I was about five. Haven't seen him since."

"Mmm, sorry. I didn't mean to-"

"No, it's fine," he assured and brought my hand up to kiss my fingers. "I'm over it. My mom was an awesome lady. I had a good life, but I've always felt responsible for everyone." He looked at me and smiled, that same weird look in his eyes as once before. "It's why I was so attached to you in the beginning, too. It's why I'm driving across town to stop my idiotic brother. I just…can't seem to stop."

"That sounds like an admirable flaw. And an adorable one."

He chuckled and smiled shyly. He pulled into a party that appeared to be in full swing. "Dang…" he muttered, throwing the car in park near the curb. "I'll be right back."

"I'm coming with you!" I said and scrambled to keep up. He threw the front door open and we were blasted with music. The partygoers eyed us curiously, but ultimately dismissed us. Mason grabbed my hand and took me up the stairs with him, pushing some guys that were smoking out of the way. The cloud blew through my face and I gasped. Not cigarette smoke…

Mason threw open several doors down the hall before reaching one where he stopped. His shoulders sagged and I felt horrible for him. "Milo, come on. Let's go."

I peeked under Mason's arm to see a smaller, thinner, shorter version of Mason, obviously drunk and zipping his pants. The girl in the bed rolled over, uncaring of who was in the room. I covered my mouth to stop the gasp.

"Get out of here," Milo slurred. "You're not my dad, Mason."

"You're right. I'm not. Your dad left and didn't come back. I'm here. Now, go get in the car."

"NO!" He swayed as he tried to put his shoes back on. The kid could only be sixteen or seventeen at the most. He spied me peeking under Mason's arm. "Who's she?"

"This is Emma," Mason said evenly and went to stand at the foot of the bed. "She's coming, too. So come on. Let's go home."

"Whatever, Mason!" he yelled. "You're such a buzz kill."

Mason grabbed him by the collar. "Car. Now."

"Get off me!" he pushed at him, but Mason was a considerable presence next to Milo. "Get off!"

"Stop fighting, Milo." He dragged him down the hall and looked back to make sure I was following. The music was so loud that Milo's protests could no longer be heard by me. I followed them through the throngs of people to the curb where he unceremoniously dumped him into the back seat.

He must've been drunker than I thought because he stayed down, his mouth open, and he looked to be a sleep. Mason opened the door for me and gave me that *I'm sorry* look. I shook my head, kissed his cheek, and climbed in. As soon as he cranked the car, we heard the sirens in the distance. He shook his head. "Just in time."

We drove in silence back to his house with an AWOLNATION CD playing in the background. Once we arrived, the kid was passed out in the back still, so Mason carried him inside and tossed him on his bed. It was the first time I'd seen his bedroom. As I was turning to leave, he woke.

"Hey, girl." I looked back at him while Mason took his brother's shoes off. "You dating my big brother, or what? 'Cause he'll just ruin you, you know. He doesn't care about anyone but himself." I stared at him. Mason had just saved his ungrateful behind and this was how he repaid him?

He let his head fall back to the bed and Mason tossed a blanket over him. He guided me away from his room with a hand on the small of my back. I couldn't believe this was what Mason's life was like. All he did was take care of other people.

We retreated back to the shop. "The sad thing?" he asked as soon as he shut the door and pulled me to him by my hips. "He'll be gone by morning."

"Can't you stop him?"

He shook his head. "He's almost eighteen, and then I won't have any way to help him anymore. The next time he gets caught, he'll go to real jail. But," he shrugged, stuffing his hands into my back pockets, "at least I can say I tried to help him."

"I'm so sorry. Between him and your mom and…me, all you do is take care of people."

He smiled and cupped my face. "Well, two of you deserve it." He kissed my smiling mouth. I circled my arms around his neck and hoped that by being here with him, his load was lighter. I could think of nothing that I could do for him, but *be there*.

A little later, he took me home. The make-out session in the front seat was another level of amazing that I had yet to experience until then. I felt like my lungs couldn't keep up with my want to keep going. I was dying, drowning, and was perfectly fine with it.

Mason dropped me off at the gate, but said that he didn't feel comfortable sneaking around. That if we were doing this, then we were doing it all the way, and needed to tell my parents, even though we knew they didn't approve.

It scared me. I was worried that my parents might do something to get Mason fired, even though he refused to have any relationship with me at all until I'd left the facility.

But he was right. It wasn't wrong for us to be together, so we didn't need to sneak. Since we'd conveniently forgotten my therapy session, he said I could come over tomorrow; we'd go for a run together and do some strength exercises. I agreed and we said tomorrow night, I'd tell my parents. He offered to go with me, but I thought it would be better with just me the first time.

"Bye, you," he said sweetly.

"Bye, you." I waved my fingers at him and went inside. Isabella thought I had been at cheerleading practice. I didn't feel inclined to correct her. We ate dinner quietly. They were talking about Mitchell and Felicia coming home again for a weekend soon. It was probably horrible to think, but I wasn't thrilled about that.

I decided that I needed to stop trying so hard to be the old me. They needed to see the changes in me and stop expecting certain things or behaviors. So, that night at dinner, I told them that I was quitting cheerleading.

Isabella's eyes were the size of golf balls. Rhett just seemed disappointed and shook his head. I had been expecting that, so I tried to explain myself. "I tried. I went to practice and it just didn't work out."

"Your physical strength will come back. It just takes time," Rhett reasoned.

"It's not my physical strength. It's the fact that it's not me. It's not who I am."

Isabella scoffed. "It's been who you are since you were five years old."

I spoke softly. "Not anymore. I'm sorry. I'm not trying to upset you. I just need to do what's right for me."

"You're giving up so easily," she said. "I expected more from you, honey."

OK, that stung. She got up, leaving Rhett and me at the table. "I'm sorry you're disappointed."

"We didn't raise a quitter, is all. I just wanted you to finish what you started."

"But I don't feel as though *I* started it." He looked at me. Really looked at me.

"I'm sorry to hear that," he whispered and got up.

I felt terrible. I really did. I didn't want to hurt them, but this was my fork in the road. I couldn't split myself in two trying to please everyone. So I went to bed early and dreaded school the next day.

When I got up, I peeled the side of the bandage off my tattoo even though Mason said I wasn't supposed to. I just had to see it. I sighed at seeing it again. It was so...beautiful. And it was all me.

Andy came that morning and I took the ride, but on the way to school, I made sure to lay out that I wasn't available anymore and didn't have any interest in rekindling any old flames between us. And I didn't want his rides to school anymore either.

"No guy in his right mind would dare try to date you," he scoffed as he pulled into the lot. "They know I'd tear their head off."

"He's not from school. But do you hear yourself? You don't own me."

"I know." He pulled into the same spot again. The one that was apparently saved for him. "I know that, babe, but everyone at this school knows that we've been together forever."

I lifted my brow at him. "Not forever, right? Everyone at this school knows that you dated that other girl."

He looked angry for a second, but then backtracked. "You sound jealous."

"I'm not," I assured him. "I think if you want to be with her, you should go for it."

He sighed and banged his fists on the steering wheel. "Damn it, Emma! Why are you fighting this so hard? Just give us a chance. You're writing us off before you even see if this can work or not."

I nodded. "You're probably right, Andy," I said softly and knew that this was hard for him. As much as I didn't like him, he had been trying hard with me. "I'm sorry. I just can't pretend. If anything, all of this has shown me that life is too short. I'm sorry."

"You owe it to me."

"No, I don't." I straightened my back. "I owe it to myself."

He shook his head vigorously. "No. I'm not giving up that easily."

He got out, leaving me sitting in his car. I sighed and got out, too. I passed the group and went straight to my locker. Andy was brooding off to the side so I assumed that they thought we were in a fight.

I opened my locker and saw a flash of blond in my peripheral. The girl I bumped into was in her locker a couple down from me. She was juggling her books and purse. I grabbed my first period book out and checked over my shoulder. My *friends* weren't even paying attention to me. Not that it mattered.

I shut my locker and went up to her. "Hey."

She glared at me with suspicion. "What?"

"Nothing. Just *hey*." With that, I walked away. Baby steps. And I had to admit, it was fun knowing that she probably wondered who had possessed my body.

I skipped through the day, avoiding Andy as much as possible. And at lunch, I skipped that, too. Going to the library to avoid lunch seemed too cliché, so I went out to sit on the lawn. There were a few picnic tables, but I just lay back. The sun was warm and it reminded me of the first time Mason had opened the blinds in my hospital room, letting me feel the sun for the very first time that I could remember.

Someone else came outside, but as soon as she saw me, she stopped. It took me a second to realize who it was, but when she turned to bolt, I remembered. "Hey!" I called. She turned like I was about to shank her or something. "Hey, it's OK. Wanna sit?"

She eyed me suspiciously, just like the girl at her locker had. I rolled my eyes. "It's OK. I won't bite."

"Why do you want to talk to me? It's over, Andy and me."

I nodded. "I know."

"So…" She looked at me and tried to will me to go on. I didn't. "What?"

"I just wanted you to know that I don't have it out for you or anything. I know my…friends made a fuss the other day, but that's not how I feel."

She pressed her lips tightly and looked to be holding back a dam. She sat roughly on her knees in the grass and pressed her fingers to her lips. "He was so devastated after…" I nodded to let her know that I knew what she meant. "He moped around the halls for weeks. He was so angry, getting into fights and always skipping class. I felt so bad for him, and one day, I caught him really upset in the gym when no one else was there. He seemed really happy to have my help. I didn't know what I could do, but I listened… One thing led to another." She sniffed and hung her head. "I felt horrible. The guilt ate at me, and I could tell everyone at school thought I was a tramp or something. I felt so guilty, but he seemed to need me so much. He was so…clingy, almost. He was with me every day, and I'm not telling you that to make you jealous," she insisted.

"I'm not jealous. I know he's trying, but…he's not for me."

"But," her eyes widened, "he dumped me for you. You have to take him back."

"No, I don't," I said softly. "I've already told him that if he wants to go back to you, he should. I don't want either of you to feel guilty about me."

"You told him that?" she said, stunned.

"Yeah," I dragged out.

"But he hasn't…I mean, he hasn't spoken a word to me since, and he won't answer my texts. I just wanted to tell him it was OK, but he won't even talk to me."

"How did you find out that I woke up?'

"He left a note on my car at work." She sniffed again.

I shook my head. "He broke up with you in a note on your car?"

She nodded pathetically. "Yes," she whined. "And he hasn't spoken to me since. And I get it, you're back, that's great. I just wanted to make sure he was OK and to tell him that I understood why he needed to go back to you. But he won't…"

"I'm sorry."

She cringed back. "Why on earth are *you* apologizing to *me*?"

"Because I know what's it like to wish things were different. For you to feel one way, but everyone else wants you to feel another."

"Why don't you hate me?"

"Like I said, I'm not who Andy's supposed to be with. He just feels guilty about me, but he'll come around eventually. When he does, if you still want him, don't worry about me. I've moved on."

"You're with someone?" she said and wiped her eye. I could tell she wanted to ask more.

"Yeah." I stood, slinging my backpack over my shoulder. "He's really great. He kinda…saved me."

She nodded, staying in her seat in the grass. "Are you happy?" She picked at a couple blades of dead grass and looked up at me. "Like, really happy?"

"I'm not sure," I said truthfully. "That's like saying, *Do you like apples?* when you've never eaten any before."

"But do you feel like you're on your way to being?"

That, I could answer. "Absolutely. One way or another."

I left her there in the grass, absolutely positive that we'd never speak again. Not that I didn't want to, but giving her the forgiveness she thought she needed to move on was what I had wanted. Now that she had it, I could almost guarantee she'd move on. She wouldn't wait for Andy to come around, because she knew in her heart that he wouldn't.

That night, I had a session that I had forgotten about, but my parents insisted on coming with me to the hospital. So once again, I got to see Mason, but not *see* Mason. Even doing our exercises, they seemed extra interested and asked him a million questions about what these exercises were doing for me and how long it should take until I didn't need therapy anymore.

They were on to us, I thought.

I texted Mason on the way home and told him I was going to tell them about us before things got worse with them. He texted back to wait, that he wanted to tell them with me. He didn't want me to deal with that alone and it was only right to tell them himself. He wanted to explain himself and show respect for them while still letting them know that I was growing up and moving on. That he cared about me sincerely and this wasn't some crush that he was taking advantage of.

I grinned through my almost-tears all the way.

That night I soaked in a warm bath, as ordered by Mason. I went through my dresser drawers earlier in a scavenger hunt sort of way. I wasn't really looking for anything in particular, just looking. I found an MP3 player and decided to play something during my bath, maybe get a little peek of the old me in that music.

But after flipping through album after album of teenie pop *I'ma-go-to-da-club-and-rub-against-you-tonight's-the-night-for-letting-loose* crap... I almost gave up, but then I came across something completely different. I waited for the song to change, to trick me into believing it was different, but it didn't. I even sat up, dried my hand off with the towel, and looked to see who and what it was. It read *Nobody Else Could Be You* by Jason Reeves.

The song was beautiful beyond words. His voice, smooth and emotional. It didn't make sense why I didn't know any of the songs in my own player, but Mason played that song at the hospital and I knew who it was. Why would my brain nitpick like that?

I listened to that whole album, and then deleted everything on the player *except* that album.

Another way of starting over.

That night while putting on one of the silk nightgowns that Isabella had left on the bed for me, I sat on the bed and turned the radio on to see what the latest music was. It was so interesting how eclectic and random the music seemed to be. Isabella had buzzed my room to tell me supper was ready, but I said I wasn't hungry. She didn't sound happy about it, but probably just thought I was skipping meals for my figure.

Whatever.

So, with new tunes that I'd never heard of streaming through my room, I set to more exploring. I'd gone through all the drawers in the desk and dressers. The closet was empty of almost everything but new clothes and shoes. I threw all the make-up away, except the colors that I thought were my speed. My love for flavored lipgloss must have stuck with me because I still found myself putting it on constantly. I had unpacked my stuff from the hospice and put the Christmas presents over on the corner window sill. It didn't seem right to open presents that really weren't for me. It seemed fitting for them to stay in the window sill. They belonged there...for now, at least.

I was going through an old purse and dumping all the trash from school and gum wrappers when a thought hit me.

I wondered if I ever had a diary. Finding something that would help me see what the old me was like would have been like Christmas, even if I didn't like what I found. And as I had the thought, an idea popped into my head.

The bed.

I crawled across the floor from my perch and slid my hand between the mattress, running it along the seam. Jackpot.

I pulled it out quickly and leaned against the bed with my back as I opened the book on my lap. The first page almost made me close it.

It's hard being gorgeous, but someone has to do it.

There seemed to be just one or two lines on each day. The first day seemed to be in August. The first day of school, I bet. I flipped the page to the next one.

Andy and I had sex in the boys' locker room again today. He has completely stopped worrying about my pleasure, and instead, is done with me the second he finds his. Boys.

I covered my stunned lips. I sounded so uncaring and just fine with it. Like it annoyed me, but not enough to do anything about it. And it brought up the unpleasant reminder that I wasn't a virgin. The fact that I gave it away so carelessly and didn't even seem to enjoy it at all made me feel so sorry for her, for the old Emma.

Daddy bought me the new Dooney & Bourke today.

The next day.

Rachel Simmons wore that God-awful skirt and everyone saw her lady-junk at lunch today. Priceless.

The next day.

The group went to the movies and saw the new Channing Tatum. The boys laughed and the girls drooled. Channing, run away with me, baby.

The next day.

If Kali doesn't do something about those cankles, I'll be forced to kick her from the squad. God...what a pig. She thinks she hides those packages of SweetTarts in her locker well, but she's an amateur playing in the big leagues.

And the next day.

Andy took me to Valentino's on the river for my birthday. He can be such a sweetie when he wants to be. Now if he'll only get me the Gwen Stefani tickets I want for our anniversary, I won't cut him off.

The next.

Misty, the Big Red Freak, was caught paying for her lunch today with a free lunch school card. I didn't even have to retaliate that she was eying Andy like a popsicle at the pep rally. One word, skank. Karma.

That was it, the final push that was too much. I threw the book across the room. Karma... karma...

What exactly was good about that girl? She was horrible and too honest and uncaring. She cared about nothing and no one but her things and her ranking among the fellow students. I got up and grabbed the pink and purple book from the floor. The radio still played softly in the background and there it was again. That song. My hands began to shake as that distinctive guitar rang out. My knees buckled and I tried to catch my breath as I knelt on my knees. *Yeah, Yeah, Yeah...*

That sound not only took my breath, it made me feel wrong. It invited feelings in me that even waking up in the hospital hadn't. I vaguely heard the door open and Isabella saying my name. She ran to turn the radio off and knelt on the floor beside me. "Oh, Emma! What's happening? What's the matter?"

"That song..." I tried to explain.

"The song...you're remembering?" she said hopefully. "Is that why you have a headache, because you're brain hurts?"

I pushed her hand away. "No. I'm not remembering." I took a few deep breaths, letting the air clean away the horrible, grimy feeling from before. "I heard that song in the hospital, too. It makes me feel...bad."

"Bad? Bad as in, you don't like it?" she said, clearly not understanding.

"No. Like something bad is tied to it. I have no idea what or why."

"Oh," she replied with disappointment. "Well...you've been home for a couple weeks now. I would have thought that you'd remember something by now."

I felt my fist clench around the book that I'd written. "Here." I shoved it at her. "Take it. This is what your daughter was like. I found her diary, of sorts. Go on, take it." She reached for it and looked at it lovingly. I rolled my eyes in disgust. "Keep it. I don't want to see it again."

"Emma," she placated and it was too much.

"I'm going to bed. Good night."

"Without any supper?"

"I'm not hungry," I said softly.

"What about cheerleading practice?" she asked, as though everything was fine and she hadn't just found me in a ball on the floor.

"I just want to go to sleep, go to school, do my therapy, survive, and then repeat." I gave her a pleading look. "Please. I know you're disappointed, but I can't do anything more right now."

She pursed her lips in the way that I was becoming accustomed to. "OK, Emmie. OK."

She left, taking that horrible book with her. I looked over at the bed *Emmie* used to sleep in. There was no way I was sleeping in her bed tonight. So I put my clothes on, took my purse and bag with me for school tomorrow, just in case, and went to the only place in the whole world lately that I felt safe and loved, just as I was.

Mason's car wasn't there yet when I walked up, so I went into the shop to wait for him. His jacket was still on the chair where we'd left it the last time, so I swung it over my torso and huddled on the couch.

It wasn't very long before I saw headlights. I hadn't turned the lights on because I didn't want to scare Mason's mom or the nurse. I figured if he didn't come in to the shop, I'd go knock on the door. But he did come in, barreling through the door with a giggling, moaning girl.

Useless Fact Number Thirteen

The average person falls asleep in seven minutes.

I stared as he slammed the door with his foot and hoisted her onto the tabletop, pawing at her shirt.

I watched the silhouette of the back of his head in the dark for so long that I knew I needed to leave before something that I *really* wanted no part of happened between the two. I could watch no longer, and stood. I started to make my way to the door, covering my eyes and wishing upon everything I knew that I could shield my ears from those horrible noises.

I ran out, and just as the tears began, hot, betrayed, and stinging on my cheeks, more headlights pulled into the driveway. The beater? I stared as Mason got out and threw his keys up into the air a bit, catching them in his hand. He saw me standing under the tree and stopped. "Em?" He moved swiftly to me and took my face in his hands carefully. "Oh, no. What happened?"

I opened my mouth to say, but nothing would come. We heard something shatter in the shop and a loud laugh, followed by that annoying giggle. He looked at me curiously, took my hand, and towed me with him. He slammed the door open and turned the light on. The guy that had been there the other night was there with a girl. She was pretty and had a little tattoo of a heart on the side of her neck. She gasped and covered her top half with her shirt and arms. He tried to cover her, too, while still trying to find out what was going on. He squinted in the lights. "Mason? I thought you said you were busy tonight?"

"My sessions ended early." He crossed his arms and gave him a look. "What the hell?"

"I think it's obvious, brother."

The girl gasped. "Baby, come on." She was so obviously embarrassed that I walked out and leaned against the side of the house. I heard her again. "Mason, I'm sorry. I figured we'd come visit, but then we got here and no one was here. He didn't say you were busy tonight. This big lug can't keep his hands to himself."

Mason laughed. "Patrice, it's fine. Normally it doesn't matter, but..." he peeked outside and grinned as he took my hand to pull me back inside with him, "I think you scared the hell out of Emma."

"Emma," she said softly and looked at the guy. "The one you told me about?"

The 'big lug' nodded and grinned at me. "Hello again, Emma."

"Hi," I said. "Sorry. Didn't mean to break up the...party. I was just..." I pointed to the couch where my purse and bag still were, "waiting for Mason."

"Wait. You were in here?" the guy asked. It was kind of hilarious to see this big, burly, leather-wearing, tattooed guy blush.

"I was waiting for him...and I thought..." I sighed.

Mason turned me to look at him. He took in my face and eyes. "You thought it was me," he stated factually.

I already felt chagrined about it as it was. Mason's head shook back and forth as my silence gave him my answer. He touched my cheek, pulling me close. "Em, you've got to know by now that I don't want anyone but you."

I bit my lip. "I'm sorry," I whispered.

"Don't be sorry." He smiled. Before I could think, I swooped up and kissed his smile. When I pulled away, he brought me back and kissed me again, a little harder and longer this time. When I opened my eyes, he hadn't moved back. He just looked at me with this look like he wanted to say so much more, but couldn't. I peeked over at the girl and guy. They stood slack-jawed, open mouthed, and silent. I cleared my throat a little and leaned back down, but into Mason's side.

His hand reached under my shirt in the back and rested there on my skin. I may have swayed from pleasure.

"Well, how about I order a pizza?" Mason said, trying to rein in the awkwardness. "Can you stay, Em?"

I nodded. "Yeah."

So we all sat dispersed on the two couches. Mason called and ordered three pizzas from his cell and then sat next to me. He pulled my legs into his lap and started massaging my calves through my jeans. "You walked here again, huh?"

"Yep. Exercise is good for you, you know."

He chuckled. "So they tell me."

"So, Emma," the girl ventured. "How are you doing? I can only imagine going through what you have."

"I'm working it all out. Some days aren't as easy as others." I looked at Mason. "But then there are these really, really great days..."

He smiled shyly and looked down at his fingers as they worked my muscles. When I looked back up at her, she was giving me this look. At first, I thought it might be jealousy or protection, but it was unbelief. Was she doubting my feelings for him, or doubting his?

But then she said softly, "We went to school with Mason."

I got her meaning. That she knew all about the horrible things Mason had been through.

He looked up at her. "Patrice-"

"And he's the sweetest, most caring, loving man I know." She looked at the guy. "Sorry, babe, but you know it's true." He shrugged and smiled. "He cares to a fault. What happens to him if you remember everything?"

Wow, so she really did know everything about my situation.

"Patrice," Mason complained in a hiss.

I didn't need to think about the answer. "It won't matter."

I took my legs from his lap and set them on the floor. I scooted to the edge of the couch, and her eyes bulged like she was imagining that I was about to bolt, but she didn't know me yet.

And Mason probably thought I was angry at her for questioning me, but she cared about him. And anyone that protected Mason, the boy who cared so much for his mother and brother that he put his entire life on hold for them, was a friend of mine.

So I went on. "I know I must seem like a liability." I peeked at Mason to find him watching me closely, his fists on his knees. "And I don't know what's going to happen. I wish I did, so much. Mason is impossible not to love-" I stopped. Crap, I just said that out loud. Her eyes softened. "Anyway, you don't have anything to worry about."

I licked my lips as they sat silently. Then she grinned and leaned forward, her hand outstretched. "Mason is so rude." Mason chuckled and touched the small of my back. "We haven't been properly introduced. I'm Patrice, and this impossible lug is Rob."

I took her hand. "Nice to meet you."

"You, too. Well, stick around, Emma." She looked at Mason with obvious affection. "I've never seen Mason so...shiny before."

I laughed. "Shiny?"

"He's glowing like a freaking lightning bug," Rob added.

I smiled, biting into my lip to keep it contained.

"Shut up," Mason muttered. The hand on my back gripped my shirt and tugged me back to his chest. I slid gently, leaning into his outstretched arm. "Leave me alone, Rob. I can glow if I want to."

Rob chuckled just as someone knocked on the door. Mason kicked Rob's shoe and nodded for him to get it. "Why don't you pay since you sneak into places and scare the crap outta people?"

Rob smiled at me and twisted his lips in chagrin. "I *am* sorry 'bout that." He got up, but Mason still reached into his pocket and pulled out two twenties. Rob snatched one and left the other. "I can get my half."

Mason smiled. When he leaned over and kissed my temple, sighing into my hair, it could have been the sweetest thing known to man. Jane Austen would have written about this moment had she not met her untimely demise at the hands of Addison's disease so long ago.

I lifted my face and his was right there, our noses almost touching. Everything went away but him and his fingers as he reached up to touch my face, his fingers moving and caressing me until my eyelashes fluttered. The corner of his mouth lifted. I reached my hand up and shook his perfect hair out a bit. "There. No more work hair."

He chuckled and rubbed it. "You don't like my work hair?" I scrunched my nose and he laughed again, but then he looked at his watch and his brow bunched. "It's kinda late for you to be walking over here," he chastised softly. "You OK?"

"Later," I promised. His brow bunched in concern. "It's OK, just...stuff."

He nodded, not seeming entirely sure. I inched closer and gripped his shirt in my fingers. He pulled my chin up and moved as close as he could get without his lips touching mine.

"I missed you today," he announced in a whisper and pulled me the rest of the way to meet him. It was a small, light brush of a kiss. I was glad because I wanted much more than that, but if he started, it would be hard to stop. And he had...company.

His eyes shifted to the aforementioned guests and he smirked. I heard Rob laughing. "OK, OK. Let's eat, yeah?"

"What about your mom?" I asked.

"I called to say I was going to be late. The nurse cooked."

I nodded. I sat there snuggled into Mason's side as we ate and laughed at Rob and Mason's ribbing. As soon as Rob said he'd be back later for a new tattoo and then left, Mason pulled me into his lap. His strong arms lifted me gently until my legs were on both sides of him as he held my face with his hands and took my mouth with force. I let my fingers slide under his shirt, but he jerked and chuckled. "Ticklish, Em."

"I remember, Yoda."

I still had his jacket on and he inched his hands inside it to be closer to my skin. I gasped into his mouth when the fingers of his other hand ventured into the waistband of the back of my jeans just barely, and he caressed the bandaged tattoo there that he had given me.

His hand still on my face reached and tugged at my hair gently to maneuver me. So instead of hanging on to his shoulder desperately, I leaned, pressing my chest to his and drove both of my hands into his hair. He groaned into my mouth and it felt amazing. Then he gently sucked on my tongue and I felt a rush of blood to my head. My lips kept time with his and soon, I was breathing so hard that I had to pull back.

His breaths matched mine as we stared at each other. "I better take you home."

"Why don't you come in with me?" I suggested and gave him a look that said why.

"Tomorrow." He smiled and rubbed my cheek with his thumb. "You can come here after school, I'll cook you and Mom some dinner, and then we'll go over at a decent hour to hash it all out." He looked at the clock behind me. "It's almost nine."

I sighed and pulled my phone out. I texted Isabella, telling her I would be there in a few minutes and that I had supper already. I was tired and was just going to go to bed. She didn't argue when she texted back, **'Ok, honey.'**

"OK. That sounds good. But...what are you going to say if they say that they don't want me to see you."

He looked down and shook his head. "I won't give up on you. I really don't want that to happen, but if they do say that..." He shrugged. "I don't know, Emma." He rubbed his head, a sign I was realizing as stress. "I still think that you should try to have a relationship with them. I don't want me to be the reason that you don't."

"I've been trying," I argued.

"Have you really? Like...really?"

I thought back. I didn't know anymore. "I'm legal anyway. I'm almost out of school-"

"This isn't about you being some teenager and needing your parent's permission, Em." He smiled sadly and rubbed my arm. "You're nineteen, an adult. This is about getting their blessing," he corrected. "Either way...I won't let you go," he insisted and touched my chin. "I mean it. I just want to let them know what's going on and hope that they understand. But by the way Isabella was so angry with me before, I'm guessing it won't work out that way. If not, we'll cross that bridge then. Maybe we'll wait for you to graduate as a way to show them respect and help them change their mind." I opened my mouth to protest and he put his thumb over my lips. "I know, I know, but you've only got one family."

I felt a cloud of doubt settle over me. "There's only one you."

He smiled. "I'm not going anywhere." He gripped my upper arms. "Anywhere."

I scowled at him. "I don't like this sensible side of you."

He laughed out loud. "Well, I'm sorry. There's a way to keep the peace and make everyone happy, and we'll find it. If we try and try and things still don't work out with, then at least we know that we did everything we could. We can be together with a clear conscience."

I nodded and twisted my lips. "As long as the end result is us together, that's all that matters."

"That's a given," he said sweetly. "And I know I seem like a stiff for wanting to talk to your parents." He looked at his lap. I squinted at the top of his head. "I know it's not normal for a guy to do that anymore, but I always-"

"I know why you're doing it." He looked up. "There's nothing wrong with being the good guy, Mason. There's nothing wrong with doing the right thing."

He chuckled. "Yeah," he said mildly.

"I know that bad boys are all the rage now, but...I want someone like you. Someone good and who I know cares about me. The tattoos do help your bad boy image though."

His smile grew a little on the side. "Yeah? You like the ink, huh?"

"I kinda love it," I said breathlessly as I traced the one on his shoulder and neck.

He stared into my eyes silently before speaking so softly, but I felt it whisper through my bones. "I never thought I'd meet someone like you." I thought about making a joke, but the tension between us wasn't the kind you wanted to be rid of, it was the kind you wanted to bathe in. I waited for him to continue, because I knew he would. "I always thought I'd be alone forever, never finding someone who saw *me*. Girls see me now with the tattoos and the shop and the crazy, tattooed biker friends and think that I'm like that, that I'm something I'm not. And then...I always thought one day that the guilt would be too much and I'd choke on it."

"Mason..."

"But you saw through that, too. I never thought I'd find someone that I couldn't see myself without."

I heard more than felt the breath as it caught in my throat. He chuckled in an embarrassed way. "I'm sorry. I know that probably scares the hell outta you, but I mean it-"

I didn't let him finish as I put my fingers over his lips. His scruff from the day made me bite my lips at the feel of it against the pads of my fingers. It felt amazingly sensual. I wonder if he realized that it was that sexy. If it was on purpose or just because the end of the day was wearing on him. Either way, it had me melting. "It doesn't scare me," I sighed each word. "Because I feel the same. You're the only one who gets me, and that may not seem like much to some people, but for me, it's all I've got."

"It's not all you've got," he argued in a whisper against my fingers before pulling them away and holding my hand hostage, "you just don't know it yet." He leaned forward and kissed my mouth in an achingly slow fashion. "Come on. I'll take you home."

I let him lift me up and tow me to his car. When we reached my driveway, I started to lean in, but he made a noise in his throat. "Don't."

"What?"

He nodded his head toward the house. "There."

I looked and saw my mother's perfect quaffed head peeking out the curtains. I looked back to Mason while rolling my eyes. "They're going to find out tomorrow anyway."

"Yes, the *right* way." I felt a scowl coming. He sighed and gave me a little exasperated smile. "I need to do this the *right* way, baby."

I felt my insides flutter a little. "Who said chivalry was dead?"

He laughed and took my hand, his thumb rubbing over my fingers. "Exactly. I'll come pick you up from school tomorrow, OK? I'll get off work early. Then after dinner at my house...we'll do this thing right."

"OK," I conceded and opened the door, but didn't get out. "Bye, you."

"Bye, you."

"And Mason?"

"Yeah?"

"Don't forget your shining armor in the back when you get out."

His laughter followed me up the driveway.

Useless Fact Number Fourteen

It's impossible to lick your elbow...and 75% of people who read this try to anyway.

I smiled happily and felt light as I hopped up the steps. The door swung open as soon as I reached it.

"Hey," I said brightly.

"Well hello, Emmie." She seemed surprised at my brightness. "How was your day? I didn't realize you had a session today." The word session seemed to get stuck behind her teeth. I smiled even brighter.

"I didn't, but I did need to see Mason about something."

She seemed like she wanted to say more, but didn't. "Well, I saved you some cake from supper." She smiled and looped her arm through mine. "It's your favorite."

I wondered what it was I was about to endure and pretend to like. I asked her about her day. She told me all about the charity auction she was helping the church set up. It was for all handmade and quilted items, and she was taking a quilting class so that she could do a square and be a contributor on the church quilt. I scowled on the inside. That seemed like an awful lot of work when they obviously had the money. Why not just donate the money for the quilt instead of doing all that work just for one quilt square?

We sat down and the dog ran in and planted itself in between my shoes. I reached down, almost on instinct, and petted it between the ears. The growly, moaning noise it produced made Isabella and I both laugh.

"That dog missed you so much, Emmie," she said as she put a slice of cake onto a delicate china plate. She put one on another for herself. She winked. "Another slice for me won't hurt, right?"

I smiled. "I won't tell if you won't."

She smiled, too, and took a bite, watching me. Waiting. I took a bite and noticed the slightly sweet taste of angel food cake, with whipped cream cheese that was really heavy, and strawberries. I moaned and she laughed. "Oh, my gosh. This is heaven on a plate."

She laughed again. "It was my mother's great aunt's recipe," she said proudly. "When we visited my mother, you kids always begged for this."

"Where is she?" I asked.

She swallowed her food and touched a locket on her neck shaped in an oval. "She passed a couple years ago." She opened it and showed me a woman and man who looked happy in their old age. "You took it pretty hard."

I sighed. "I wish I remembered. I wish I knew her."

She set her fork down and touched my hand. She stood, took both plates in her hands, and looked down at me. "Come with me. Let's see if we can jog your memory."

I waited for her to come back from the kitchen and then followed her into the den. She showed me scrapbooks and leather album after album of pictures of the whole family. Of us as kids, on vacation and in school plays. Some of us playing football in the yard together. Tons of professional portraits. We sat there for hours. The ones of me when I was little were fascinating to me. I was such a normal girl, awkward and strange in my own skin, but happy. As the years progressed, I became more and more prissy and smiley. My hair got blonder and blonder and the skirts got shorter and shorter, but I still looked happy. Not fake like I did with those pictures of Andy in my room, but really happy. I could tell the old me really loved my family. I wanted to remember so badly. I wanted to feel for one real second what it was like to feel so confident in her love for this family.

Isabella cried through some stories of us as kids, just normal things that every family goes through. I didn't cry though. I was in a weird place in my head. When it was late, Isabella said I should go to bed. I nodded and thanked her for showing me.

She smiled. "Come back to us, Emma. We're waiting for you."

She walked out, the little dog following her closely, like she hadn't just dropped a bomb in our den. That one sentence broke my heart into a million un-pick-up-able pieces. I stared at the walls, lined with photos and events of people that I didn't know and couldn't remember. It took this, this one innocent little slice of strawberry cream cheese cake with my mother, who just wanted her daughter back, to see that I would never be welcome there. No matter how hard I tried, they would always be waiting for Emmie.

So that was that. I guess I'd just live here until graduation and then leave. Maybe by my leaving, this family could finally grieve their daughter and get some peace. And I wouldn't feel so obligated to be someone that I wasn't, or feel guilty that I was disappointing people just by being me.

I went upstairs and took Mason's coat off. I still had it on and slung it across the chair, fully intending to wear it the next day. It was like a letter jacket to me. I would wear it with pride, and though it was too big, it was *his*.

A small piece of paper fluttered from the pocket when I let go and I bent to retrieve it. I felt my lips part when I realized what it was. It was the note I'd given Mason with the kiss lips in lipgloss. He carried it around with him? I felt the smile tug hard at my lips. Man, my big softy was turning me completely to mush.

I returned it to the pocket and climbed into bed with a heavy mood, but a light heart. It hurt to know the truth sometimes, but at least I knew and could make plans for my life. And tomorrow, when Mason and I told them we wanted to be together, I knew they'd be angry, but I was past the point of return.

I stayed up to late hours of the night before going to bed. My Calculus and Science homework made my brain strain behind my eyes. If I didn't have two tests coming up, I wouldn't have done it at all. Even though I could barely keep my eyes open, I wasn't stopping until I was done.

I'd only been in bed for about an hour when I heard a noise in my room. I sat up and looked around, thinking that Isabella had come in or something, but the room was still and dark. I heard it again. I pushed the covers back and stood. The window was rattling. I almost smiled, thinking Mason was coming to see me or something, though sneaking in the window didn't seem like his style, but it wasn't Mason. It was Andy.

The window was locked and he was attempting to jiggle the lock free from the outside. When he saw me coming toward him, he smiled this sugary smile and said, "Let me in, Emmie."

"No," I answered in a loud whisper. He still heard me because his face completely changed. He was no longer sweet. "It's late, Andy. Go home."

"I know it's late. That's why I'm coming in the window. Open it," he commanded through gritted teeth.

"What are you doing here?"

"I've missed you. I thought I'd come over and..." the new grin was a dirty one, "show you just how much."

"Go home."

He banged the side of his fist once on the glass, causing me to jump. "No more games. We talked about this. You need to give this a chance. You're throwing everything we had away because you think you got a second chance at life or something. What we had was good."

"I did get a second chance at life," I said louder and didn't care who heard. "And I'm not taking this one for granted. I'm sorry that you're taking this so hard, but I am not the girl that you used to love. I'm not her. I don't want to be her. I don't care about being popular or dating the captain of the football team."

"You don't know. You haven't given it a try!" He was talking loudly, too.

"Go home."

"I want to make it up to you, the way I hurt you before the accident," he begged. "I need to. If you'd let me, I know that you would understand that what we had isn't worth just throwing away."

"I'm seeing Mason now." His face morphed into an ominous anger. "Just go home, Andy. I'm happy. Don't you want me to be? I don't want things to go back to the way they were."

He sneered. "This isn't over," he promised and practically pressed his face to the glass. "Prom is coming up and I'm taking you," he ordered. "Do you hear me? You at least owe me that if nothing else."

"I don't owe you-"

"Yes, you do!" His face fell a little. "Do you have any idea what you're doing to me?"

"No," I said softer and moved to stand right in front of the window. "No, I don't. Go home, Andy. I'm sorry."

"I'll pick you up tomorrow in the morning," he spouted and turned to go. "Be ready. I'm not kidding, Emma."

"Go home!" I said harder.

"I am, but know this; you owe me, Emma. You belong with me just like you always have."

He left and I sat staring at the darkened, streetlamp-lit window for a long time before finally crawling back into bed.

If Andy thought I'd cave under his threats, then he didn't know me as well as he claimed to.

I was slicking on some mascara when Isabella yelled up the stairs for me. I grabbed all my things from the bed and put my lipgloss on as I went down the stairs. I stopped in my tracks at seeing Andy in the doorway. He grinned, in a *gotcha* kind of way. "I wanted to make sure that you knew I was here to pick you up...as planned."

I decided now was a good a time as any to put the kibosh on dear old Andrew. I marched myself down the stairs right past him. He hurried, yelling a goodbye to Isabella, and caught up with me. "Glad you're seeing things my way, Emmie. We wouldn't want your parents to... Where are you going?"

I went past his car and straight to Mason's as he sat near the curb. I climbed in and made a point to wave at Andy before turning back to Mason. He eyed Andy in my driveway with a strange look before putting the car into drive. The short drive to school was over before I could think. He smiled at me and leaned over, patting my thigh slowly. "Have a good day. *Learn* something."

"Are you implying that I'd sabotage my high school education because I'm too preoccupied with you?" I said sweetly.

"No," he grinned, "I'm implying that you'd do it to avoid seeing that tool with legs."

I laughed so hard that I buried my face in his shoulder. "Ok. You got me."

"Just say the word if he gives you any trouble," he said ominously. "I'll tattoo something really nasty on his forehead in his sleep."

I smiled. "Like what?"

"A pile of steaming-"

I covered his mouth laughing. "I get the point. Thank you."

"Anytime," he mumbled against my hand and pulled me to him. He pulled my hand down and held it between us. "Anytime," he repeated, so close that his breath blew the hair at my cheek. "Your hair looks really great down like that."

"Thanks." I looked down at our hands entwined between us. "Are you sure you want to do this with me tonight?"

He lifted my chin. "Is that doubt I hear?"

"No," I assured. "Just worry. What if they try to do something drastic? Like get you fired?"

"That'd be an awful lot of work on their part," he mused. "You think they'd go that far?"

"I don't know. Are you willing to risk that?"

The look that spread across his face melted bones and didn't apologize for it. He growled his words in a delicate way, "What do you think, Em? Do I look willing to risk it?"

I took a much needed breath and swallowed. Loudly. "Well..."

He licked his lip as he took my face in his hands. "There's no point speculating on something until you need to, right? For now, just..."

He kissed me softly at first, and then proceeded to kiss the breath right out of me. When it was done, I was clinging to his collar, playing my damsel part very well. The smile he wore showed his enjoyment of my current state. He brought my hand up and kissed my palm. "Have a good day, Emma."

"Is this how you'll send me off to school every day now?" I asked in a whisper.

His smile grew. "Don't press your luck, Miss Walker."

I giggled as I exited. I shut the door and then leaned in the window. "Thank you."

"You're welcome," he said with a cocky smile.

I cocked my head to the side. "I meant for the ride."

"Well...you're welcome for that, too."

I shook my head and laughed. "Bye, you."

"Bye, you."

I looked back once more over my shoulder before he drove away. He was still watching. That thrilled me in odd places. He waved and somehow made even that look sexy. I turned and ran right into the trio. Cookie spoke first. "Oh, my gosh. Did you break down or something and he gave you a ride?"

I bristled and decided I was on a roll this morning. This chick needed to be taken down a notch. Or ten. "Why? Because he doesn't drive a Beamer?"

"He-" she began.

"Not finished. He's not some bum who gave me a ride. We are totally together." Their faces screwed up. "That's the man I'd marry if he asked one day." I didn't stop there. "And don't ever say anything bad about him again. He has more goodness in him than most of the people I know all combined."

"Yeah, but..." she said and looked to the others, "can goodness buy you things?"

I pushed through the middle of them. It looked like I had better get used to being a loner, because I refused to play *the old me* anymore.

"Emma!" she called. "He's cute and all, but you screw guys like that, you don't marry them!"

I shook my head as I burst through the front doors of the school. And those words were from my so-called friends. I scoffed and made my way to first period. I ignored Andy's pleading looks. I focused on my work. I wanted to graduate. That was my new mission in this school. I wasn't giving up, I was just facing facts. Finding Emmie was no longer a possibility. She was gone. So getting out of this place was my new priority.

The teachers seemed pleased by my attention and questions. When I raised my hand to answer once, the teacher even waved her hand at me and said, "Go ahead. The bathroom pass is by the door," and moved on. I had to wave to get her to see that I wanted to actually answer the question. I thought her eyes were going to pop out of her little head.

Everyone could see that I was a different girl. That didn't stop my friends from shooting their pleading, pathetic looks at me. I thought avoidance and ignoring would be the best course of action with those three, but it seemed like...maybe not. I hated it. I didn't want them to feel so tied to me. They thought I needed to be their leader, to help them function in high school, but I needed to set them free.

Useless Fact Number Fifteen
An octopus' testicles are located in its head.

I headed outside to eat lunch in the grass, and saw them intercepting me. I knew the needed showdown was inevitable. I held my little box of chicken strips in my hand and smiled as the trio approached. "Good, just who I wanted to see."

"Really?" Kali scoffed. "We thought you hated us. Did I do something wrong?"

"Something wrong? Like what?"

"We didn't come see you in the hospital." She looked at them and back to me. "We wanted to, but thought you'd be mad at us."

"For the life of me, I can't imagine why I would be," I said, exasperated.

"Look, Emmie...you're a little exhausting." I felt my eyebrows rise. "Well, the old you was. You always called the shots and without you here to tell us what to do, we were scared of making it worse. We called to check on you and your mom said you were just sleeping. That's all she would ever say. We didn't think it was right to go and see you when you didn't even know that we were there."

I nodded. I understood that. "I'm not mad at you, I'm just not...who I was. I'm not interested in being anyone's leader." She opened her mouth, but I stopped her. "Or anything else. I just want to focus on school, graduate, and then see what this world has to offer someone who can't remember her life."

They didn't laugh at my joke. They just looked dejected. "It's not our fault that you don't remember us. Everyone in school expects you to still be our friend. It looks like you're rejecting us."

"Sorry," I spouted and pushed through them for the second time that day. "I'm just here because I have to be."

"Don't be like that, Emmie!" Cookie yelled, causing eyes to jerk to our location. "You need us just as much as we need you."

"You don't need me!" I yelled back and smiled. "You have brains in your heads! Use them. Don't peak in high school. Do something with your lives. High school's almost over anyway."

Their mouths fell open, but I just rolled my eyes and took my spot in the grass. I floated the rest of the day until I walked home. I walked past Andy's car, and he reached over and threw the door open. When I didn't come, he revved the engine and glared at me over the steering wheel. I shook my head and kept going. When I came in, I could hear voices in the kitchen. It sounded like Rhett was home. He and Isabella were in there and they were going back and forth about my college applications. Apparently, Isabella had sent them off without my knowledge while I was in a coma and had gotten back a couple of packages today.

She had also opened them and planned to enroll me in Brown without asking me. She was going to surprise me with it later and surprisingly, Rhett was on my side about it. That doing something that extreme without talking to the person was going too far. I agreed. I wanted to burst in and ask, 'How dare you?' But I didn't.

When I heard her huff and leave through the other doors, I went in. "Hey, there."

He turned and looked drained. At seeing me? At dealing with Isabella? "Hey, Emma. How was school?"

I hopped up on the counter and took a peach from the basket. "Oh, you know. It sucked royally."

"Is that right?" he said and watched my every move as I took a knife from the block and sliced a piece off the peach, sticking it in my mouth and licking my finger. "What sucked about it?"

"I just want to graduate, but everyone else wants me to..." I shrugged. "I don't know. They just think my priorities are off or something. Like wanting to graduate and refocusing after everything that happened to me is wrong."

He glared at the peach in my hand.

"What's the matter?"

"My daughter hates peaches."

We stared at each other. My daughter, he said. My daughter... Not, *you* ate peaches...

He turned and walked out without another word. It stung more than I ared to admit, but hadn't I kept them at arm's length? Hadn't I done verything but spit on the memory of their daughter? So, I guess I deserved 1at.

I tossed the peach into the trash and once again, made the walk to 1ason's. My stamina was getting better by the day. I didn't cry, in fact, I idn't do anything. I was numb in a strange way about it.

When I arrived, Mason was just getting in the car. "Hey," he said in urprise. "I thought I was coming to get you."

"I couldn't wait," I heard myself say.

"Uhoh," he muttered and beckoned me to him. He wrapped his arm round my side and pulled me to his shop. He shut the door and sat on the ouch, pulling me into his lap. He took my face in his hands slowly, as if :sting my mood, and kissed me before settling back.

"So…what happened today? And you never did tell me what happened 1e other day, either. Whose face needs rearranging?"

I tried to laugh, but failed. I sighed and said, "It was just…everything. .n avalanche."

And I told him *everything*. About Andy taking me to school every day, bout him trying to kiss me and me telling him we were just friends, about 1e note in my locker, about the horrible retaliation of my friends, about how ;abella was so awkward and almost mad at my inability and want to be just ke her daughter. And then I told him what Andy had told me, what had set 1e off, and what those girls had said about karma. That the trio had begged 1e to come back and be their leader because they didn't know how to 1nction...Andy coming to my window...and how Rhett had said his daughter ated peaches.

I was so ashamed. It was the first time that I felt like a teenager, spilling 1y guts about high school problems to my…boyfriend. I rolled my eyes and :offed at myself for that one.

Mason was angry, that I could tell, and I knew it mostly had to do with Andy. "So, anyway," I finished, "that's why I was coming over. To tell you all about the crappy week I'd had, and about my epiphany."

"I'm glad you told me," he said gruffly.

"Are you mad about Andy?" I guessed. "I only let him drive me to school because Isabella wouldn't drive me. And after that stunt at my house, I want nothing to do with him."

"No, it's fine. I just want to hurt him, is all," he confessed and twiddled with my fingers. "And not because he drove you, but because he's a complete tool. And he hurt you…but so did I, so…"

"You didn't hurt me like he did. And besides, I'm thankful to him." He lifted an eyebrow in question. "If he hadn't just laid it all out there for me like that, I wouldn't know what I know now. I wouldn't know without a doubt that I want absolutely nothing to do with the old me."

His eyes squinted. He cursed softly. "What?" I asked.

"Em, I probably should have told you this before, but you had so much going on. I worried about piling too much on you. Then we were kinda…fighting or whatever, and then it just felt like I'd waited so long that it was too late to tell you without you being upset. And now…I just have to tell you. I don't want you to hate yourself, the old you." He took my other hand. "Promise that you'll listen to me and not run out until I'm done?"

Run out? "What's this about?"

"Promise me," he commanded softly.

I nodded slowly. He stared at me carefully and then closed his eyes. "There's more to my story than I told you that night, and it…kinda includes you."

My heart jumped. "Whatever it is, just tell me."

"I became a therapist to take care of Mom and worked for a while, but decided to open the tattoo shop instead, so I could work from home." He pointed around the room. "My shop. I don't use it as much now, but I've always wanted to open it full time."

He waited so I asked, "What happened?"

"I swore off drinking and partying after the accident happened, but my brother took the opposite route. He started partying hard, which you know. One night, I heard about this party that he was going to…" He gulped and gripped my fingers tighter. I waited, completely baited. "He was there and he was so toasted. I watched and tried to be nonchalant so he wouldn't know that I was there. I lost him once, and went upstairs to find him. While I was searching the bedrooms, I found a girl..."

I knew there was something he wanted me to grasp, but I just wasn't getting it. My lips parted and I waited for the punch-line.

"She was plastered. I asked if she was OK because she was crying. She said she broke up with her boyfriend that night because she found out he'd been cheating on her. She'd known about it for a while, but actually caught him in the act that night at the party. She said…she was done with being the girl who lived for everyone but herself. That she needed a change, and the next day, she was going to tell her friends and family that she was done with that guy. That she wanted to be a different person. That…" He smiled and rubbed my arm. "That she was spoiled and needed to be responsible for herself. I know she was drunk, but I believed her."

My heart started to beat fast. Really fast. He took my face in his hands, his thumbs rubbing across my cheeks. "Emma…I only met you once before your accident, but it was enough to make me completely adore the girl you wanted so badly to be."

I felt my lips fall open. "That girl…was me?"

"I know what you're thinking. I know it sounds…creepy or whatever, but just listen. You talked to me for hours that night." He smiled again, taking a tear from my nose with his finger. "Eventually, I said I was going to go get you a bottle of water. That I was going to help sober you up before I took you home, but…when I came back, you were gone. I looked all over for you because I knew you'd been so upset. I was worried about you, but you vanished. Later that night on the news, I heard about the accident. I don't know how I knew, but I *knew* it was you. And I felt guilty and responsible and cursed all over again."

"Why?" I breathed.

"Because I shouldn't have left you alone. I knew you were upset. I should have made sure you got home safely, but I didn't. So I called the hospital and asked them about you, telling them I was a therapist. They said you weren't going to make it, that your parents were sending you to a hospice. *My hospice.* It was like…fate. So I vowed to take care of you, because I already failed you once."

I covered my mouth with my hand to hold in the sob. He closed his eyes, still holding my face. "God, help me, Emma. You'll never know how sorry I am, for everything. I just feel like, from the start, things have been hard for you. I'm so sorry. I just wanted you to know the truth. I don't expect you to forgive me-" He stopped so quickly, as if he knew that I was barely holding on by a thread.

"Mason, no," I protested softly, more to myself than to him. "You were the one person in my life that didn't lie to me. That didn't expect anything from me."

"And I don't expect anything now," he assured. "I know that I didn't tell you, and I'm sorry, but to me, it didn't seem like a lie, it felt like...a necessary omission. Emma, I'm so sorry. I never, ever wanted to hurt you. I didn't want you to come back into your life with the last memory anyone had of you, other than the ass that ran you over, with you drunk at some party. And when you woke up, you couldn't remember anything and were upset, it just made me even more sure that you didn't need to see that last night of your life yet. You needed to accept that you weren't the same girl, Emma, and not have some memory making you doubt that you could be different, that you could be whoever the hell you wanted to be." Every time he stopped talking, he gritted his teeth so hard that I heard it. He went on. "And you're not the same. You're *you*, Em, and making sure that you saw that, even with everyone else doubting you and wanting you to be something else...I felt like I was the only one on your side. But," he gulped painfully, his face agonized, "I was wrong. I should have just told you and let you decide for yourself." Even though he looked away, he still held my face. He stared at the wall. "Good ol' Mason strikes again."

That statement almost made me stay.

Almost.

I ached for him. I got it. I understood that he was looking out for me, but my heart just couldn't handle anything else. I leaned in and kissed his cheek as slowly as I could move. I wanted to savor this. I needed to remember exactly what this felt like. If another coma struck me down, I wanted to keep this somehow.

His face was so smooth today, like he shaved just for me. I squeezed my eyes shut at that thought. When I leaned back, his eyes were squeezed shut, too.

I pulled away, letting his hands fall from my face to his lap. He didn't try to stop me, which I was glad for. He didn't open his eyes either. I looked back once more as I opened the shop door. He was a magnet, pulling and begging me to come back without even trying. But my head needed clearing and I had some things to think about. So I made myself walk out the door, closing it softly behind me, and started my walk home. The tears started with the click of the door and didn't stop until I was home. They weren't gut-wrenching tears because I didn't even really know what they meant.

Was I angry with Mason? Yes. Did I understand why he did what he did? Yes. Was I done with him? I couldn't imagine that. What was I going to do now? I had no clue.

No, the tears that I cried were just something that needed to be done. I had gone through the mourning stage. I mourned the old me and I was accepting of my place in this world now. Now...I just kind of missed her. I missed Emma because I wanted to ask her a million questions. I wanted to live in her head for just a day to see where she was coming from and what she would have done in my place.

I wiped my face with the wrist of my sleeve as I made my way up the long driveway and stopped at the front door. It was then that I heard it. The beater. I turned to see Mason's car passing the gate and felt my lips fall open.

He followed me to make sure that I got home safely in the dark, even after I left him there like that. I felt a little piece of the doubt and hopelessness that had surrounded my heart since I woke up break off and fall away. To have the love and protection of someone like Mason was a once in a lifetime thing. I had no doubt that whatever happened, I'd never find someone like that again.

Useless Fact Number Sixteen

On average, people are more scared of spiders than death.

I pushed my way inside the door, only to be met head-to-chest by the butler. "Miss," he said briskly.

"Hey...man." Dang, I couldn't remember his name.

His brow lifted pompously. "Hanson."

"Hey, Hanson. Sorry I ran into you." He stared. "What's shaking?" I said wryly and started to make my way past him and up the stairs.

"Have you been crying, miss?"

I stopped and turned. "Uh...it's just windy out. Thanks, though."

"Are you certain?" He stepped toward me just a bit. "Not that I'm calling you a liar, but you don't look windblown, miss."

I sighed and ran a hand through my hair. "You caught me, but I'm fine."

"Was it your parents? Or that young man that you go to see?"

I squinted. "What?"

"That has caused you to cry."

I smiled at his candor. "Neither. Both. Just...a collection of lots of things." I sat on the bottom step and pulled me knees up to my chest. "Would the old me have come in crying when she had a bad day?"

He pressed his lips together and put his hands behind his back.

I laughed silently and stood. "I didn't think so. I'm going to bed, Hanson. Night."

"You know, miss..." he started a little too carefully, "just now you've spoken more words to me than you ever have which had nothing to do with some chore you wanted me to do for you."

I felt my breath catch. "I'm sorry, I..."

He smiled. It was reassuring and sincere. "When I overheard your parents say that you'd woken up and couldn't remember anything, honestly, I thought you were pulling a prank." I grimaced. He wasn't the first person to suggest that. "But seeing you since you got home, watching your eyes show such so honesty, hearing you speak with your parents... You were always a tight-knit family. You were always respectful of them, but you also always got your way." He smiled a little wider. "And now, you're still respectful, but you worry so much about letting them down. No offense, miss, but the young woman who used to reside in your bedroom wouldn't have cared about that and she certainly wouldn't have said she was sorry for running into me."

I let that soak in. "I feel like all I do is apologize anymore."

"You don't have to apologize to me. Or anyone, for that matter. I can only imagine what it would be like to wake up and not remember my life, but the only explanation that comes to my mind is...a second chance. Most of us don't get those."

I swallowed and nodded. He nodded his head once in return and made his way from the pristine foyer. I stood there for who knew how long before finally making my way to my room. The stairs no longer caused me such shortness of breath and it felt good to have a piece of normalcy back.

My cell buzzed in my pocket. I pulled it out reluctantly and read the text from Andy asking—well, not really asking, but more like stating, that we were going to Prom together on Friday. He said his tux was black with cream. I could get a swatch and match the color if I needed to. I shook my head.

He was thick-headed, that was for sure. I plopped down on my mattress and kicked my shoes off the side. I let my cheek press into the cool surface, calming and resting my senses. I felt like I was on a precipice that was the most important I'd faced so far. It was all I could do to hang on and see what happened when the cliff gave way. I couldn't face my parents tonight and didn't know if I was surprised that they didn't call me down to dinner or not. I was surprised, however, that Hanson knocked on my door with a tray of fruit and a slice of apple pie for me. I took it gratefully and smiled at him as he shut the door. How had he known that solace and food was what I needed?

I ate, took a shower, put on some cute sleep shorts and a tank that matched to a T, and then lay on my bed and looked up at the dragonflies. My father must've been the one to put these here for me, too. My father who was angry with me for liking peaches.

I knew that wasn't fair. I knew that wasn't *really* the reason, but it was all I had right then. I was still on top of my comforter with the lamp on when Isabella came in, and it didn't escape my notice that she didn't mention my missing dinner. "Emmie, I got you something."

I looked down the length of my bed at her and raised my eyebrows. "You did?"

"Uhuh," she said and grinned. The dog had followed her in and sat by her feet. Yeah, the dog missed me all right. Isabella had a bag draped over her arm. I knew it was a dress. A freaking prom dress.

"What is it?"

"Well," she stalled and swung the dress bag up so quickly that I jumped. "Tada!" she squealed and unzipped the bag, revealing a gorgeous-beyond-belief cream dress.

I felt sick. "You talked to Andy, huh?"

"Of course. He called me, said you had worked everything out, and that you had agreed to go to prom with him. So I went to his house today, got a swatch to match his tux, and went right to Macy's!" I made a face. "Well, honey, I had to go to Macy's on such short notice. If you had given me more time, we could have gotten you fitted at Vera Wang-"

"That's not what I meant." I sighed and looked at the dress. "I'm not going with Andy. He shouldn't have told you I was."

She stood still for a few seconds before lifting her arms in surrender, the dress draping and flying like a flag of guilt. "Then who are you going with?" I squinted and looked away. "You're going, aren't you? Aren't you, Emma?"

"I don't know." Why should I?

"You have to. You'll regret it if you don't."

"No offense, Isabella, but how would you know that? I think I'll survive without Prom on my résumé."

"I know because I never went to mine," she explained softly. "And I always regretted it."

"Why didn't you go?" She looked at me strangely. "What?" I asked, but then I understood and sighed. "We've had this discussion before, haven't we?"

She nodded. Then she tossed the dress on the chair and sat on the bed beside me. "We were too poor for me to go."

My lips parted. "Really?"

"Mmhmm. My father was so upset about it, but none of my five sisters got to go to Prom. It was just never something that fit into the budget, no matter what we did." Her lip quivered a bit. "I suppose it's why I'm so hard on you about things. I never want you to live like I did, never want you to have to tell your daughter that she can't go to Prom one day."

"I know what you said to Mason," I blurted and looked right at her. I wasn't angry and I was just wanted all my cards on the table.

"I did. I said those things and probably a few more things that he was too much of a gentleman to tell you about." I waited. She stared at the carpet before I saw her lip tremble. I was so shocked at the sight that I could do nothing but stare. She turned to me, her head shaking, tears on her cheek, and I lost it.

"Ah, Mom," I whispered and put my hand on her knee. I noted how soft the fabric of her white slacks was. "I'm-"

"You called me Mom." Her voice was high and her eyes were wide. "You called me Mom," she repeated, as if to break me from my stupor.

"I did," I admitted quietly. "To be honest, this is the first time that you really feel like it."

She laughed a little. "Because I'm crying like a goon?"

I laughed at that. Goon. "No, because you're facade is down and you're being real with me. You're not asking me to do anything for my future or how I'm doing. You're just being...you." I squinted and stared into her eyes. My own eyes glazed over and I let it all come out. "I wish I could remember you, so badly. I can almost, almost grab onto some memory when you look at me like this."

"Oh, baby," she cried. "It doesn't matter." She pulled me to her and for the first time, I latched on. She smoothed my hair and I felt like someone's daughter. *Her* daughter. I started to spill my guts.

I told her all about what Andy had done to me, and my friends, and lastly, Mason. I didn't spare her the details at all, and she was peeved about the tattoo, let me tell you, but the part about him knowing me one night before the accident made her very quiet. I didn't know what that meant. I missed him already and I told her so. She didn't scold me about seeing him behind their backs, or about the party I'd been to that night that would ultimately be my demise, or that Mason and I were going to tell them we wanted to see each other regardless.

No. She just absorbed.

I lay back and pulled the pillow down. I patted it for her and she smiled before lying down next to me. We both looked up at the ceiling and I reached over to turn the lamp off. The dragonflies practically swam in the dark above us and she told me about them without my asking. "You used to get so mad at your brother when you were little. He would pull the wings off dragonflies and you'd throw an out-n-out hissy fit, say they weren't hurting anything, and that they were pretty and harmless, that they didn't deserve to die."

"Well...they don't," I said and she laughed before rolling toward me a little to get closer. I put my head on her shoulder, still looking at the ceiling. She went on.

"So when your father bought this house, you said it would be amazing if you could have dragonflies for pets." I smiled against her shoulder. "Your father...being the big softy he is, knew there was no way to keep them as pets, but he searched high and low until he found these." She pointed to the ceiling. "You were our only child that was never scared of the dark. You never had nightmares. You never came and asked to sleep in our bed. It was because of them. It was more than just plastic bugs on your ceiling. It was more than that."

I nodded. "It was." I felt myself tearing up again. "He's mad at me."

She knew who. "No, he's mad at himself. I don't have any doubt that you two will find your way back to each other. You always had this connection. He's... He's sorry, baby. He's so sorry."

I didn't want to talk about Rhett anymore. He didn't want me, so I just closed my eyes and snuggled closer under her arm. Before I knew it, I jolted awake a tiny bit when Rhett pulled a blanket over us both. I closed my eyes so that he wouldn't know I was awake. He leaned over me and kissed Mom's forehead. Then he kissed mine before rubbing my head. "My girls," he muttered. "Back together again."

He plopped down in the chair next to my bed and rubbed his face hard. "God, what am I doing wrong?"

I held in my tears just barely and closed my eyes again to let sleep claim me.

✖

In the morning, he was gone and so was Mom.

Mom. I smiled. It felt so good to embrace that. I got ready for school, though I didn't want to go. I skipped breakfast and half expected Andy or Mason, or both, to be waiting for me, but they weren't.

So I walked and that was fine. When I arrived, the trio waved and kept going. I felt good that maybe at least one fire had been diffused. Now, if I could just get Andy to take a hint and then figure out about...Mason. Sigh.

Andy was in his car and watched me go past. It was beginning to be beyond his wanting to help me. It was creepy. So I steered clear of him all day. I hadn't done my homework the night before since Mom and I had a cry-fest, so I just took notes and listened. All anyone talked about was Prom anyway. I was glad that they had moved on from talking about me. Though I was tired of Prom already and I hadn't even gone yet.

I wondered if Isabella...Mom was right. Would I regret not going? Was that one of those things that I needed to do to feel...normal...

I pulled the list from my purse and on number four wrote *Prom*. Ok. It was settled. I didn't really have a date, but I was going. So I muddled through the day just like that, and the next, which wasn't too hard since Rhett had a work dinner. I convinced Mom to watch a movie with me and we ate in the den. She even went and put on yoga pants.

Yoga. Pants.

It was like seeing the Pope wearing a Christmas sweater.

The next was P Day. Prom. Mom threatened to pull me out of school early to have my hair and nails done because that's apparently...what people did. Not I. I said I could do my own and wasn't interested in being tortured pre-Prom. It was actually kind of nice, because after lunch, half the student body was gone. We basically did nothing the rest of the day. We watched the Dicaprio version of Romeo & Juliet in English if that's any indicator.

That night, I almost changed my mind. It had been two days since I'd seen Mason. I had picked up the phone so many times to text him, but didn't. I didn't really know why. I wasn't really mad at him. I was confused, but not about him. I knew I wanted to be with him, it was just a matter of kicking away my pride and going back over there. To be honest, the reason I think I left was because I felt cheated once again. Even Mason got to know a piece of me before the accident. I wanted to know her and it wasn't fair that I was always the one out of the loop. I doubted he'd come here for me. He probably thought I hated him.

A horrible pain went through me at that thought. He probably *did* think I hated him. I just left and didn't look back. He probably thought I hadn't thought of him at all since I left when the reality was the opposite. But if I hadn't had that fight with Mason, would my mom and I have resolved our issues? If I hadn't been sulking in my room, she wouldn't have come to see me and talk, now would she?

Gah, all of this made my head hurt. Maybe I could just skip Prom and go see him instead... No. What if he was angry with me? I hadn't thought of that. What if he was upset that I had left and wasn't interested in reconciling? He had done so much for me and I just walked out on him. He hadn't texted me either or come to try to talk. I bit my lip and threw myself back to the bed.

Oh, no. That was it, wasn't it? He was done. Well, I'd have to figure out how to make it up to him then. I'd have to-

"Emma!" I jolted up to find Isabella in my doorway. "What in the blazes are you doing not getting dressed!"

"What?"

"You're going to Prom," she commanded and pulled me from the bed with a wide grin. "Oh, just...everything that I thought you'd miss and now you get your chance." She burst into tears right there.

It may have been wrong of me, but I just couldn't break her heart. I'd give her this night and then tomorrow, I'd go get Mason back. I'd tell her that I was absolutely done with Andy, and Mason and I were absolute. If he took me back...

I pushed that away and let her practically rip the shirt from me. The bra came next and she placed a strapless bra on that was basically cups and nothing else. It was magic for all I was concerned. But I couldn't dwell on that because she was putting the dress over my head and twisted my hair up before I could even think. I slipped my heels on and looked at myself in the mirror. The dress was a soft cream and had a strapless top that bunched at the high waist to cascade down the front. I had to admit that I looked beautiful, even if it was wasted on no one.

I leaned in and brushed on mascara and some blush. She turned me to her and I mirrored her mouth as an 'o' as she put on my lipgloss. She cried again and didn't even wipe her face, just rushed me out my bedroom door and down the stairs.

She took a couple pictures, but I finally waved her off and begged her to stop. My cell phone rang in the little black clutch around my wrist. I frowned and pulled it out. She must have put it in there, because I didn't even have anyone to call me anymore. I answered. It was Mrs. Betty and she was pretty upset. "I just thought you should know, child."

"Should know what?" My first thought was Mason was hurt, but why would Mrs. Betty call me if that were the case? "Mrs. Betty?"

"Mason was fired today."

Useless Fact Number Seventeen

Apples are more efficient at waking you up than caffeine.

My breath stopped. "What? What for?" I turned to glare at my mother as she came back in. How could she? "You called and got Mason fired?" I yelled at her. "I thought that we-"

"No, it wasn't her, or your father," Betty corrected. "The doctor found a note in Mason's pocket..." my heart skipped a beat, "...from you. So they fired him for fraternization and misconduct."

Oh, no. Oh, no. Oh, no. This couldn't be happening. He got fired because of me? I slammed the phone back into my purse and started out the door.

"Wait!" I heard behind me. "I'll drive you."

I didn't wait to see why she was driving me or how she knew where we were even going, but I followed her out the door. We didn't make it to her car. Mason was there on the curb, his back to us as he leaned on his car. She clutched her purse and smiled at me as she turned to go back. "I am so confused-"

"Just go. We'll talk later," she assured. She reached over and tucked a piece of hair behind my ear. "Everything happens for a reason. I want you to remember that."

I wanted to say more, but I stepped out in the driveway. "Mason," I called softly, but he heard. He heard and stiffened. He didn't turn. That didn't give me any encouragement, but I stepped toward him anyway. "Mason, I'm sorry."

He turned and blew his breath out, looking at me up and down. "God, help me." His face solemn, he turned and came up the curb slowly. "You're just as beautiful in my dreams, Em, because I have to be dreaming right now."

I didn't know what he meant, but it didn't matter. "I'm so sorry that you got fired for me." Wait. "Or," I shook my head in frustration, "because of me."

"Because of you..." He licked his lips and shook his head, taking another step toward me. "How did you even know what happened?" He looked back at my arms and shoulders. "And why are you dressed like an angel?"

I looked down at myself and couldn't help but smile. "Oh, sorry. It's prom tonight..." I gulped at the look on his face. "Mrs. Betty called me and I'm so sorry."

He smiled sweetly. "You're sorry that I carried your note around with me everywhere I went and some jerk found it who'd been looking for any reason to fire me for months?"

"But I thought...that I left it in your pocket and..."

"No," he corrected and took the last step between us. "No, Emma, I put that note in my pocket on purpose. Just like I have every day since you gave it to me."

"But I thought you hated me-"

His hand moved swiftly toward my face, but I wasn't scared. I didn't flinch as he gripped the back of my neck and pulled us together all the way up and down. "Don't ever, ever say that again." His breath coasted across my face. "I don't hate you—why would I?"

"Because I left," I said lamely.

"I lied to you, Emma. I knew you'd leave."

"You didn't lie," I reasoned. "You omitted. And you were right. If I had woken up, knowing that the reason I was there, the very reason that I couldn't remember anything, was because of some stupid thing I did. Some completely stupid and pointless thing... As my therapists, I'm glad that you didn't tell me. I've had a really hard time forgiving her." He wiped under my eye and looked like he wanted to say something, but I went on. "I hated that I couldn't have a clean slate with you. I didn't want you to know her, but now I see that it wasn't her fault. She wanted to be different, and I'm not sure if she was strong enough to pull it off or not, but I am." I closed my eyes as he caressed my cheek with his fingers.

"Yes, you are." He lifted my chin and I waited to open my eyes, savoring his touch and how calm and connected we were in the dark in my front yard. I opened them and waited. "I've never met anyone who recovered as quickly, who was so determined to be a better person, who believed as hard and as wide open as you."

The wind blew his hair as I stared at his face. It was cool and I felt it waft over my bare shoulders and blow my gown around my feet. His hair fell across my forehead and I saw my hand move to fix it for him. He closed his eyes. "You just wanted to tell me that you're sorry I got canned?" He opened them and I knew everything was about to come to a head.

"No," I whispered and toyed with the button if his shirt. "I missed you."

"I was giving you space," he explained in a rumble. "I wanted to come and beg you to forgive me every second since you left, but I wanted you to come back because you wanted to. Because you wanted to be with me, and if you didn't, then I would have to deal with that. I would just spend forever remembering what it was like to be in love with this amazing girl."

I heard it, I did, but I couldn't dwell on that. I was too busy damming the tears back and feeling guilty. "Baby, what's the matter?" he asked, looking completely confused as he rubbed my arm in his warm palm.

I took a deep, shuddering breath. "It's my fault you got fired. How are you going to take care of your mom, now? I'm not worth that!" I insisted. "I'm sorry."

"Stop right there." He gripped my upper arms firmly. "You are worth it, number one. Number two, I have the shop and always did well with it. It's what I wanted to do anyway."

"Then why were you working at the hospice? I know you said you got into it because of your mom, but..."

"I did, but I planned to quit and open the shop full-time. But...then you happened."

I threw my arms up, dislodging his hands. "So I'm to blame for that, too! First I ruin your chance to work at the shop like you wanted and now I get you fired."

He smiled. I glared back at him as he came and took my arms again. "That's the shakiest, most self-deprecating argument I've ever heard. You're just looking for any reason to take the blame for everything, aren't you?'

I squinted and looked away. "Maybe."

He pulled my face back to him, something I was getting very accustomed to. "You can't take the blame for my choices. I chose to keep working there to take care of you and I chose to carry the note you wrote me because I missed you. And now, I get to open my shop back up full-time and nothing would make me happier. They did me a favor by firing me. That jerk who runs the place hated me anyway."

"Well...I'm still sorry. I just..." I huffed. This was it. The conversation had run out, the stalling was done, the topic, shifting.

He instigated. "I can't believe you're here with me right now," he said in a low voice. "I thought you were gone forever."

"I was afraid that after everything you'd done for me, you'd think I was ungrateful and spoiled."

"Emma-" he complained.

"One minute, I feel so old and outdated because of everything I lost, and then the next, I feel young, naive, and stupid." He sighed guiltily. "But I don't feel that way when I'm with you. I don't feel like I have to find the balance, I just feel like me." He nodded and squinted a little. It was so cute. "What are you doing here, Mason?" I ask, not unkindly.

"Ruining your Prom, apparently," he answered wryly. I half smiled. "I couldn't go another night without knowing if you hated me or not. Good or bad, I had to know. And I'll tell you this," he knelt in the grass in front of me, "I'm sorry, Emma. You'll just never understand how sorry I am. Sometimes I just feel like I have to take care of things, even when it's none of my business. I've taken care of things for so long with my family, and when I didn't, awful things happened. I'm sorry that I overstepped-"

"I forgive you," I made sure to say loudly. He just stared at me. "If you'll forgive me."

"No," he said and twisted his lips. "You didn't do anything wrong so there's nothing to forgive."

"I still feel guilty," I muttered. He stood and lifted my chin once more.

"Don't," he begged. "Please. Would it be all right if I kissed you? Because these past couple days, I thought you'd never speak to me again, let alone let me kiss you again."

"I'm not really sure what kept me away," I said truthfully. "I wasn't really mad, I guess I just...didn't want you to see the old me. She feels like something that I have to reconcile or apologize for. I hated her, and for you to tell me that there was a chance that she maybe wasn't so bad, made me question everything, every decision I've made. Except you."

His eyebrows lifted, his brow bunched. I wanted to kiss the spot there. He spoke softly, rubbing my cheek. "I can't wait for the day that you figure out that you and she are one in the same. That you don't have to compartmentalize your life. That there's bad and good in everyone and we *choose* who we want to be. You are not your past, you are your future." He moved achingly slow to kiss my top lip. "If the angel before me is having doubts about the goodness of her soul, what hope is there for the rest of us?"

A small chuckle fell from my lips. I shook my head and gave him a look that said, *Kiss me, like, yesterday.*

He pulled me up to meet him and we both groaned when our tongues collided. I'd more than missed him, I *needed* him. It wasn't a dependency, it wasn't weakness or a failure, he was an addition to my very soul. And I laughed into our kiss as I realized that this was what love was. I could live without him, of course I could, and I could function and get on with my days if he wasn't here, but I didn't want to. I wanted him right where he was, in my space and in my life.

His hands tugging and pulling at my hips brought me back to earth. My arms were wound around his neck, my elbows on his shoulders, and he plundered my mouth with not a care but to feel me against him.

It was then I realized that I had been going about my new life completely the wrong way. The things we should focus on in any life shouldn't be what we've lost, but what we've gained.

When his hands shifted, one coming up to wrap around my waist, and the other going lower to pull me against him, I gasped into his mouth. He pulled back a little, keeping his hand where it was, and said, "Sorry, but gah, woman, that hiney is amazing in this dress."

We laughed against each other's lips. "Well," I said coyly. "Hiney."

"Yeah," he started and squeezed again, "I thought your jeans were going to kill me, and then you come out in this dress... OK, we've got to stop talking about this."

I pushed his chest. "Shut up."

He smiled, staring at my face. "Your gorgeousness is wasted on me tonight." He looked down at his jeans. "Did someone ask you to Prom?"

"No, except Andy." His jaw clenched a little. "I was going by myself, but I don't want to go now."

"It's on your list, isn't it?" I scowled at his perceptiveness. "Number four. You're going." I opened my mouth to protest and he covered my lips with his thumb. "Emma Walker, will you go to Prom with me?"

I pulled his hand down. "You do not want to go to Prom, Mason."

"Sure I do," he said with a smile. "I never went to mine. I thought it was lame and I was too cool."

"Really?" I said, trying not to sound too hopeful.

"Really. Will you go with me?"

I felt my heart melt a little more. "Mason."

"I can help." We turned to find Mom on the porch. "Come on, Mason. The girl got all dolled up to go and you need to get up to speed, boy.

She beckoned him to her, flicking her wrist in urgency. He looked at me, as if in permission.

"Your call," I said, thinking he'd back out and I'd get to as well, but he smiled at me and took off in a sprint. I watched them go inside in a hurry and made my way inside. In six minutes flat, Mason and Mom came through the den. Mason must've been wearing one of my dad's tuxes. She had her arm in his and looked at him proudly. I could have kissed her.

He looked down at himself and shrugged bashfully. "Fits pretty good," he said modestly.

"You look good," I told him and smoothed the front with my fingers. "Really good."

"No time for that," Mom insisted. "You're already late. But wait, let me get some pictures."

I thought Mason would moan and complain, but he came right up behind me and put an arm around my waist. He leaned in, brushing his face against my hair. "You smell amazing. Like, seriously amazing."

I turned my face to let his nose rub my cheek. "Mason, let's just stay here," I told him breathlessly.

He chuckled, huskily and dangerously. "Oh, no, absolutely not. I'm not to be trusted with you alone right now."

I sank into his chest as Mom got the camera and pretended she couldn't hear or get what was going on.

"Smile, Emma," she said softly and we stared at each other. And I did smile because for the first time in a long time, I felt normal. She only took one picture and then came to hug me to her. "Oh, Emmie. Emma." She leaned back and cupped my cheek. "I never lost you, Emma." I felt my brow bunch in confusion. "You were always here. You've always been you. I'm sorry if I ever made you doubt that."

I shook my head, feeling the tears threatening to spill over. "It was me, not you. I understand now."

She smiled and then turned to Mason. Her smile changed just a bit. "I don't have to explain that I will hunt you down and chop your-"

"No, ma'am. I get it," he said quickly. I chuckled and bit my lip. "I'll have her back by midnight," he said gentlemanly.

"I trust you," she told him and winked at me. "It's Prom. Stay out as late as you want, but text me, Emmie."

"Ok," I told her. The old me probably loved having such a lax mother. "I will."

"Here," she said and scrambled to her purse, pulling the keys out. "Take the Rover."

"No," I said and softened my tone. "We're fine," I insisted. "I want to take the beater."

Mason chuckled a little. "Beater," he repeated.

"It's a term of endearment," I assured him. "I love your car."

"If that's what you want."

"It is. I want complete normalcy."

"OK," he said and grinned, swinging his arm out. "Your chariot awaits."

He opened my door for me and I knew that it wasn't just for show for my mom. He was just that way. We drove the short distance to the school and he once again came to open my door.

We could hear the chatter of teenagers and the thump of music from the car. "Ready?"

I took his hand. "Yeah."

He smiled. "Number four, here we come."

I laughed and let him lead me all the way to the doors. It was everything I imagined a cliché, cheesy high school event to be when he opened the gym doors. The clutch around my wrist banged against my arm as we stopped and stared. "Wow," I said and looked around. "It's so..."

"Mysterious?" He leaned closer and spoke against my ear since it was so loud in the room. "Magical? Enchanting? Fantastical?"

"None of the above," I laughed out the words. "Oh, my..." I looked up at him, so close. "Want to get out of here?"

He laughed. "Absolutely."

In the parking lot, we stopped before getting in the car. I leaned against it and he leaned with me. "Well, that was a waste."

"Nah, it wasn't," he insisted and looked down at my dress. "It's never a mistake for you to look this beautiful. I'm not ready to take you home yet."

"Well," I said coyly and gripped the front of his tux. "I can cross number four off now."

"So let's make a number five." His smile was causing me difficulties. "Come on. Get in."

"Where are we going?"

He moved slowly until he was taking up all of my personal space. I leaned against the car door because I *had* to. "I'm gonna take you to all sorts of cheesy places to fill your list. And when you feel *normal enough* for tonight, I'm going to take you somewhere and kiss you until you can't think or move or breathe."

My breath caught. I whispered in a stupor, "We can skip to that part."

His grin was smug. "No. I want you to feel like your life was complete and your memories intact with everything that you wanted to do. Tonight is all about you, Em. Whatever you say goes. So, where we going first?"

I bit into my bottom lip and tried to think. He gripped my chin and tugged with his thumb and I looked up into his hazel eyes as he owned my very being. "Surprise me."

He accepted the challenge with a tilt of his head and a nod. I pulled his collar and shivered from more than the chill in the air. He wrapped me in his warm arms and rubbed my bare arms as he pulled back. "Cold?"

I shook my head 'no'. "I'm just affected."

He started to laugh, but we both looked toward a car door a couple rows over. I felt Mason stiffen and felt my own fingers grip his lapel tighter without my permission as Andy glared at us. He was alone.

"Look at you," he said angrily, but his eyes took me in, head to toe. Mason turned and stepped in front of me. "So beautiful. In that cream dress...that matches my tux so perfectly."

"Stop talking to Isabella about things that aren't true," I said harshly. "I never said we were going together."

"You belong to me," he said low, but we heard. He glared. "You may not remember, but you were mine and it's not fair that you just-"

"We broke up," I said loudly. "Before the accident, we broke up."

His eyes squinted. "No...we didn't."

"Yes, we did!" Mason stood still as my shield and I gripped his hand. "I know all about the night of my accident."

His eyes widened, wider than I'd ever seen them. "All about it, huh?"

I didn't nod. I didn't acknowledge him. He just turned around, got in his car, and left with his tires squealing on the pavement. Mason turned and tried to hide his scowl. "You OK?"

I nodded. "Jackass."

There was that hint of a smile. "Come on, Em. Don't let him ruin tonight. Let's get out of here."

"OK. Number five."

He helped me in and ran to his side. When he slid in, he took my hand in his and moved it to the gear knob as he shifted. Then he laid them on his lap and kept looking over at me, as if to see if I was really there.

Useless Fact Number Eighteen

It is illegal in the state of Kentucky to marry your wife's grandmother.

When we pulled into the movie theater, I laughed so hard. "You are not taking me to see a movie in a prom dress."

He grinned, pulling his jacket off, then his vest and tie.

"Oh, yes, I am." He got out and came to my side. He opened the door and took my hand. After I was upright, he wrapped his jacket around my shoulders. "Let's go."

"Are you serious?" I yelled and laughed even more when an older couple walking by gave me the stink-eye.

"Dead. Serious." He gave me a look that said, *I have a plan here*, and towed me to the ticket counter.

"Can I help you?" she asked, looking about as bored as I did in math class. Her braces were green — neon green — and her glasses had a *Hello Kitty* right in the center, between her eyes.

"Two tickets, please," Mason told her and pulled his wallet out.

"To what showing?"

"Doesn't matter," he said, his eyes smoldering as he looked back at me. "We don't plan to watch it anyway."

She cleared her throat as she pulled out two tickets and handed them to us. "Ooooookaay," she drawled and smiled condescendingly. "Enjoy your movie."

I thought I heard her say, "Weirdos," as we walked away, but I didn't care. My heels were killing me as we stood in line to get candy. He asked me what I wanted and I went with the classic M&Ms. He got a box of Reese's Pieces and a big Dr. Pepper for us. When we entered the theater, it was completely empty, which was weird.

He sat us in the back row and took a big sip of the drink before offering it to me. I giggled a little, taking a sip of his drink where his lips had just been. We nibbled our candy, sharing back and forth. The commercials started, the lights dimmed, and I shivered when I felt him turning me by my chin to face him, knowing what was coming. He took my lips before I could even think and I fumbled to lift the armrest between us. Once it was out of the way, I scooted over to practically be in his seat with him.

He tasted like sweetness and chocolate and...Mason. He always had this smell and taste to him that I couldn't really pinpoint. Clean and manly.

No one came in and I was so happy because I didn't want him to stop. He plundered my mouth with his and my body with his hands. His fingers inched their way into my hair and across my side and hip as he pulled me against him.

But when the Bonanza theme song started, we both stopped and looked at each other. He took the tickets out of his pocket and looked at them. Under *Theater 3* it read *Bonanza Throwback Marathon*. I could have kissed that ticket attendant.

He rolled his eyes. "That girl-"

"Did us a favor," I said sweetly and wrapped my arms around his neck again. "No one is coming in here for a Bonanza marathon. Nobody." I kissed his jaw and then his neck.

He puffed out a breath and groaned a little. "I guess you're right. Thank you, weird ticket girl."

I giggled and leaned my head back as he ravaged the spot under my ear. "Ah...Mason," I breathed.

He chuckled against my skin. "You're killing me with that."

He didn't wait for a response as he took my mouth again. I sank into him and gasped when I felt him lean down and his fingers encircle my ankle. His palm grazed my skin all the way up past my knee to my thigh, where he squeezed and gripped to pull me closer. I gasped into his mouth again.

"This is as far as I'm going," he assured. "This OK?"

"You don't have to stop there," I said, brazen and bold.

He stopped for a split second as I opened a couple buttons and slid my hand into his shirt, examining the tattoos that I knew were there, but couldn't feel or see. "Yes, I do, Emma," he almost growled before kissing me fiercely again.

My hand roamed inside his shirt as his roamed my leg. He pulled me to sit in his lap, my legs on either side of him. This was quickly becoming my favorite spot. This way, he was able to use both hands, pushing my dress up as his palms explored my legs up and down in an agonizing assault. But, true to his word, he went no further. He did torture me mercilessly though. When he leaned me back and kissed the center of my chest above the strapless top of my dress and then moved his way up my chest, nipping into my shoulder, I felt like sparkly igniters were about to go off in that theater. And then he was back to my mouth, pulling me against him, forcing more embarrassing noises from my throat. He ate those noises and sucked them into his mouth, making his own every time. It was a vicious cycle that I played right into willingly. I begged for time to stop, for the lights to not come up, for us to be able to stay there for hours and hours until our lips were blue and our hands ached from gripping each other too hard and too long.

Our lips didn't disconnect until the lights came back up and the credits rolled. My lips actually hurt. I touched them and smiled. He helped me stand and took my face in his hands. He smiled, rubbing his thumbs across my cheeks, and leaned in to kiss me. "Thank you."

"For what?" I whispered.

His smile was kind of bashful. "For letting me be the one that you trust."

"I trust you," I told him, "of course I do. The way you take care of your mom... I don't think there's a sweeter guy on the planet." He smiled in embarrassment. "If anything, after tonight, I trust you more."

His eyebrows rose. "I drag you into a movie theater to make out," he rubbed his nose against mine, coyly, "and it takes everything in me to not let my hands keep going up those legs of yours...and you trust me more?"

"Yes," I whispered, unable to play into his joke.

He moved forward and took my bottom lip between his right before we heard, "Hey, I need to clean."

We turned to find a pimply, red-headed boy with a broom that was bigger than he was. I giggled as we walked past him and went to Mason's car. Once inside, he asked for my list. I rolled my eyes, pulled it from the wrist bag I'd thrown between the seats, and gave it to him. He pulled a pen from the visor and wrote: #5 *Make out at the movies*. Then wrote : #6 *Dance in a field*.

Then he crossed out number four and number five. He pointed to number six. "This is next. Now. You up for it?"

I felt myself smile. "You wanna dance in a field with me?"

"Of course I do," he said in a low voice. "And it's a perfectly *normal* thing to do, go dancing with your boyfriend."

I felt a girly sigh go through me. "Really?" I asked in mock condescension to cover it up. "A field?"

"Don't knock it 'til you try it," he said and smiled as he pulled out of the parking lot. "Especially since you were deprived of dancing in that dress tonight."

"It's just a dress," I reasoned.

"That...is not just a dress."

I smiled as I turned to look out the window.

We were almost out of town when my phone rang. I fumbled to answer it, thinking it was Isabella. "Hello? Isabella, I'm-"

"You are my constant source of torture," the low voice said. I felt my heart skid a little.

"Andy?" I saw Mason's head turn toward me.

"You have to know what you're doing to me, right? You just have to." He seemed to be talking to himself more than me. "You're all I can think about. You're all I have nightmares about. You're all that consumes my conscience. This ends tonight. I...can't do this anymore."

"Andy-"

"You weren't supposed to come back," he confessed and my heart officially stopped.

"What did you say?"

"You were dead!" he yelled. "You weren't supposed to come back!"

I took a shaky breath. "Tell me what you mean by that."

"I'm at the bridge, Emmie," he said softly. "Come save me like I couldn't save you."

My heart kicked up into fourth gear when I heard the line go dead. "Go to the bridge, Mason."

"What happened? What did he say?" he asked, but he was already turning around. It made me want to kiss him for just trusting me and doing what I asked instead of asking questions first and trying to stop me.

"He's gonna jump," I told him. "He... I think he had something to do with my accident."

"The bridge..." he muttered. "That's where your accident was."

I looked at him. "I didn't know that."

He sighed and banged his fist on the steering wheel. "Emma. If he confesses that he ran you over and then left you in the road to die, he won't have to jump. 'Cause I'm gonna kill him."

I didn't say anything to that. What *could* I say?

I could see Andy's car on the road after we made the short drive to the bridge. The moon was full so the road was lit brightly with the eerie light. I could imagine how beautiful that full moon would have been had we gone to the field instead, but this wasn't beautiful.

Mason turned off the main highway and I could see the bridge. This was the road that went out of town and lots of the kids lived out on this road.

Mason took my hand as he stopped the car behind Andy's. We could see him pacing the highway. Mason looked at me and took a calming breath. His jaw worked as he ground his teeth. "I'm going to call the police, OK? And I'm coming with you."

"I want you to." I gripped his fingers tighter. "I don't want to be alone with him."

"You won't be. Ever," he growled and got out, almost running to my side of the car. He pulled out his phone and quickly dialed 911. He gave them the address and then hung up. He took my hand again and led me past Andy's car onto the street. Andy was still wearing his suit, but had taken off his jacket and his tie was loose. His hair was a mess and he appeared to be talking to himself.

When he heard us approach, he jerked around toward us. "You came." He seemed relieved.

I spoke slowly. "I want to know what happened the night of my accident."

His face scrunched. "Oh, God, Emma. Oh, God, I never wanted this."

"What do you mean?" I asked, though Mason was standing in front of me, a statue of protection and anger. He was silently begging me to let him loose on Andy.

"You did break up with me," he confessed, quietly, his eyes haunted. "I was such an ass. You caught me that night with...it doesn't matter." He grabbed at his hair. "You'd told me so many times that you were through with me, that you'd had enough of my crap, but I knew you'd take me back. You always did and no one ever knew what was going on. You were so good at pretending everything was fine. But that night at the party after you caught me, it was different. I knew you weren't coming back to me. I knew everything was going to be different after that. So I was coming to your house to beg you to forgive me, to take me back, to please not let it change us. That I was sorry and it would never happen again, and I meant it."

Mason scoffed, but stayed silent. I knew Andy meant what he said; it was all over his face that he realized that whatever happened that night was a catalyst for us. But it didn't matter.

He scowled as he said, "My phone rang and I reached down to answer it from where it'd fallen from the middle console. It was you. You were calling...for some reason, and when I leaned back up, it was too late to stop."

I covered my mouth with my hands to keep the sob inside. No, no, no...I changed my mind. I didn't want to know. He continued anyway.

"I got out and there was so much blood, Emmie. So much blood. I checked your pulse and didn't find one. All I could think about was my parents and football and what everyone would say-"

"You son of a-" Mason growled and started toward him.

"I know it was selfish, OK, but I thought you were dead!" Andy yelled and held his hand up as Mason reached him. Mason gripped him by the shirt collar and reared back to punch him. "Go ahead! Hit me! Go ahead!"

Mason hesitated. Andy didn't even fight back. He lifted his jaw and wanted him to hit him.

"Why did you leave me there?" I heard myself say.

His face fell. "I thought you were dead."

"But she wasn't!" Mason defended.

"I'm not a paramedic! How was I supposed to know?"

"You're the reason she was in a coma," Mason kept the growling going. "If she hadn't have laid in the road and had a brain bleed, she might have been OK. But now we'll never know if you stole all that time from her or not."

"Whatever," Andy muttered and looked at me. "Why were you calling me, Emma? Why?" I stayed silent. "It's your fault this happened. Your fault that I've been eaten alive with guilt."

"Shut your face," Mason commanded and shook him. A song broke out and my breath caught in my throat. I began to shake and watched as Andy pulled his cell phone from his pocket. That's why that song haunted me. He had been reaching for his phone before he ran me down...

Mason looked back at me and I was frozen. That song...that song played through my brain like it was *that* night. I couldn't remember anything else and for once, I was glad. My body shook so much that my vision bounced. Mason squinted in indecision before pushing Andy back against the car. He pointed in his face and said, "We are not done yet."

He made his way back to me swiftly and ever so slowly reached his hands toward my face. "Em, baby," he soothed. "Breathe for me, OK. Just in slow and out slow. Deep breath in."

I obeyed and tried to get a grip on myself. I was due a freak out, right? I hadn't had one in a while. He was still going with his pleas for me to calm down and relax, so I touched his cheek. "I'm OK."

He made a noise low in his throat. "You are not OK."

I could hear Andy mumbling behind him, but kept my eyes on Mason. I nodded as I told him, "I promise. I'm...all right."

He sighed harshly. "Emma, I need you to do something for me."

"Anything."

He looked kinda haunted and gulped. "Keep me from killing this guy."

"Mason-" I began to explain all the ways about how he was better than that and Andy wasn't worth it, but we heard a crash.

We turned in time to see Andy's car as he pushed it off the side into the steep ditch, and watched helplessly as it crashed into the water. I looked at him with a million questions in my eyes as he looked back at me. He smiled, a ghost of a tear on his cheek. "One less thing for my parents to have to deal with," he said, as if that explained everything.

Mason must've understood more than I did, because he said, "You don't have to do this."

"Yeah," Andy sighed and looked at my face with a smile that was more sad than anything. "Yeah, I do." He began to walk backward to the railing and my heart jumped into my throat. "Emma, you'll never know how sorry I am that I hurt you. I loved you, I did, I was just an idiot and I let idiots tell me how to run my life."

"Come on, man," Mason tried to stall and moved forward a few steps. "Let's just talk for a minute."

"I'd give anything to go back and not answer that phone. Why did you call me, Emma?" he yelled. "Why? I'd give anything to go back to that night. Anything! I'd have passed you on the road, picked you up, took you to your house and we'd have made up. We'd have made out in my car like we did a million times before and we'd be together now!"

"Andy, no," I denied.

"That's why I needed to make it up to you. That's why I've been so obsessed about seeing you and trying to be together because I didn't know any other way to make it up to you! I needed you to forgive me, even if you didn't remember. I needed you to let me know that you were OK. But you saw right through me, right through my bullcrap. Just like you did that night at the party when you said we were done. I knew it was hopeless. And then tonight...this guy..." He slung his arm out toward Mason, who had inched forward a little more. I clung to his back and watched the train wreck happen in front of my eyes. "I knew we were over. You looked at him like...the old you used to look at me." He rubbed his head. "God, Emma, I wish you all the happiness that you deserve." He smiled a little and another tear slid down his cheek. "Which is a lot."

He was only feet from the rail and Mason didn't wait any longer. He took off slowly after him in an easy manner, with his hands raised, nonthreatening. But it was too late...

"The night of your accident..." Andy's back hit the railing and I saw his shaky breath. "Damn, Emmie, I died right along with you."

And then he pushed off with his foot on the bottom rung, pushing himself over the railing, and let himself fall. I heard my plea, my useless cry for him to stop, but it was beyond too late.

Mason ran to the railing and looked down for long seconds. I couldn't move. I was stuck to my spot in utter disbelief. And then my feet moved without my permission, this need to see for myself blazing through my veins.

I stared down at the raging water below and watched for nothing and everything. There was no Andy, nothing to show the horrible thing he had just done. I felt beyond wretched. I didn't condone what Andy had done, in fact, it pissed me off so badly I couldn't think straight that he'd do this to his family, but the fact that he was just gone and there was nothing left of him, nothing to show how sad and desperate he'd been...broke my heart for him.

I stared at that water...

I didn't even see Mason come to me, but I felt his hands on my face and jolted aware. The police lights whirred behind his head and I wondered how long I'd been like that.

"It's over, Em." Mason pulled me to him and let me bury my face in his warm neck. "It's over."

"Mason," I whispered and pulled away a little. He looked worried, like I was about to run. I shook my head. "I'm not going anywhere," I reminded him, just like I told him before. "I just want you to take me home."

"Miss," a deep, brusque voice said. "You can't go home until we get a statement."

I sighed as Mason groaned in frustration and turned to the policeman. We both told them everything, from seeing Andy at the school, to the phone call, to coming there, Mason going off on him, and everything Andy said. Everything. Then how he jumped.

At some point, Mason must have called my mom, because she and Rhett showed up a few minutes later, and when they got there, she pushed the policeman aside and hugged me to her so hard. She pulled Mason, who hadn't left my side, into the hug, too. "Thank you for calling, Mason."

"Mom," I squeaked and she kissed my head as she began to sob.

"Oh, Emmie. What happened here?" She lifted her head and looked around. "What happened?"

I looked at Mason and he gave me a *sorry* face. "I couldn't tell her over the phone," he said in apology.

"What? What couldn't you tell me over the phone?" she asked in a high, aggravated voice.

"He... Andy, he..." I tried. I couldn't. There was no way.

I felt Mason's mouth on my ear. "I'll do it, baby. You just sit here and let me take care of it."

He moved me to sit in the open door of his car in the passenger's seat. I vaguely heard him as he and my parents discussed what had gone down. What Andy had done. How he just jumped, throwing his life away. He didn't say, however, how his last words were that he blamed me, that I was somehow responsible for not only my own coma and amnesia, but for his guilt as well. I felt my face crumple and my chest wracked with sobs that didn't belong there.

It wasn't my fault. It wasn't my fault that he wasn't paying attention and ran me over. It wasn't my fault that he thought I was dead and left me there. It wasn't my fault that I woke up after he assumed I would be in a coma forever. It wasn't my fault that I was a different girl who couldn't be who he wanted me to be.

It wasn't my fault that he jumped.
It wasn't my fault that he jumped.
It wasn't my fault that he jumped.
It wasn't my fault that he jumped.
It wasn't my fault that he jumped.
It wasn't my fault that he jumped.

Useless Fact Number Nineteen

Heinz ketchup leaves the bottle at twenty-five miles per year.

My chest hurt so badly and my lungs begged for air. I felt a hand on my cheek and looked up, ready to fall into Mason's hazels, but it was Rhett. He seemed confused and that just made me hurt even more. I turned away, pressing my cheek to the cloth seat, and saw out of the corner of my eye as he moved away and Mason took his place. I wrapped my arms around his neck, pressing our chests together, and let loose.

"What's wrong? Are you OK?" Rhett asked and tried to get in my line of sight. "Talk to me, Emma!"

"Rhett," Isabella tried, "just hold on. Emma, baby, talk to us. Are you going to be all right? Do we need to take you to the hospital?"

I shook my head, silently begging them to stop. I heard Mason say, "Just give her a minute, OK? She just needs a minute."

My chest ached with something I'd never felt before, and I was so confused by it, but it wasn't going away. It started small and the more I cried, the more it grew. It was like a slow burning fire that grew to an inferno. Mason understood and he held me to him so tightly and he whispered all the things people say when something awful has happened. But more importantly, he said he was there for me, that he wasn't going anywhere, and to take my time until I knew that it wasn't my fault. He stayed right there and never moved an inch. The police came to talk to my parents, and he let his hands smooth and soothe me up and down, and didn't ask me to speak. Just like in the hospice when everyone was freaking out over my 'breakdown',

Mason knew it was just what I needed. He understood that I was in my own head and I was safe there. I'd come back when I felt like I could.

That made me fall in love with him all over again.

And I realized that I was in love with him.

His neck was my favorite place to hide and I stayed there until I felt him putting me in his car. I didn't look around. I just closed my eyes and felt him take my hand after he put the car in gear. The short ride ended and I felt him get out and lift me, carrying me close to him. My parents chattered and argued behind us. Rhett wasn't happy that Mason was "taking over" in this situation.

Isabella convinced him to leave us alone for a while.

When Mason sat with me in his lap, I opened my eyes to find us at my house. We were on the couch in the den and Mason's jacket was back around my shoulders. I looked up into his face and he cupped my cheek with his warm, calloused palm. "You don't have to stay," I said, but didn't mean it. "I'll just go to bed."

"Not a chance," he replied firmly. He sighed and let his thumb brush under my eye. "I'm so sorry. No one should ever have to..."

"My baggage just keeps getting heavier and heavier," I said pathetically.

"Stop it," he ordered in a whisper. "I told you, I've got broad shoulders." He held my chin and looked through me. "It wasn't your fault. You can't take responsibility for someone else's choices, remember? You told me that." I bit into my lip hard. "Maybe...maybe I shouldn't have provoked him."

I shook my head so violently that my hair came down from its pins. "It wasn't *your* fault. He called us and practically said he was going to jump. You turned around, even though you didn't like him, and you tried. It wasn't your fault. And it wasn't mine either," I said through gritted teeth. "I don't care if he said I called him. It wasn't my fault."

"No, it wasn't, Em. It wasn't."

He moved me to straddle his lap and rubbed my back as he leaned his head back with me. I curled up on his chest and in his arms like I was home, like I was safe, because I was. Before I knew it, I had cried myself to sleep and woke when I heard a scuffle in the room.

I started to lift my head, but someone kissed my hair. "It's OK. I was just checking on you."

Rhett.

"Go back to sleep, baby," he said softly and pulled Mason's jacket off my shoulders only to replace it with a blanket to cover us both. I pulled it up to my chin and laid my head back down on Mason's shoulder. He hadn't moved an inch and his mouth was opened just a bit. Rhett left the room and I watched him go.

I closed my eyes and begged for sleep to come back.

When my eyes opened, I half expected Mason to be gone, me to be in my own bed and scarred from a horrible nightmare. Instead, it was real, I was on Mason's lap, and was scarred from a horribly real experience.

I waited for the tears. I waited for the sobs to overtake me once more, but they didn't come. I felt guilty about that for a split second before I remembered what Mason had reminded me last night. You can't take responsibility for other people's decisions and choices.

I took a deep breath and looked up to find Mason watching me, waiting to see if a breakdown was coming. I reached up and pulled him down to me, keeping my hand wrapped in the hair at the back of his neck. I kissed him slowly and with as much love as I could put into it. He kissed me back just as slowly, and when I pulled back, I licked my lips. "Thank you."

He shook his head and leaned forward to kiss the corner of my mouth. "You don't have to."

"Yeah," I sighed. "Yeah, I kinda do."

We looked at each other and I knew there was really nothing to say. What happened yesterday was unspeakable, unthinkable, and unstoppable. Filling the space with empty words was pointless and I appreciated that Mason didn't try.

"Go home," I told him and laughed at his face. "Go home, Mason. It's Saturday. Your mom's nurse goes home this morning and I need a shower and...you're in a tux." I laughed sadly.

He looked down at our clothes and grimaced. "Yeah. You're sure you're OK? I know that your parents are here and that you're fine, but...are you *OK*?"

I nodded slowly. "I'm OK. I'm going to take a shower, sleep through lunch, eat dinner with my parents. Normal stuff."

He licked his bottom lip. "OK. Can I, uh...can I see you later?"

"Of course," I scoffed and gripped his shirt front. "Maybe I can come over and we can get some dinner instead?"

"I've got a better idea." I twisted to find Isabella...Mom standing there. "How about you come here for dinner, Mason? And bring your mother."

I squinted and looked back at Mason. He seemed to be waiting for a confirmation from me. I shrugged. "Yes, ma'am. Thank you," he answered politely.

"That way we can all get to know each other a little better," she explained hurriedly.

So that's what we did. Mason went home, I slept the day away trying not to think, and that night, he brought his mom over for dinner. Rhett had a 'meeting' but I was sure it was more than that. He didn't like Mason and me together, and seemed to be struggling with the fact that the daughter he once had was gone. I understood and tried not to be too hard on him. It stung though to know that I was the reason that he was gone so much.

Mason's mom was the funniest lady. She had my mother busting a gut over an old Monty Python episode. My mom's blush was hilarious and we all had a good time. I tried to participate, but still felt raw from what happened. Everyone just let me be, which was a Godsend all its own. Mason's hand gripping mine under the table was all I needed. The next night, they came for dinner again and I felt a little bit more normal, like the wound was trying to close.

Mason came to take me to school the next day. I kissed him when I got out. As he drove away, I turned to find a school that hated me. Everyone knew what had happened to Andy and thought me heartless. One, for coming to school only two days after what happened, and two, for kissing my boyfriend on school property. Like it was sacred ground in memory of Andy and I wasn't allowed to live my life on it.

They didn't care that we hadn't been dating. They didn't care that Andy had been practically stalking me. They didn't care that he had been the one to run me over and leave me in the street to die. None of that mattered. All they could see red for was that he had blamed me. Apparently, one of the officers had done an interview and spilled all the gory beans about that night. He was now on probation, my mom said, but it was pointless. It was out there and there was no taking it back.

So that week was hell. I just ignored and avoided everyone. Mason dropped me off and picked me up every day, narrowly avoiding an altercation with a guy from the football team who made a snarky comment about "Andy's amnesia whore". I was barely able to keep Mason in the car. That kid didn't realize that I probably saved his life.

On Saturday, I woke and went down for breakfast. Mason and I were spending the day together. I really wanted to discuss what was going to happen after graduation, which was only days away. I didn't want to go to college, but he was adamant that I at least look at my options. So all those packets my parents had for me were going to be put to good use today.

The kitchen was empty and I grabbed a yogurt from the fridge for breakfast while waiting for the coffee to brew. I heard the steps coming and turned to tell Isabella good morning. My brain still fought with me on that, calling her Mom half the time and Isabella the other, but it was Rhett.

"Hey," he muttered and looked at the cup in my hand. "Yogurt, huh?"

I looked at it, feeling guilty, and then back to him. "Emma didn't like yogurt, did she?"

He shook his head. "No."

I felt my heart break once more. "I'm sorry. I'm sorry that I'm not her. I'm sorry that you're so disappointed in me for that, and I'm sorry that your daughter is gone. I am so sorry that you lost your daughter that day."

I set the yogurt down and grabbed my purse on the way out to Mason's. I was just so numb at this point that I didn't even cry. Once I reached Mason's, he was already climbing in his car. He looked back at me with a smile, but it drained away. "What happened?"

"I left. He wants his daughter, not me." He got my meaning immediately and pulled me up, gripping me tightly to him.

"Oh, Em. I'm sorry. What happened?"

"I'm not their daughter anymore. They lost their daughter in that accident. I can't give her back to them." A sob finally came and took my breath. "I don't even know who I'm supposed to be now."

He pulled back, wiped a tear from under my eye with his thumb, and smiled. "You're the girl that I'm falling madly in love with."

I felt all the breath leave me. My mouth fell open, but no words escaped.

He chuckled. "A speechless Emma. That's really cute."

I reached up to take the beautiful lips that just said they loved me. Me. Not her, me. It wasn't long before we heard an engine pull up. Mason eased away, taking one more pull from my mouth before setting me back.

I peeked over to find Rhett. "How did he know to find me here?" I wondered aloud.

"Emma," Mason chuckled, "I think it's obvious."

I looked up to his face. "Because it's obvious that I'm falling madly in love with you, too?"

A puff of happy breath left his lips before the smile appeared. "God, I hope so."

He pulled me up to him, even with Rhett there, and brushed my mouth with his.

I let my hand slide slowly from his cheek before walking to Rhett slowly. "I'm sorry," he said, his face pinched.

"You don't have to be sorry that you miss her."

"No. I don't have to miss her, because she's right in front of me. People change. You're a teenager. Teenagers change every day, and instead of being happy to have you back, I chose to focus on all the things that didn't matter." He worked through something in his head. His face changed several times before he spoke again. "I'm sorry that I made you doubt that you were my daughter." He held in a sob and pulled me to him. My head fit under his chin and I felt it shaking. "I'm so sorry. Please forgive me, Emma."

I closed my eyes and felt my lips smile for the first time in days. "There's nothing to forgive."

After he left, I sat on the trunk of Mason's car with him. He was so relaxed, but not. He seemed like he had something he wanted to say and I waited for that. He finally said softly, "You've got to go, Em."

"Go where?"

"College. You've got to get out of this town...away from me, and do something for yourself."

"I don't want to leave," I muttered quietly. "I'm just now figuring out who I am. I'm not ready to start reinventing myself yet."

He sighed and rubbed his face. "I just want to protect you."

"From what?"

"From my life." He shook his head. "Oh, God, help me...you're going to think I'm such a shallow idiot."

"I wouldn't think that," I insisted quickly and turned all the way to look at him, my leg under me. "What?"

He swallowed hard and looked at me full on. "I want to protect you from...me. I won't ever be able to buy you some fancy house."

"Don't want one," I shot back.

"College? No funds for it."

"That's what student loans are for."

He seemed to visibly steel himself as if gearing up for a fight. "I'm dirt poor. All my money goes to helping my mom."

I sighed. "And it's the sweetest thing I've ever seen."

He sighed, too. "My car breaks down half the time I take it from the curb."

"It's a small town. Biking is good for me anyway."

"Ahh!" he yelled in frustration and laughed sadly. "I'm trying to do the right thing here. I want you to have everything you ever wanted."

"I want you. And then I want to talk about what I might want later. Whatever happens, I'm not worried." I put my head on his shoulder and he seemed to relax a little. We sat there just like that for a while in silence.

"What are you thinking about, Em?"

"I just wonder what the old Emma would do now."

"It doesn't matter. The old Emma is gone." He shook his head. "I thought I wanted her to come back, for your sake, for your family's sake, but I'm...selfish and glad that she didn't." He took a deep breath through his nose. "Because it's not the old Emma I'm in love with, it's you."

I turned and looked up at him. He waited and smiled a little.

"Ask me what plans I had for my life," I said and felt the first of what I knew were many happy tears slide down my cheek. "Ask me what I wanted to be and how I was going to get there. Ask me how many kids I was going to have and what color the shutters on my red-brick house would have been." I touched his arm. It was really warm. "I'm sure I knew all of those things. But none of that matters now. Ask me what I want now and all I can picture is you-"

He moved in swift. His hand moved to the back of my neck and he pulled me to his lips that were warm and moist.

I sank.

I drowned.

I gave in.

And I was wide awake.

THE END

Epilogue

To say the last week of school was the definition of hell was the understatement of the century. The old me didn't matter anymore, none of the facts about my accident mattered. I was the brunt of all of their misplaced anger. For some reason, Andy's passing with only a few weeks left of school, on Prom night no less, was too tragic for them to ignore. It was on the news, there were memorial posters and signs everywhere, Andy's locker was covered with letters and trinkets that people left him. And that was fine. People should remember him, but instead of focusing on what they should have been, the fact that a teenager ran someone over, left them there to die, and then committed suicide, they focused on me.

Mason even tried to come to class with me, but I assured him no one was causing me bodily harm, they just hated my ever-loving guts. Words I could handle, and did. Now, with only three days left of school, I was just ready to start a new life that had nothing to do with the kids in this town. They could leave and go to their fancy colleges, as long as I didn't have to see their judgmental faces anymore.

Rhett — yes, I still called him Rhett — wasn't happy with my decision to take a year off and figure out what I wanted to do. He thought a year off was a year wasted, but I was just in a coma a few months before. Was it really that much of a stretch that I take a little time for myself to figure things out? Mom was very supportive and we spent every Sunday night together for a girl's night. We watched movies and ate junk. My sister, Felicia, even came home this week to spend some time with the family before my graduation. There was still a big awkwardness there, but she was trying. And I was trying to be a part of the family...because I was.

I was Emma Walker, always have been, always will be.

Epilogue
-*Part Two*-
Mason

I was waiting on the curb for her. She practically sprinted from the doors like the sexy, sweet girl that she was. I grinned and opened my arms as she bounced into them. I leaned down and kissed her easily before opening the passenger door for her. "I've got a surprise for you."

"What?"

I laughed and got in my side. "It's called a surprise for a reason, Em."

She punched my arm playfully and giggled when I reached under her thigh to tickle her. I could see that she was about to retaliate, so I surrendered.

The radio played a really great Killers song and I turned it up. She put her head on my shoulder, letting her fingers run across and trace one of the tattoos on my arm. I couldn't keep the smile off my face. Emma was graduating even after everything she'd been through. And not just that, she was number twenty two in her class of two hundred after missing months of school.

She worked her ever-loving buns off. I was so proud of her it was ridiculous.

We went past my house and then her house. She gave me a curious look, but didn't say anything. Just smiled and enjoyed the ride. She trusted me and that was something that I felt like I hadn't had in a long time. Trust.

Milo was still Milo. He hated my guts and that wouldn't change. Emma and I had gone to get him one night this week and I vowed to never do it again, but I knew that was a lie. I'd do it as many times as it took. He was my brother and I loved him, even if he didn't reciprocate. And Emma was a trooper as always. She fawned over him when he threw up on the curb and then again when I had to stop to let him throw up some more. He didn't even push off her efforts like he did me, and she seemed so eager to help, so it was a good partnership, I guess.

And she was good with my mom, too. Every day after I picked her up from school, she went and read the same chapter to my mom in her book. Every. Day. Same. Chapter. Mom couldn't remember that she'd already read it a million times, and she couldn't remember Emma's name, always calling her Mariah.

I took Mom to the doctor and went through her daily life like we always did at her check-ups. When I told the doctor about Emma, about how Mom always calls her Mariah, he was very intrigued. I explained it all and he in turn explained what fascinated him about it.

He said, "It's not that she calls her by the wrong name, it's that she calls her by the same wrong name every time." I must've looked confused because he explained further. "She never met this Emma before the accident, correct?" I nodded. "Then she shouldn't be able to remember her at all. She remembers her every time she sees her."

I got it and it gave me hope, but he quickly shot me down. "Don't get too excited. It doesn't mean that anything is changing in her brain, it doesn't really mean anything. It's just fascinating how the mind works. When little miracles like that happen, we just take them as they come."

I agreed and when I told Emma later, she cried. I knew she would. She felt close to my mom in a way the rest of us never could be. The fact that my mom had some kind of weird connection with her was amazing. It made me fall in love with her a little bit more every time I saw them laugh together, or when Emma pretended that she hadn't seen that daggum episode of *The Price is Right* a hundred times already, or when Mom freaked when she saw me and didn't remember me being this old, Emma would bring her some hot tea and the photo albums.

God, thank you for her. I loved her more than any man had a right to.

So now, as I drove her to my surprise and held her small hand in mine, I didn't have any doubt that I'd marry her one day, and she'd go to college to be whatever she wanted to be, and she'd have a little girl that looked just like her and had my eyes. I wasn't going to ask her to marry me today, no, but I *was* going to ask her one day. And she'd say yes because she loved me, too.

We drove for almost two hours, talking about everything but where we were going. She had school tomorrow and we were going to be late getting home so, even though she was nineteen years old, an adult, and didn't really need their permission, I asked her parents' permission anyway out of respect. They were warming up to me more and more every day, especially after what happened. I thought they'd hate me after that, but...the opposite seemed to be true.

When we pulled into the apple orchard, she looked confused, but amused. "Apples, huh?"

We pulled further into the field and she saw all the cars first, and then the booths and rides. Then the huge sign tied across the poles that said, **"Dragonfly Festival"**. She gasped and looked at me. Her eyes were wide and awe-filled. "How did you..."

"I have my ways." I grinned as I pulled into a parking spot and came to her door. She looked up at me like I was more than I was. More than a poor boy that had nothing to offer, more than a tattooed guy who always had to prove he was *something* from judging eyes, more than I deserved.

I took her face in my hands and then took her mouth. That mouth that owned me, that mouth that made me forgot who and what I was and made me feel like I was better than all that. Her whimper as she went to her tiptoes and the way she gripped at the hair on the back of my neck had my pulse rioting in my ears.

As I pulled away, she held on tighter and slipped her tongue past my lips. My eyes rolled into the back of my head and I turned us to press her to the side of the car. She laughed happily into my mouth and that was it for me. I took another long pull from those lips and then leaned back. "OK, we've gotta stop."

She laughed at me and fell back on her feet from her tiptoes. "Is this my surprise?" Her voice was light and happy.

"Maybe," I said coyly and grinned at her as I locked her door and shut it. "I have a lot of surprises for you tonight."

"I need to call Isabella."

"I handled it. It's all good."

"Really?" I nodded. She bit into her lip and took my hand with both of hers. "Thanks."

"Welcome, baby."

We played every game there, we rode all the rides, I watched as she got sparkly dragonfly temporary tattoos on her hand and arm, and she ate enough cotton candy to hyperactivate six small children. We ate corn dogs and greasy fries for supper.

Then the lights went down along with the sun and a live band started to play cover songs. They shut off all the street and spot lights, and all that was left was the twinkling string lights strung above the field. I couldn't have imagined anything better. When she sighed at it, I almost laughed. I pulled her to me, holding her hand on my chest, and led her as the band played.

I leaned down and put my mouth to her ear. "Do you know what we're doing right now?"

She laughed. "Yeah, Yoda. Dancing."

I nodded, my nose rubbing her cheek. "Yeah, dancing. In a field. You can cross off number six now."

I heard her breath catch a little. "Oh..." She pulled back just enough to see me. "Was this part of my surprise?"

I nodded. "We're going to put a hundred things on that list, and somehow, someway, I'm going to help you cross them all off."

She smiled, her eyes welling. "Thank you. This is better than anything you could buy me. You know that, right?"

"Hey," I chuckled. "It was just too good to pass up. Dancing in a field and dragonflies. Two birds, one stone."

She laughed and pulled me down to kiss her. My hands moved to her hips, and we swayed, moved, pulled and frustrated ourselves for hours out there as the band played in the dark.

When we finally walked back to the car, I was physically restraining myself. The ride home was going to be torture. It was after midnight and we had a long ride home.

"Are you going to be OK to drive?" she asked as I opened the creaky door for her.

"Course. Besides," I growled and nipped at her bottom lip, "I want you so bad right now that I won't sleep for a week."

"Hey, it's your fault," she said and laughed. She reached around me and stuck her warm hands into my back pockets, knowing exactly what she was doing. She kissed my neck. "You're the one with hands that-"

"Uh huh," I groaned. "You've got to stop."

She laughed. I felt my scowl in place, but that just made her laugh more. She wrapped her arms around my neck. "I love you. Thank you for this."

"You know the first time I really, seriously fell in love with you?"

She shook her head. I pulled the note she wrote me all those weeks ago, the note I've kept in my pocket ever since. Her...tribute to the Useless Facts book I'd gotten her. Her smiled turned a little shy and she laughed under her breath. "You're still carrying that thing?"

"I told you, it was the first time I knew that you were going to be mine. I carry it with my every day because I love you."

She opened it and laughed before reading it out loud, "Turtles can breathe through their butts." We both laughed as she continued. "I just wanted you to see what you were giving a young, impressionable mind to read. I can't stop reading it. It's addictive. Thank you so much. P.S. I miss you when you're not here - Emma." She folded it back up and put it back in my pocket. "That's still true," she muttered softly.

"I'm glad." I let my hand move to her back pocket, her backside under my palm, and my fingers of the other snuck inside the back of her jeans to touch her tattoo. She loved to touch my ink even when she couldn't see them. I could see the appeal now and I couldn't wait to see her tattoo again. "All in all, I just want you to be happy again, whatever that looks like, Em."

She smiled a sexy smile and kissed my lips. "You don't have to try so hard, Mason," she said against my lips. "We're there."

Six Months Later
Emma

"We'll be here," I assured him. "Of course, I wouldn't miss it."

Dad smiled. Yes, not Rhett, Dad. He hugged me to him, snuggling me under his chin, and then leaned back. "Thanks, baby. To be honest, your old man is a little nervous."

"Why, Dad?" I chuckled and put my arm around his waist as we moved around the pool in the back yard. "You're the CEO and you've been that for a long time. There's nothing wrong with stepping down and letting someone else take over for a while."

He laughed. "That's a nice way of putting early retirement."

I looked him over. "I'm really glad that you're doing this. You and Mom could use some time to yourself. You've been through a lot."

"Coming from you," he said wryly and kissed my forehead and whispered, "that's just ridiculous."

"Your going away party is going to be great, Dad. And surprising Mom with a trip to Mexico... She's going to flip!"

"I hope so. And I also thought I might surprise her by renewing our vows while we're there."

"Aw, Dad." I smiled, but felt my eyes cloud over. "You're going to make me cry." We approached the driveway and I hugged him around his neck. "That's the sweetest thing ever."

He took a deep, deep, deep breath. I started to wonder about it, but he pulled back and his smile was small, but happy. "Oh, I think I've heard sweeter things."

He patted my cheek, and the little familiar ache to wish to remember him doing that before assaulted me. I still had days when all I wanted was to remember, but then I remember who I used to be and how Mason and I wouldn't be together. But sometimes...I wish I could remember what it was like to be this man's little Daddy's girl and look up to him as he bent down to be at my level. To know exactly how to tug on his strings to do anything that I wanted... But I loved my life now and I wouldn't change anything.

"I'll see you tomorrow afternoon then," I told him and kissed his cheek before walking toward the driveway. "Tell Mom I'll come and help!"

"Mason's coming, too, right?" he yelled across the yard. "I could use some extra muscle with the tables and chairs!"

I smiled. He was hiring a company to handle all of that for him. He was just trying to show me that they understood that Mason was my other half.

"Of course!" I yelled back before climbing in my Mini Cooper.

I'd only been driving for a couple of months now. Learning to drive was interesting. My dad took me to a Driver's Ed class, but that didn't teach me how to drive, it just taught me the rules. So Mason took me to an old grocery store parking lot and turned me loose. He guided me along and told me what to do, but let me learn for myself. After a week or so, I was driving myself, but only back and forth from the house to Mason's mostly. Now, I'm good and feel confident in driving anywhere...mostly. Mason took me to the city a couple times. Once in the daytime to go to an art festival. He asked me if I wanted to drive back home. I refused. Never, ever, ever would I drive in this road-rage infested place.

The Jason Reeves CD blared through my car and out the windows. It felt so good to be independent and making my own decisions now. Able to stand, literally, on my own two feet knowing that my fate was my own.

The bridge came into view just as he sang *I know I'm lost in crazy, but you are the one that saves me...*

Andy's face, haunted, comes smashing into my mind. Leaning my elbow on the open window, I rested my head on my palm. I hated to admit that Andy's face still flashed through my mind at the oddest times. It wasn't really guilt because I knew that it wasn't my fault. I'd toyed with going back and forth over the guilt factor, but in the end, it was just facts. Andy ran me over. Then he left me there in the road, his girlfriend of years, and pretended he knew nothing about it. He let my parents go through all the toil and pain of pleading for someone, anyone, who knew something to come forward. He did all that just to save himself from trouble. Then when I woke, he dumped his new girl without a second's thought for what that would do to her. And he did all this for himself. Everything he has ever done was for him, and his suicide was for him, too.

My new therapist told me to imagine what Andy had gone through and understand why he felt the need to kill himself. I understood completely. He was eaten alive with guilt, he told me so himself, and he knew there was no way out of it but to confess and take responsibility. I couldn't imagine living with the guilt for six months of knowing that I'd not only ran some over, therefore putting them in a coma, but that I'd left them there to die. The weight of that must have been awful. But the difference between us was that I would never have left someone to die in the first place.

When I started to feel guilty, that's what brought me back. Andy made his choices and they were bad ones. You can't take responsibility for someone's else choices.

Andy's mother came to see me one day right after graduation. She said she wanted to tell me that they had lied to the police before. Andy had called and left a message on their answering machine at home, telling them the entire thing, everything that happened, and then told them he was going to end it. He said that he felt like his insides were boiling and it was getting worse every day. When she closed her eyes in agony, I wanted to burst. But then she said it was her fault. Hers and her husband's because they spent so much time telling him that he needed to be perfect and make them proud that Andy never felt like he could come to them. They failed him, she said.

She said they'd gone to the police and given them the tape of Andy, though it didn't change anything. The investigation was *open and close*, but she wanted to make sure everyone knew that it didn't matter what Andy had said in the buckling of his grief, it wasn't my fault. She told me they had sold their house and were moving. They knew what the town thought of me, but really, most of that had died down to nothing. People didn't want to dwell on things and I was more than willing to let it all go.

After pulling into Mason's drive, I knocked but pushed my way inside without waiting. "Hey," I said to the nurse. "Everything good today?"

"Same old, same old," she muttered and shrugged, smiling.

I nodded and went through the hall to Mason's room. He was lying on the bed with bare feet, his arms behind his head with his eyes closed. When I pushed the door to, his eyes popped open, almost comically. He smiled, but that changed to a smirk when I peeled off my jacket and threw it across the chair.

"You look happy to see me," I whispered and kicked one shoe off.

"I *am* happy to see you." His grin widened as he sat up on his elbows to watch me.

I kicked off my other shoe. "I'm happy that you're happy."

I heard his laugh as I flicked the light switch, settling us in darkness. I moved across the room to him. I let my hand guide me, running it up his leg, across his stomach and chest to his neck. I let my weight fall on him and loved how his hands gripped my hips to pull me against him. I settled my lips over his and he wasted no time in sucking my tongue into his mouth. I shivered, much to his delight. I felt his grin against my cheek before he put one hand in my hair and pulled me to him again, harder, my breath exploding from me as his lips slid and coaxed me to melt.

Soon, the tables turned and I was under him, mind, body, and soul.

The sounds of his breaths as they moved across my skin were the only sound in his room. And it was the only sound I needed or wanted. His hands held mine hostage to his bed above my head. Being completely out of control was something that was only fun with Mason. And it *was* fun.

He tortured me in ways I never knew I even wanted to be tortured. I knew I wasn't a virgin, but as Mason said, if I couldn't remember, my slate was clean and it was as if it never happened. So all these experiences, all the things Mason did for me and my *normal* list, all the little things he did to me to make my breath catch...they were all new, all sensual, all swoon-worthy.

"Mason," I groaned, begging him to find my lips again.

We still hung out in the shop a lot, but had started migrating to his bedroom, too. It was more convenient since it was becoming pretty close to impossible to keep our hands off each other. Mason, my ever-protective good guy, remained the sweet, gentle, amazing man that I fell for. If not more so.

My parents had gotten over their aversion for him for the most part.

I tried to get an apartment between the local college and home. No one wanted me to live by myself even though I was perfectly capable and healed in every way. Even Mason seemed to not like the idea. I planned to start living on my own -of course that meant spending all my time here with Mason, I knew- and then I'd start college next year. Community college. And I planned to be a counselor. With all my knowledge of both sides of the high school coin, I thought it was fitting that I try to make sure that school kids understood that tragedy is inevitable. It will happen to you one day, in some form or fashion. Does that mean that we lock up our hearts and look over our shoulder every minute? Does it mean that we keep the seat belt extra tight and never deviate from the plan? Does it mean we always do what everyone says is right and don't do what we know we should because it's in our bones and speaks to us like nothing else? Does it mean we never skip class or take a gamble? Does it mean that we answer our phone every time it rings for fear of something epic being on the other end of that receiver?

No.

We let the freaking phone ring. We skip Geometry every once in a while. We try a new hairstyle and don't give a rat's behind if it's picture day. We tell our parents that we need a year off of school, but we plan to go next year, and we mean it with all our heart. We kiss the butler on the cheek out the door to our boyfriend's. We open our arms to the one who can make our heart melt and our chest sigh because love is about not just a feeling, but our reaction. It's a mixture of souls, sighs, needs, wants, and got to have. It's a balance of sweet and sexy. It's something that's out there for everyone.

And I wanted the kids who came through the school halls after me to know that. So, I'd start my classes soon, after some much needed time off.

But now, as he nudged my face up with his to reach the space under my chin, I wasn't thinking about any of that. I pulled him back to my lips, tasting my own lipgloss on him. He pulled back just a bit, and when he licked his lips, his tongue touched my lip. "What flavor is that?" He tongued his lip again in investigation. "It's new."

I smiled at his perceptiveness. "It's peach."

He grinned. Even though the room was dark, I could feel the tilt of his lips in the dark. "Peaches," he growled. "You taste amazing, Em."

He covered my mouth with his again, pressing me to his mattress as he hovered over me on his elbows. Our bare feet tangled and rubbed together at the foot of the bed. His bare feet with his jeans on were sexy and that's how we usually hung out in his house.

His palm hooked under my thigh and pulled it up to press me against him. His phone rang on the dresser and he ignored it. I bit into his bottom lip to thank him for that. He groaned into my mouth before kissing me harder. His phone rang again. He leaned back with a sigh.

"Daggum it," he growled before reaching over and yanking it off the bedside table. He sighed again. "It's Rob, which only means one thing since he called me and didn't text."

I knew. "Milo."

"I'm so sorry about-" he began.

"Hey," I stopped him, putting my fingers over his lips. "I knew what I was getting into with you."

He made a growly noise in his throat. "But that little jerk has ruined too many nights for us, especially lately. It's getting to be once a week I have to go find his sorry behind. I wish I could I just..." he shook his head, his nose rubbing mine, "let him go, but I can't."

"I'm with you, and I'm not going anywhere," I reminded him. He needed reminding even after all this time. He still fought his own self-loathing. He still fought his guilt. He had grown by leaps and bounds these past few months, but every now and then, a peek at the old Mason who hated himself would shine back through.

His sigh this time wasn't in annoyance but relief. His entire body sighed. "Gah...I love you, Emma."

"I know," I whispered and pulled him to me, wrapping my legs around him and my arms latched around his neck. I kissed his lips once, twice, before pulling his forehead to mine. "But Mason, you have to stop thinking that you're a burden for me. That you're holding me back or making me unhappy. You're not. Milo and your mom are a part of your life, each in their own way, just like my family is a part of mine. I want every piece of you, Mason. If it takes ten more years of chasing Milo and he finally decides that he wants to come home for good, wasn't it worth it?"

"Of course it was," he said softly. "I just hate that you're carrying the burden with me."

"Love isn't a burden, Mason."

His breath was deep and I could tell it was the last one he needed. "Baby, I love you," he said against my lips.

"I love you."

I barely got the words out before his tongue slipped past my lips. I pulled him tighter to me when his phone rang once more. He pulled back and kissed my nose. "You ok here? You can come with. The nurse is here."

"I'll just stay with your mom. I'll make some fettuccine for her while you're gone."

He smiled and rubbed his nose against mine again. "Thanks, Em." He scooted to the edge of the bed and started to slip his boots back on. He looked over his shoulder and chuckled before saying sternly, "Gah, don't lay there looking all sexy like that."

I laughed and sat up, putting my chest to his back and my arms around his neck. I put my lips to his ear. "I'll try to tone it down, Mr. Wright."

He groaned and reached up to cup my cheek. I felt it all the way to my toes. But then he pulled me around to his lap before I could say anything. He let his fingers caress and move against my cheek. His eyes, though it was almost dark in the room, held mine and I knew there was something he wanted to say. More than that, it was something that was going to change things. His lips parted to speak, but he held on to his thoughtful silence for a few seconds longer. Then he said, "Baby, I love you. And I love how you love me. How you love my mom. And...I want to take you somewhere this weekend." His eyebrows rose in question. "Would that be all right?"

"Of course," I said like he was silly. "I'll go anywhere with you."

His eyes closed and he smiled before opening them again and holding me still while kissing my mouth just once, achingly slow. "You make me happier than I thought was possible."

I grinned and combed through his hair. "Then we can check number nine off my list now."

He chuckled happily. "See, this is what I'm talking-"

His phone rang. He groaned while I smiled wryly. "I'll be right here. Go."

"Bye, you." He kissed my top lip before standing me up.

"Bye, you. Be careful."

He nodded, turning to look at me once more on his bed. His smile held something different. I couldn't wait for him to explain it. I assumed he had something to tell me and he'd tell me this weekend. I knew he was going to ask me to move in. I practically lived there anyway since I was there all the time. I knew that was what was on his mind. He put his head down on his way out, his smile still shining.

I stood and combed my hair out with my fingers as I made my way out. I forgot my phone and turned to get it, bumping it off the bedside table in my bumbling in the dark. I pulled the string to turn the lamp on and reached down to get it. That was when I saw it. On the shelf under the end table, beside our stack of useless fact books, was a little red box.

A ring box.

My fingers snapped out to grab it before I could stop them. My fingers gripped the lid and I shook my head at myself, scolding, "Emma, what are you doing?"

I put the ring box back on the shelf and stared at the closed lid. The more I stared with my knees to my chest, the more my vision waved and blurred. My lips went so wide that my grin actually hurt as the tears fell from my chin.

He was going to ask me to marry him this weekend.

It was then that I realized I didn't care where we were going, all I could think about was how I was going to compose myself with him until then. Because just thinking about Mason on his knees before me, accepting me for who and what and everything I was, asking me to be his for the rest of our lives, taking me into not only his life but his mother and brother's as well, wanting me to be his one and only girl, as he'd said to me once more, was more than I ever thought I was going to have.

I wiped my face and grinned as I stood. I couldn't wait for this weekend.

When he asked me if I'd be Mrs. Mason Wright, there was no question what I was going to say.

Do turtles breath through their butts?!

A. Million. Times. Yes!

Stay tuned for *Wide Open*, Milo's story, and see how all these pieces finally get put back together again.

Expected Publication : Winter 2013

Thank you

The irony from the fact that I developed a tumor in my head while writing a book about a girl who was in a coma from a head injury has not escaped me. Between all the spinal shots from when I broke my neck and now all the tests and doctors visits from this, writing this book was challenging. I was late on my deadline and release date, which is something through twelve other book releases I've never had to deal with before. But with the weight off of my shoulders, I finished the book at my own slow pace and I kinda missed writing that way. No deadline.

I'm so glad it's out and finished now, and I have a few people to thank for motivating and sending me love in the form of texts, emails, Will Ferrel pics, and goodies to check on me and keep me cheery. Jen Nunez, *points finger* you and me, me and you, you know! Amy Bartol, you are the queen of sarcasm and wit and I miss you like an insane person. Georgia Cates, my southern bell, Mwah! Anne Eliot, those flowers were better than ANY flower ever, on the planet. Mandy Twimom, blogger #1, I heart you for always being awesome when I need something. Mary Smith, you're the sweetest and I thank you for all the blog love. YATR, same goes for you. I notice all the sharing, I see it, thank you. Candace Selph, you and your formatting skills are amazing and just...thank, thank you! Cynthia S, Mwah, mwah, mwah!! There are a few fans in particular that I see and notice every day. You comment, you share, you post, you send me messages asking me how I'm doing. I heart you the most! Just to name a few: Marcia W, Maggie T, Jenny & Mike B, Stacey B, Kathryn J, Kimberly S, Kathryn G, Jody D, Liz J, Nanette B, Kerry H, & Bridget T. ((HUGS))

Playlist

(theme song) Nobody Else Could Be You : Jason Reeves
Lover of the Light : Mumford and Sons
Forest Whitaker : Bad Books
Stubborn Love : The Lumineers
Black Chandelier : Biffy Clyro
The Way It Was : Killers
Nothing Left To Say : Imagine Dragons
Slow and Steady : Of Monsters and Men
Heart Skips a Beat : Olly Murs
Every Teardrop Is a Waterfall : Coldplay
ON Our Way : Jason Reeves
Harbour Lights : A Silent Film
Heartbeats : Royal Teeth
Living Louder : The Cab
Give Me Love : Ed Sheeran
Sleep Alone : Two Door Cinema Club
(Mason's Therapy Jam) Keep Your Head Up : Andy Grammar

Shelly is a *New York Times* & *USA Today* Bestselling author from a small town in Georgia and loves everything about the south. She is wife to a fantastical husband and stay at home mom to two boisterous and mischievous boys who keep her on her toes. They currently reside in everywhere USA as they happily travel all over with her husband's job. She loves to spend time with her family, binge on candy corn, go out to eat at new restaurants, buy paperbacks at little bookstores, site see in the new areas they travel to, listen to music everywhere and also LOVES to read.

Her own books happen by accident and she revels in the writing and imagination process. She doesn't go anywhere without her notepad for fear of an idea creeping up and not being able to write it down immediately, even in the middle of the night, where her best ideas are born.

Shelly's website:

www.shellycrane.blogspot.com

Turn the page for a preview of the next novel
by Shelly Crane...

SMASH INTO YOU

ONE

It was a case of mistaken identity.

The worst kind.

The kind that ended with appalled, parted lips and evil glares.

The girl was cute enough. Cute wasn't the problem nor the solution for me. I needed to blend and be invisible in the most plain-as-day way and girls like this, girls who just walked up to guys because they had hope somewhere deep inside them that I would fall for that pretty face, were the opposite of plain-as-day. Those kinds of girls got guys killed. At least the kind that were on the run.

She had mistaken me for a normal guy.

And this girl who approached, who could see that I was already surrounded by two, which was more girls than I knew what to do with, must've thought I had a hankering for something sweet. Because when she spoke, her words were soft and almost made me want to get to know her instead of send her packing. But I couldn't stay in this town. It was better to hurt her now when she wasn't invested than it would be to leave one day without a trace.

The girls who were currently soaking up my attention - that they thought they had - they'd move on to their next prey and forget I ever existed. But sweet girls got attached and asked questions.

Don't stop running...

I swallowed and stared bored at her as she finally made her way to me from across the hall. She tucked her hair behind her ear gently and smiled a little. "Hi, uh, can I just-"

Showtime. "Honey, that's real sweet, but I'm not interested." I slid my arm around one of my groupies. I didn't even know her name, but they were always within arm's reach. "As you can see I have my hands full already, but thanks for offering."

She scoffed and looked completely shocked. I took her in, head to foot. She *was* cute. She had a great little body on her and her face was almond shaped. He lips looked...sweet. She was not the kind I wanted within ten feet of me. She was still standing there. I had to send her packing.

I grinned as evilly as I could muster and felt a small twinge of guilt at the vulnerable look of her. I looked away quickly. I didn't even want to remember her face. "Run along, sweetheart. Go find a tuba player, I'm sure he's more your speed. Like I said, I'm not interested."

She didn't glare, and that was a first. Most of the girls who approached a guy were confident, I mean that was the reason they thought they had a chance, right? But she looked a little...destroyed. When her lips parted, it was in shock, it was to catch her breath. I continued my bored stance, though at this point, it pained me in my chest.

But I was doing the best thing for this and any other girl. People who got involved with me were collateral damage when Biloxi came around. He was a ruthless bastard and if he found me and knew someone cared about me, or worse, that I cared about someone, he'd be all over them.

So when she turned without a word and swiftly made her way down the hall, I was thankful. I probably saved her life, though she had no idea. She thought I was an ass, but I was really looking out for her. That's what I told myself as I watched her go. That I had hurt her feelings for a reason, and that she'd get over it.

A slender hand crawled over my collar.

"What's this from?" she asked in a purr and slid her thumb over the long scar from my ear all the way to my chin. "Mmm, it's so sexy."

It followed my jaw line and it was not sexy. Unfortunately, it wasn't the first time some girl had said as much and it pissed me off to no end that they thought that, let alone said it out loud.

It was my reminder of what happened when I let my guard down and it was anything but sexy.

I bit down on my retort and sent her a small smile that showed her I was listening, but she had to work for my attention. "Is that right?"

"Mmhmm," she said and kissed my jaw. "I have a little scar, too." She pointed to the place between her breasts. "Right here. Wanna see it?"

I managed a chuckle. "Is there really a scar there?"

"Pick me up tonight and you can find out," she purred, making her friend giggle.

"Don't think so. Busy."

"Ahhh, boo." She pouted and let her other hand hook a finger into my waistband. "Well here's something to keep you company tonight."

And then she pulled me down by my collar and kissed me. I tried not to cringe away, but her lip gloss was sticky and sweet. When she tried to open my mouth with her tongue I pushed her away gently with my hands wrapped around her bony arms.

"Let's keep this PG, honey. Settle down."

She giggled. I knew she would.

It was the last week of school. It was my last week to pretend that I was still *in* high school. The next time I made a move to evade Biloxi, I'd enroll in college because I was getting too old to be a high-schooler. I didn't know where I was going. I would have graduated from high school years ago, but at the rate I was going, I didn't know if I would have *actually* graduated or not. School was not a place of learning for me, it was a cover, a place to blend in and be normal until Biloxi found me and then I'd be gone to the next place.

This was my life. No time or want for girls, no parties, no movies, no parents.

This was my life, but it wasn't a life at all.

TWO

Six months and one lonely birthday later...

College sucked.

The big one.

I had only been going to class for a couple of days and was already dreading the long classes. It was part of my cover. I practically chanted those words in my mind as I trudged everywhere I went. But one thing remained the same. Desperate girls ran rampant and I still wasn't interested. Every once in a while, they were good for a distraction if need be, but mostly…not interested. There was this one chick, Kate, who would not take no for a answer. She'd 'found' me over the summer when I was apartment hunting and hadn't 'lost' me yet, no matter how hard I tried. To get her to go away one time, I'd even given her my phone number. I was going to ditch it in a couple weeks anyway when I undoubtedly had to move again, so it didn't matter, right?

Wrong.

The girl was as annoying as a Chihuahua all hopped up 'cause there's a knock at the door. The texting and come-hithers in text code were nonstop.

And now, as I stared out into the dark rain to see a POS car sideways in the road, I knew the world hated me, had to, because someone had just smashed her car into my truck.

I got out and braced myself. It wasn't easy to pay cash for new cars every time I needed to skip town. It was hard living when you couldn't be who you really were. Finding people to pay you under the table was almost impossible these days.

I groaned and glared at the beauty standing at the end of my truck. "Look at that!"

"I'm so sorry," she began. I could tell she really was, but I was beyond pissed. "I'll call my insurance company right now."

That stopped me. "No!" I shouted and she jolted at the verbal assault. "No insurance."

"Well," she pondered, "what do you mean? I have good insurance."

"But I don't."

She turned her head a bit in thought and then her mouth fell open as she realized what I was saying. "You don't have *any* insurance, do you?"

"No," I answered. "Look. Whatever, we'll just call this even-steven, because you did hit *me*."

"Even-steven my butt!" she yelled and scurried to jump in front of me, blocking my way. "And what a cute butt it is."

Even through the noise of water hitting metal, I heard her intake of breath. The rain pelted us in the dark. I hoped no one came around the corner. It would be hard for them to see us here in the middle of the road. She might get hurt. Then I wondered why I cared.

"Look, buddy," she replied and crossed her arms. It drew my eyes to her shirt. My eyes bulged 'cause that shirt…well, it was see-through now. She caught on and jerked her crossed arms higher. "How dare you! You're on a roll in the jerkface department, you know that!"

"My specialty," I said and saluted as I climbed in my truck. "Get your pretty butt in your car and let's pretend this never happened, shall we?"

Because if cops and insurance were brought into this, I'd be on the run sooner than I thought.

She huffed. "Excuse me-"

"Darlin'. Car. Now." She glared. "Like right now."

She threw her hands up in the air and yelled, "I knew chivalry was dead!" before climbing in her car and driving away. She didn't know it, but I was being as chivalrous as they come. I made sure she got out of the rain and back into her car, even though she didn't like the way I did it, and I got her as far away from me as I could.

In my book, I deserved a freaking medal for being so chivalrous, because people that stuck with me didn't live long.

Just ask my mom.

Oh, wait, you can't. She died long, long years ago saving my life. I refused to bring anyone onto this sinking ship with me. If it finally did go down, I was going down alone.

Publication Coming 2013

CPSIA information can be obtained at www.ICGtesting.com
Printed in the USA
LVOW061503140513

333774LV00003B/502/P